ZANE PRESENTS

DADDY'S MAYBE

support, listening ear, and faith in my work. Victoria Christopher Murray, a kind and giving person.

Many, many thanks to Alisha Yvonne, Yolanda L. Gore, Jihad & Maurice, Markisha Sampson, Lt. Col. Logan, my KPFT Family, Ron Reynolds, Marlo Blue, John Brewer, Luke Jones: you all make my days easier so that I can focus on writing at night!

Special thanks to my super agent, Sara, and a world of gratitude to my Strebor family, the dynamic duo Zane, and Charmaine, for having faith in my work. Special thanks to the publicity Queens led by Yona Deshommes at Atria who help spread the word about my work.

But my deepest gratitude goes out to you, the reader! I'm so honored to have your support. There were so many book clubs that picked up *Daddy by Default*, *Football Widows*, and *Party Girl*. I know you have many, many choices right now; I'm so humbled and grateful to have your support. Here's a special shout out to some of those book clubs: The bible of AFAM Lit: Black Expressions book club. Sisters are Reading Too (They have been with me from day 1!!) Special thanks to Divas Read2, Happy Hour, Cush City, Girlfriends, Inc., Drama Queens, Mugna Suma, First Wives, Brand Nu Day, Go On Girl, TX 1, As the Page Turns, APOOO, Urban Reviews, OOSA, Mahogany Expressions, Black Diamonds, BragAbout Books, Spirit of Sisterhood, Renascence Men, Ella Curry and so many more!

Also huge thanks to all of the media outlets that welcomed me on the airwaves to discuss my work: "Inside Her Story" with Jacque Reed on the "Tom Joyner Morning Show," Yahoo Shine, Hello Beautiful, *Essence*.com, the *Huffington Post–Fictiondb*, *Houston Chronicle*–Guest Blog, Junebugg Blog, Onnix Blog, Author Tuesday's presents, Northparan.com, The Book Depository.com, *Black Pearls Magazine*, S&S Tipsonlifeandlove.com, nextreads.com,

The *Dallas Morning News*.com, Interview-KFDM-CBS Beaumont, TX, 3 Chicks on Lit, Clear Channel Radio News & Comm. Affairs, KIX-96 FM, KARK-TV Little Rock, AR, KPRC NBC, Houston Beyond Headlines, Artist First radio show, The Mother Love Radio Show, It's Well Blog Talk Radio March 7th.

If I forgot anyone, and I'm sure I have, please charge it to my head and not my heart. As always, please drop me a line at rekcutp@hotmail.com or sylkkep@yahoo.com. I'd love to hear from you.

Warmly,
Pat

offices, along with other benefits. Mario had a premium membership.

"I've been in touch with your attorney and he's frustrated too. I think the press coverage will help. Trust me, I see cases like yours more than I care to admit," I said.

But still, he seemed nervous. When he looked like he didn't want to leave, I waited before I said anything else.

Mario's eyes darted downward. He sighed really hard. I knew exactly what he was feeling and what he was going through. I remembered the feeling of hopelessness, the feelings of frustration, and then, downright fury.

"This is gonna be a helluva battle, but it's not impossible," I said quietly.

When he started shaking his head, I knew he was probably fighting back tears. Few words could describe what a man was feeling at a time like that. I only knew because I'd been there. I knew what it was like to want to scream at the top of my lungs that the kids not mine and I shouldn't have to pay!

I reached over and patted his back a couple of times.

"We're gonna work through this. You gotta hang in there, buddy," I said.

"That's easy for you to say. " He choked on his words a bit.

"Ain't nobody threatening you with jail, man! These fools trying to threaten me with jail time if I don't pay!"

After he sat, I took my seat. I waited for him to turn to me. It took a few minutes, but he looked at me, blinked back tears and said, "I ain't never spent a day in my life behind bars."

"Well, I have. And I can tell you, it's no fun! Not only is it not fun, but it's even worse when you're in jail for not paying child support, when you know damn well you ain't fathered no child!"

His eyes narrowed as he zeroed in on me. Recognition etched

itself into his features. His bushy brows crept inward like they were being pulled together by an invisible string.

"So you've been to jail..."

"For not paying child support!"

His eyebrows were nearly meeting in the middle of his forehead. He looked around the office. I watched as he took in the pictures of me with the mayor, the governor, and other lawmakers. Then he looked back at me. He looked bewildered.

"But you're famous, aren't you?" he asked.

"I'm not famous, not really, but what I have done is built a solid reputation on the shoulders of the many men I've helped. And I was able to help them because I've already walked in their shoes," I said.

"You went to jail?"

"Boy! Did I?" I leaned back in my executive leather chair and told Mario my story. I told him how I spent months behind bars and was literally held hostage until I came up with the money to pay back child support. I told him how it wasn't until the press got involved and exposed my situation that I finally brought attention to the greatest injustice any man could imagine, much less experience.

"So you didn't even know this chick," he said more than asked.

"My case was extreme. But still, it was a form of paternity fraud. A woman had it in for me, and specifically targeted me. She knew the system, knew how to work it, and basically got away with it."

"But how? Wasn't she breaking the law?"

"Yes and no. See, part of the problem is the law isn't set up to recognize and punish paternity fraud. The concept is still relatively new, but once I got a state representative to hear me out, he was able to author legislation that helped my case."

"You get your money back?" Mario asked.

I shook my head. I didn't want to discourage him before we even got started.

"So this bitch intentionally set out to finger you as her kid's father, and nothing happened to her?"

"It took some time, but my name was recently cleared. Now we're about to work on the next phase of this nightmare," I said.

"Whoa! Wait, we're talking some years," he balked.

"Again, my case was extreme. Yours, textbook, you're gonna be okay and it won't take half the amount of time mine did," I said.

Mario looked at me like he didn't know whether to believe what I said. I noticed the distant thoughts running through his mind. His eyes told me he wasn't trying to hear me talk about years. He was desperate for resolution, and he wanted it immediately.

"Man, I don't have *years*. Hell, I barely got months," he said.

"Listen," I started with as much calm as I could muster up. "I can't promise you a quick process, but I can promise you that you won't have to go through this alone like I did."

He blinked quickly.

"I could yank that trick by the neck and squeeze all the life from her sluttish body," Mario said. There was no mistaking the rage in his eyes. It looked so familiar to me because, for years, I saw the same thing when I looked in the mirror.

Before he could turn to leave, a loud crashing sound pulled our attention toward the front door. A crazed man burst into the office.

"Yo, Parker. Man, you gotta come outside. I didn't know where else to go. I can't believe she called the law, man. I can't believe this shit!" Collin Rivers was tall and usually looked more like a banker than someone on the run.

Collin stumbled into my office, breathing hard; his hair disheveled, and body drenched in sweat. His T-shirt clung to his body like another layer of skin.

"Collin, calm down. What's going on?" I looked through the windows, trying to see what or who had chased him into our office.

"All I did was go over there and try to talk to her. That's all I was doing. I just went over there to try and talk to her. That's all, man, I swear," he stumbled all over himself.

I wanted Mario to leave before I started talking to Collin, but things moved so fast, it was hard to keep up.

"Collin, man, calm down. Here, let me get you some water," I said.

"I don't want no damn water, Parker. Man, you don't hear what I'm trying to tell you. One minute I'm trying to talk to her, the next thing you know, I'm flying down 59, a trail of cop cars behind me."

My eyes got wide. And that was when we heard it.

"Come out with your hands where we can see them!"

My head whipped toward the door.

"Is that someone on a bullhorn?" It looked like the Fourth of July with colorful lights dancing outside my storefront office.

"Parker, they was chasing me like I stole something," Collin said.

LACHEZ

There was a running joke around 1307 Baker Street. Apparently, the digs were so nice there, people didn't mind going back. Yours truly was not one of *those* people. I looked around and I wondered what the standards were if *this* place was considered the Cadillac of the Harris County Jail System.

"Say, baby girl, whatchu know good?" Peebles asked as she pimp-strolled into the day room downstairs.

"Just counting down the days, ready to spring up outta here; you know the drill," I said.

Jail was *not* the business, regardless of how much nicer this facility was supposed to be than the other dumps. Here at 1307 Baker Street, there were about 250 females. Each dormitory was designed to handle forty-eight inmates.

The day room was where the TV and several chow tables were. There was a door that led outside for recreation. Upstairs there were twenty-four sets of bunk beds. The shower area consisted of four shower heads with hot water, porcelain sinks and toilets. There was a cold water fountain upstairs and down. Unlike 1200 Baker and 701 San Jacinto, there were windows that actually allowed us to see the sun.

There was nothing in the county lock-up but a bunch of hoes, thieves, and backstabbing haters. There weren't any violent offenders here. These inmates were charged with multiple DWI, theft, minor drug possession, fraud and shit like that. I had no plans to come back, and I couldn't wait for my two days to come. Of course, I tell all these haters I have two weeks left, 'cause when you a short-timer and everyone knows, you might as well have a massive target on your forehead.

"So, you out in a couple of weeks, huh?" Pebbles asked like she was suspicious. She was a thirty-four-year-old black chick accused of passing a slew of bad checks. Pebbles was short and petite, but she ran the yard. "You ain't one of 'em lying and shit about their day, right?"

"Oh, never that! I ain't fixing to lie on that," I said. All the while, I'm wondering why Pebbles is all up in mines.

Pebbles was always in the middle of some mess, so I stayed clear of her. I didn't need any trouble, especially when I was so close to getting up outta here.

When a ruckus suddenly broke out on the other side of the day room, Pebbles jumped up and rushed over there like her life depended on it. I didn't care if the building crumbled or burned, I just wanted out. As the crowd swelled, I eased up out of there and headed back upstairs. When they locked the joint down, I didn't want to be anywhere near the melee.

Two days later, when I sprang up out of there, I expected something like you'd see in the movies. You know, where the wide gate slowly opened and loved ones waited with a stretch limo stacked with all your favorite foods and drinks.

But the scene for me was nothing like what you might find in a movie. Processing started in the afternoon, but I wasn't released until 2:45 the next morning! I was pissed! I had no money, nobody to call, and no one was waiting.

"How the hell am I supposed to get home?" I asked the guard.

"Hell if I care. Hop the bus." He shrugged.

I started to read him up one side, then down the other, but thought better of it. I didn't need any more trouble. What I needed was to find my way over to my girl Toni's until daybreak so I could holler at my mama Darlene's hateful behind.

I grabbed my bag that held what little property I had. I was waiting with the rest of the females who were released. We stood and waited for them to open the door.

We walked a short distance and lined up to get on the bus. The only information they gave us was that we were being dropped off at the Greyhound station. After that, we were on our own.

"Lachez!"

I whipped my head toward the sound of someone calling my name just as the line started to move.

The smile on my face must've been priceless when I saw my girl, Toni, standing there leaned up against a sweet whip. I scrambled to get out of line and ran toward Toni like we were long-lost lovers.

"Guuurrrl, what are you doing here?" I screamed.

We must've been quite a vision the way we hugged, laughed and screamed like two fools in love.

"Shit! I'm here to scoop your ass! I remember what it was like six months ago for me and I didn't want you to have to go out like that!" she said as the hug wrapped up.

I couldn't remember a time I was so happy to see her.

"Damn, you right on time!"

"Yeah, I didn't want you trying to hook for a ride to my place," she joked.

"Umph, after what I've been through, I wouldn't mind turning a trick or two." I laughed.

"Girl, you know I got you, right?" she asked.

I had no idea what that meant. It was one of Toni's bright ideas that got us both sent to jail almost two years ago, so I was not trying to be on any revolving door type of mess.

"Listen, we're gonna head to the house, rest up, then I've got some plans for us later," she said after we settled into her car.

Toni looked good, reminded me of the good ol' days when we were running the streets and running men like they were both going out of style.

"What you done got us into now? I ain't even been out a good five minutes and you already got plans? Really, Toni?"

"Now you know good and well, I couldn't let my girl get out without any fanfare, right? You know that wouldn't even be my style," she said as she navigated the streets.

"I just wanna see my kids. You know Darlene done made me rattle off a long list of impossible promises just so I can see my own damn kids."

"Girl, let's not worry about any of that right now. Let's get you to the house, cleaned up, and rested. Tomorrow, when you feel like rolling over, we can hit a few corners."

I nodded.

Toni turned up the music and we rode in silence the rest of the way home. I had so much running through my mind. My life was a mess, and I knew I had much work ahead, 'cause I needed to get a grip real fast-like, so I could make it do what it do.

EBONI

"Ummm, is that Shawnathon?" Ulonda Swanson, my bestie and partner in crime, asked as she craned her neck to look over my shoulder. She had good reason to be worried if she thought she spotted my baby's daddy, Shawnathon McGee. He was a certifiable fool who was just short of crazy!

Ulonda and I sat outside on a near perfect afternoon. We were having lunch at Maggiano's Little Italy restaurant near Houston's Galleria Mall. I whipped my head around just in time to see that fool jump out of his Escalade. He left the truck right there in the middle of the parking lot, running, with his door wide open.

I scrambled to get up out of my chair but couldn't move fast enough. One second, his truck screeched to a sudden stop, the next, he had bum-rushed me at our table outside on the restaurant's patio.

But Ulonda sprang into action just as fast.

Heads turned, and other customers screamed at the crashing noise as glasses, dishes, and silverware went airborne. Shawnathon fell into a table and as he did, he hurled insults and swung wildly in my direction.

"You bitch!" He scrambled as he struggled to get to me.

But as usual, Ulonda blocked his path.

"I hate yo' low-down, connivin' ass. You gold-digging trick!"

My eyes grew wide; shock and horror invaded my features as I cowered down behind Ulonda. My heart raced and its beating sound pounded loudly in my hot ears. I felt my blood boiling. Nervous energy rushed through my veins.

"Five hundred feet!" I screamed. "Five fucking hundred feet! You need to quit! You know you in violation!"

"I'll show you a violation, you bitch!"

"I got yo' bitch, you punk! Why don't you pay your damn child support! Pay up and quit hiding behind your pre-paid lawyers!"

I felt a sense of relief when two big burly men approached and pulled Shawnathon up from the wreckage of the collapsed table.

By now, the customers had gone from shocked, possible victims, to nosey whispering spectators. I couldn't blame them, though. This was some reality TV type-drama, and it was my life! But I was done being embarrassed.

These kinds of run-ins had become more frequent. We still kind of ran in the same circles, so it was never a surprise when Shawnathon tried to go off on me in public.

"Shawnathon! You need to quit!" Ulonda yelled. "Somebody, please call 9-1-1!" she screamed as she looked around at the crowd of people who were shamelessly gawking. Ulonda had jumped in front of me and that seemed to piss him off even more.

"Ulonda, my beef ain't with you!" he said. "Move, lemme at her!"

"What's the problem here?" one of the big men finally asked. I guess he was no longer star-struck.

"The problem is, *boys* shouldn't front like *men*. Then when it's time to step up, their punk asses wanna cry and whine like a little mama's boy!" I screamed. I served up much attitude because I knew that hit close to home, and I didn't give a damn.

Shawnathon shot deadly daggers in my direction. His face was twisted and he looked more like a demon than the handsome superstar staring back at me.

"Sir, we need you to calm down," the other man said. One of his big, beefy arms held Shwanathon at bay as he struggled to keep still.

"I'ma catch yo' gold-digging ass, and when I do, ain't nobody gonna be able to save your trifling ass!" He pointed a crooked finger in my direction. "Bet!" he said.

"So you threatening me now?" I asked. "Now you tryin' to threaten me?"

"Oh, it ain't no threat! I'm just keepin' it one-hundred, ma! Just keeping it one-hundred!"

"Yeah, well, you better get your buster ass out of here before the law comes! 'Cause I don't want you to go to jail, sorry-ass. I need you free and bouncing that basketball so I can get my paper!" I said while twisting my neck.

"Sir, we're gonna have to ask you to leave," one of the men said.

Ulonda was breathing hard. My pulse was still racing and a part of me hoped the police would come and catch his behind. Maybe a few days in the Harris County jail was just what he needed.

Shawnathon stood up straight and shook his head. He looked like he wanted to spit on me. Suddenly, Shawnathon turned to leave, but not before he tossed me one last, nasty look over his shoulder as he rushed back to his running truck and hopped in. He peeled out of the parking lot, careened around the corner, and left a chorus of honking horns in his wake. In his rush to get away, he had cut off several other drivers. But just as quickly as the drama had started, it was over.

"Let's go!" Ulonda screamed as she pulled a bunch of crumpled bills from her purse. She dropped them on the collapsed table, and tugged at my arm to steer me out of the gate and into the parking lot.

"We not paying for the damage his stupid behind caused. Let's bounce before we gotta ride downtown to answer a bunch of questions."

It was times like this I was glad for my girl and her quick thinking. I was still somewhat discombobulated from Shawnathon and his latest antics. My legs wobbled and my hands trembled as I stepped over the mess and followed Ulonda to her car.

"You guys need to fix this. He can't be flashing on you out in public like that," she said. "It's so not a good look!"

"I don't know how it's gonna get fixed when that punk don't wanna pay child support," I said. "It makes no sense. He thinks I'm supposed to feed, clothe, and take care of his children by my damn self when he helped to make 'em?"

"Men are a straight trip!" Ulonda said. She hit a button on her keychain and unlocked her car doors. We slipped into the car, buckled up, and Ulonda cranked it up. I felt like 50 percent of Thelma and Louise as she put the pedal to the metal and zoomed away from the scene just as we heard sirens blaring in our direction.

"See, that's what I'm talking about! You would've been laid out on the sidewalk with your skull cracked open by the time they arrived," she hissed. "There's gotta be something you can do to get him to leave you alone!"

"Girl, he ain't never gonna leave me alone. He wants me to walk away, always flashing that damn note in my face like that's supposed to prove something. I wish he'd just pay up and quit fighting it!"

At the light, Ulonda turned to look at me. "You okay?"

I bounced my head back on the headrest and started to laugh. It wasn't that she'd said anything funny, but it just dawned on me. That fool literally crashed our lunch, all but threatened to kill me with his bare hands, in a crowded, public place, but it wasn't until he was gone, and we were safely in her car and around the corner, that she finally thought to ask if I was okay.

"Girl, you know you my dawg, right?" I asked.

She started to laugh. "I don't know how much longer I'ma be your dawg with that loose cannon running around. Eb, if looks could kill..."

"I know, right!" I said, cutting her off.

Ulonda shook her head. "That fool was fired up! He looked like he wanted to snap you in *two*!"

"I'm surprised he didn't have his *note*," I said. "Usually he's waving it around like it's his *get out of jail free card*!" I said.

"Well, he should know by now that's not gonna help his case. I mean, what kind of deadbeat refuses to support his own flesh and blood, because of some lame note?"

"As drunk as we were, girl, I can't even believe he thought that would hold up in a court of law, but whatever, let him hang on to his little note; meanwhile, my ass gonna be laughing all the way to the damn bank!" I said as I wiggled in my seat. "I worked too hard to snag a rich man to not get paid!"

"I *heard* that, girl." Ulonda pulled one hand from the wheel and reached over to slap high five with me. "But on the real, though, you need to start packing some heat. That way, when you see him coming, you can put your finger on the trigger and tap his ass a couple of times; bet he won't be so quick to run up on you like he ain't got no fear!"

Blank stare.

"Ssss, oh yeah, my bad; I forgot about *that*," Ulonda said, looking like she was trying to think fast. "Umm, mace! You can get mace!" she yelled.

"You know, that's not a bad idea," I said. Since a felon can't get a license to carry a firearm, I'd have to settle for the next best thing.

And she had a point. Besides, I knew for sure Ulonda wouldn't always be there to act as a human shield between me and Shawnathon.

The restraining order did very little to keep him away, so it was obvious that eventually, I'd have to take matters into my own hands.

Lord knows, I needed to be ready the next time he decided to jump bad on me.

SERENA

I was so stressed the hell out! I couldn't even focus on the pleasure I was supposed to be getting. JahRyan Cox sucked on the inside of my right thigh so hard it was like he was trying to draw blood. I couldn't stand men who made such a big production out of eating the coochie.

If you're gonna do that shit, then do it, dammit! Don't be dancing around the issue. Either you ready to eat, or don't sit at the table!

And if he didn't stop moaning like a *bitch* in heat, I was gonna get up and put him up outta here. What was sucking on my cellulite doing for him? Maybe he was one of them fetish kind of freaks or something.

JahRyan was okay to look at in the face. Nothing too pretty, he had average features, big brown eyes, wide nose and thick lips. But it was his body that offered promises. He wasn't tall, but he was thick and stocky with ripped abs and swollen muscles. We had been kicking it for a little more than a year.

I rolled my eyes again. The fool pissed me off even more. I fumed as he gnawed on my left thigh. That mess tickled, and I was not in the mood to laugh. I thought I'd be screaming in ecstasy, releasing some of the pent-up frustration with orgasm number two, but no.

"Damn, your skin so soft," he eased up to say.

The minute he moved his suction cup-like lips away from my

thigh, I grabbed his head with both hands and tried to steer it where I needed it to be. But the fool resisted.

"Hmmm, aren't we eager?" He chuckled.

Eager? I wanted to tell him, for as long as you've been sucking on my damn legs, I coulda busted three nuts and been in a deep, comatose sleep by now, but I held my tongue.

I shoulda known this was a bad idea, but I needed something more than what my battery-operated *friends* could provide. Sometimes human contact was in order.

"Uh, your skin," he said, again.

I sucked my teeth. Enough with the soft skin! Again, I grabbed his head and tried to move him closer to the target. He was nowhere close! But what did he do? He pulled his head beyond my grasp.

"Lemme drive this car," he had the nerve to tell me.

JahRyan could handle me on most days, but sometimes he behaved like he didn't know this job was dirty when he signed up. He knew I wasn't one of those little girly women who enjoyed letting the man take control. I needed a man who understood my need to run the show!

When he eased back down, and cupped each of my breasts, I thought, okay, now he was talking! But suddenly, that fool started sucking on my thigh again! I had had enough. I could show him a whole heckuva lot better than I could tell him!

"Get up!" I screamed.

His head popped up like a Jack-in-the-box. All of a sudden, he looked perplexed, like he was lost.

"What's wrong?"

"I need you to go. I ain't got time for this shit," I hissed at him.

His eyebrows bunched together and he turned my nipples loose. He didn't do it because he wanted to, but when I moved to get up, he had little choice.

"Serena, what's wrong with you?"

"I got a rabbit with my name on it. I called you 'cause I needed to cum. You sittin' up here acting like a high-school boy about to get down for the first time," I snapped in his direction.

"Girl, as wet as you are, you trying to tell me you 'bout to get up from here?" he asked, like the idea seemed preposterous.

"Watch me," I said, as I wiggled to get from under him.

"Serena, you be trippin'. My dick is rock hard!"

"You shoulda thought about that while you were sucking on the body parts that didn't count!"

"Girl, if you leave me hanging like this," he threatened like my words didn't mean anything.

But by then, his threats were talking to my back. I stormed into the bathroom, locked the door, and turned on the faucet. I pulled out my toy and checked to make sure the batteries were good to go.

Unfortunately for him, the sound of running water did very little to drown out the loud, vibrating noise. Just as I was trying to concentrate, the fool started knocking on the door.

"Serena! Are you doing what I think you're doing in there?"

I didn't even bother to answer. I closed my eyes and bit down on my bottom lip. I tried to focus.

"Ain't this some shit! What's that noise?" he barked.

I squeezed my eyes shut tighter.

"Open the damn door!" He pounded louder.

Bliss was in reach. I eased my tool to the spot and tried to relax. It wasn't easy with all the banging and hollering going on outside the bathroom door, but I was determined to do what JahRyan refused to do earlier.

"That's fucked up, Serena!" I heard him say. It sounded like he kicked the door.

But by then, nothing else mattered. That elusive sensation

started to dance in the balls of my feet and I knew I was well on my way.

After JahRyan left, I tried to catch my breath. My body was coated with a thin layer of perspiration, no thanks to his sorry behind.

When I walked out of the bathroom on shaky legs, the only traces of him were the rumpled sheets and the pillows strewn across the room. I didn't care. He should've handled the business and I wouldn't have had to take matters into my own hands. That should teach his ass for next time.

I slipped on a robe and took off downstairs. My kids were away so I could get some and that fool acted like he didn't know what to do.

"Umph, bet next time his ass'll make it do what it do," I muttered as I grabbed a snack and turned on the TV.

The moment I turned the TV on, my eyes focused on the image on the screen. Suddenly, all of my previous frustration washed over me like a heavy wool coat in the middle of a brutal Texas heat wave.

I eased a cigarette between my pursed lips, which formed an airtight seal around the filtered end. My hands trembled when I flicked my lighter on. I brought the flame almost to the tip of the cigarette, and sucked on it in short but hard bursts.

This clown had me wound so tightly, I was a nervous wreck. As I removed the cigarette from my mouth, I inhaled deeply, and allowed the smoke to flow smoothly into my lungs. I closed my eyes and instantly, my body started to relax. Finally, I was able to concentrate on what this fool was saying. The TV was blaring so I wouldn't miss a single word.

"If you're tired of these laws that unfairly hold men hostage, join our fight! We can change these outdated, useless laws and hold these women accountable!" the man on TV yelled. "Paternity fraud is wrong; it's a crime, and it should be treated as such!"

"Who done died and made his ass the sheriff? Talkin' about crimes and shit! What a fucking loser!" I screamed while I grabbed the cigarette from the astray and placed it back between my lips. I sucked in another long drag.

I watched and listened as he talked about the latest case he was involved with. What was he now, some kind of vigilante for whacko baby daddies? He was nothing but a hypocrite! Look at him, standing there in his expensive-ass suit, dressed to the nines, while my ass was over here struggling to make ends meet!

He made me sick to my stomach and I was even more disgusted over the way people seemed to hang on to his every word.

Thank God my cell rang when it did. I might've thrown something at the damn TV.

"Mom, can I spend the night at Latrice's house again?" Semaj yelled the minute I answered.

I was glad she was finally coming out of her shell. Her separation from my ex-husband, James, whom she was named after, had been a difficult time in our lives.

But after a couple of years she seemed to be blossoming. Except here lately, she'd started asking questions about her *real* father! I needed the break that spending the night at her friend's house provided.

Now here she was, interrupting my serenity. Why did kids have to be so damn worrisome? I rolled my eyes and finished my cigarette.

"Mommm," she whined in my ear.

I looked at her daddy on the screen and decided it was time I knocked his cocky ass down a few notches!

PARKER

"Why are all these damn reporters parked outside our house?"

That was how my lovely wife, Roxanne, greeted me as I dragged myself into our house. She stood near the blinds in our living room and peeked outside.

"Did someone kill somebody or something? They're like a bunch of maggots," she said as she left her spot and turned her attention to me.

"You look a mess! What's wrong and why are you so late?"

"It gets crazier and crazier every day." I hated bringing work home and Roxanne hated hearing about the drama from my office most days.

But today she stood in front of me with her hands planted firmly on her hips like she was talking to our two-year-old instead of me.

"What now?"

"A guy shot a woman, took police on a high-speed chase and decided to run into my office instead of surrendering to the police."

Roxanne's eyes grew to the size of grapefruits as she listened in horror.

"Oh my God! Are you okay? Who is he? What about the woman? Is she okay? What happened?"

Her questions were coming faster than I could handle. Suddenly, her stance softened, and she rushed to take me into her arms. Roxanne showered my face and head with kisses.

"I wasn't expecting you to say nothing like that! I can't believe how crazy people are nowadays," she sobbed. "Are you okay?"

"I'm fine. I'm fine. I try to tell these guys, violence is never the answer. I know how they feel. I understand their frustration, but violence doesn't solve a damn thing!"

"Who is he?"

She guided me over to the sofa.

"Where's the baby?" I realized I'd been home for a few minutes and he was nowhere to be found.

"Oh, he's napping. He was extremely fussy so I put him down early."

I looked at her cross-eyed. Putting our son, PJ, down early meant we'd be up all night.

"It's not what you think. I'm taking him to the doctor tomorrow. I think he's picked up a bug or something, so I think he'll sleep right through the night."

"Oh, do we need to take him to the emergency room?"

"No, it's nothing like that. I'm monitoring his fever. I think we can wait until tomorrow." She patted the sofa between us. "C'mon, now tell me what happened today."

I started the story at the beginning, or at least what was the beginning for me.

"Collin Rivers rushed through the door like he was running from someone, and he was, but I had no idea it was the law! After I heard the police on a bullhorn, I talked to him, and he told me what he had done."

"Wait, he's the guy who kept getting arrested over his child support, right?" Roxanne asked.

I nodded.

"What happened?"

"Well, this last time when we finally got the child support payments to stop, he found out he wouldn't get any of his money back and I think he snapped."

"Why did he think he'd get money back?"

"I do the best I can to explain to these guys how the system works. It's still far from perfect, but we've come a long way. I did my best to drive it home to Collin. 'Man, you know regardless of how it turns out, you need to write that money off as a loss,' I'd tell him, but it's like he had his mind set on a recovery anyway."

"So he shoots her?" Roxanne asked.

"Babe, by the time they get to me, many of these men are way past angry. I told him to stop communicating with her. I told him to let his attorney handle the rest, but he was determined."

"Is she...?"

The horror on Roxanne's face told me what she wasn't brave enough to ask.

"No, she's gonna make it. But now, he's looking at even more jail time."

Roxanne leaned in and wrapped her arms around my neck. I could feel her heart racing against my chest.

"Baby, I'm fine," I told her.

"Yeah, this time, but Parker, these men are crazy and I don't want to be on the receiving end of a bad phone call. PJ and I would be lost without you. I know the work you do is important, but the risks," she said.

"Cases like Collin's are rare, Roxy, and you know it. You also know there's no way I'm gonna jeopardize my safety, no matter who I'm working with."

I eased out of her embrace so I could look into her eyes. The last thing I needed was Roxy being a nervous wreck at home when I left the house. I was able to help other men because the home front was calm and solid for me. If my home life went off the deep end, everything would be ruined.

"Look at me," I told her.

Reluctantly, Roxy looked me in the eyes. She sniffled as she did.

"You know the work I do is important. It's my life's mission, and it's what allows us to live comfortably. You and Junior are my world, but this is how I provide for you guys, for us."

She blinked back tears.

"I need you to stay strong. What would I look like, closing up shop because my wife is afraid something bad will happen to me?"

She chuckled a little, but I could tell she was still afraid.

"I hate having to worry about whether one of these crazy women or men will haul off and do something stupid to you," she said.

"And you shouldn't have to. I don't want you worrying about any of that. That's why the courts have started doing referrals much earlier and we're able to intervene before the men even think about losing it. Hey, how long have I been going through this?"

I slipped my hand under her chin and tilted her face upward.

"How long?"

"Too damn long." Roxy chuckled. She was still sniffling.

"Yeah, but long enough that you know I know what I'm doing, right?"

She nodded her head slightly.

I had gotten through to her.

"Now let's eat. After the day I've had, I'm hungry. I don't wanna have to think about Collin until it's time to go back to court," I said and moved to get up.

Roxanne tugged at my leg as I stood.

"What do you mean, time to go back to court? What's that got to do with you? You going to court for him still?" she asked.

I turned to look back at her. "He's still a client, Roxy. What sense would it make for me to drop him now? Besides, I'm sure the police are gonna call me in to question me about his surrender and all that stuff."

For a moment, she remained stoic on the sofa. I was hungry and not in the mood to keep this conversation going, but Roxy could be like a dog with a bone when she wanted.

The moment my cell rang, I used it as an excuse to leave the room.

"It's my attorney." I held the phone up toward Roxy as if she could see the caller ID. Then I walked out of the room to take the call.

"Parker Redman here," I answered.

"Parker, I'm ready to talk about that lawsuit. We just got the green light, so let's meet to get our ducks lined up," William Smith said.

For a moment his words didn't register. We had been battling for years and now he was saying we could move forward? I wondered momentarily if my ears were playing games on me.

"Parker, you there?"

"Yes, I'm here."

"Did you hear what I just said? The judge has ruled in our favor. We can move forward with our lawsuit. I say let's go after all of those bastards. The Attorney General, the county, hell, the city even!"

"So we're really gonna do it?" I asked.

"Listen, a federal judge said after what you've been through, we can sue any damn body we want! Let's meet tomorrow. I'll come by your office. Oh, and Parker, this might be a good time to call some of your media buddies. We want this thing to go viral."

"Okay, I'll see you in the morning."

I must've looked pretty crazy as I stood there with the cell phone held tightly clutched to my chest. Roxy snapped her fingers in front of my eyes and pulled me back from my thoughts.

"What now?"

"Nothing. I mean, it's nothing bad. I finally got the go-ahead to file suit against the state and the city for the paternity fraud with Serena and Lachez," I said.

I looked into Roxy's eyes and it made me wonder whether she was up for yet another fight. But even the fear I saw wasn't enough to make me throw in the towel after all I'd been through.

EBONI

Shawnathon McGee was mean-muggin' me like I was supposed to be scared. It was obvious he didn't know who the hell he was dealing with. As I stood outside our house in my pajamas and robe freezing my butt off, I was pissed. But I was not about to let him get the best of me. No, not this time.

The officer looked at me like she didn't understand what I said.

Her partner had Shawnathon hitched up near his truck. I wanted them to throw his butt in jail! I was tired of him and his antics. Someone needed to put a stop to his childish behavior before this thing got out of hand.

"I'm telling you what the fool said. He was banging on my door and windows. I was scared for my life!" I eyed Shawnathon from the corner of my eye. He stood several feet away as he talked with the other officer.

All of our nosey-ass neighbors were outside. They stood and gawked like they didn't have anything better to do at midnight. The old hag across the street even had the nerve to plop down in her rocker with a bowl of popcorn. All I thought was, they'd better be glad the law was out here; otherwise, I'd give all their nosey behinds something to stare at.

I didn't like any of my neighbors; they couldn't mind their business to save their sorry lives. Just like now, was it really necessary to be outside all up in our business? Quite surely there was something else they could've been doing.

"So, Mrs. McGee," the officer started.

"I am not married to that fool. My last name is Brown!" I snapped. I knew she was not trying to be funny.

"Oh, Ms. Brown, so your..."

Was she trying to clown?

"Ex-fiancé," I finished her sentence.

"Yes, your ex-fiancé. How do you spell his name?"

"It's like Johnathon, except you replace the John with Shawn," I said.

She jotted it down in her notepad, then looked back up at me. Who didn't know this boy's name in this city?

"Okay, so Mr. McGee, he's your ex-fiancé. What exactly did he say to threaten your life?"

I rolled my eyes and sighed. I was so sick and tired of going through this mess with Shawnathon I wanted to scream. All he had to do was pay his child support on time, and we wouldn't have a problem. But could he do that? Hell no! Her question took me back to that moment when the loud, booming knock made my heart feel like it was about to leap from my chest.

"Open up this goddamn door!"

I rushed into the twins' room, but they were still sound asleep.

"I know what you did, bitch! I know what you did!"

Shawnathon had a short fuse. We never really got along good once I got pregnant and wouldn't have an abortion. True enough, he did say from day one that he didn't want any kids, but I knew a kid was the only way to get what *I* wanted. I craved a life on easy street! It wasn't really about him. This plan had been in motion long before he came onto the scene.

Once I got pregnant, Ulonda and I felt like we were on the run. We were so scared he'd come and try to push me down a flight of stairs or anything so that I'd lose the pregnancy. He hated me so much because I wanted to keep the babies.

After the kids were born, his rage seemed to be off and on. He'd come over and would try to smooth things over. Sometimes I got weak and even gave him a little taste. After that, he'd hook me up and we'd be good to go. When that happened, it made me think we had a chance, that we could make it. But all of that changed when Elisa came into the picture.

Once he got with her evil ass, it was like I was suddenly invisible. That was okay, though. I had something for his ass! You can best believe that!

"Ma'am? Ms. Brown?" The officer looked at me like I might need some kind of medical attention.

"Ouch!" I yelled. A bright light was flicked into my eyes, damn near blinding me on the spot. "Why'd you do that?" I asked. I rubbed my eyes with my hands.

"You weren't responding and your pupils were dilated, so I was trying to make sure you were okay," the cop said.

"I'll be a lot better when you guys arrest that bastard!" I said.

I tried to look in Shawnathon's direction, but the officer stepped to the side and blocked my view.

"Let's focus on our discussion here. My partner is taking care of him," she said. "Finish your story about what happened."

"He's extremely violent. That's why I have the restraining order. I figured once he found out about some of the things that happened in our relationship, he might get upset, so I didn't want to be a sitting duck," I explained.

"Do you have a copy of the order?" she asked.

"Yeah, it's in the house."

"And what does the order stipulate?" she asked.

"He's supposed to stay away from me! Isn't that enough? If he's supposed to stay away from me, I don't understand why he's here," I said. The more I listened to her talk, the more pissed I became.

"Are you gonna take him to jail or not?" All this other mess was not helping the situation.

"Ma'am, we need to get his side of the story. Once I listen to your side of the story, then we'll talk to him and see what happened."

"I'm trying to tell you what happened! He's not supposed to be here! Why won't you listen to me?" I felt myself getting flustered.

"Ma'am, if you don't calm down, I'm going to have to restrain you," she said.

The moment those words fell from her mouth, it hit me. He had gotten to her, too!

She knew exactly who Shawnathon was! After all, he was a hometown boy from the Third Ward who'd made it big. He had been a basketball phenom who was a local star at Madison High School, Texas Southern University, and then he was drafted in the second round for the Houston Rockets.

Couple that with the fact that he had a winning personality, he was real slick in the mouth, and women, young and old, loved his dirty drawers. I should've known when she was asking about how to spell his damn name!

They fell for anything that flowed from his mouth. If he wanted, he could sell water in a rainstorm. I may not like him anymore, but he was fine as all get out, too. When we used to go out to eat, the waitresses would fall all over themselves to wait on us so they could gawk at him.

He was the type who not only looked good, but he knew how good he looked, and he took full advantage of his popularity. He may have been fine, but I knew for certain I was a dime piece myself. So while he was walking around thinking he was Denzel, I was turning heads myself. Besides, this wasn't my first rodeo. I'd been connected to some pretty high-profile men; as a matter of fact, those were the only type Ulonda and I were interested in.

But I had no idea snagging a rich man would be this much trouble either.

I already knew we were headed for trouble, but I never thought things would get as bad as they were. I listened to the officer run down a bunch of crap about why she couldn't do anything to Shawnathon. I wanted to tell her to save it, that I'd been down this road before.

The more she talked, the more images of others just like her popped into my head. After a while, they all started to look and sound the same.

He's so much better-looking in person!

On TV, he looks smaller.

His eyes, they're so dreamy!

And that smile, could it be any brighter?

Yes, everyone loved Shawnathon McGee. But if they thought that was gonna make me ease up on what I had in store for him, they had another thing coming!

I glanced over at the officer who was supposed to be interrogating him and it looked like Shawnathon was busy throwing around his autograph! I was fit to be tied!

"Just tell him to go home and leave me alone," I finally said to the officer, who was treating me more like a criminal than the person who called for help.

Ulonda's words rang loudly in my head. She was absolutely right. This experience made me see firsthand that no one was gonna protect me from that fool!

LACHEZ

"Yes, Darlene. I am doing everything I'm supposed to be doing." I rolled my eyes as I listened to my mother question me like she was a special state prosecutor.

"So I thought I was seeing the kids yesterday. Why are you talking about this weekend?"

As I talked to Darlene, I watched Toni walk out of her bedroom wearing a T-shirt and some panties. I wasn't hating, but I only hoped I could bounce back like she did. Toni had her shit together. From her place, to her ride, and her gear, her shit was tight. Right now, I didn't have a damn thing of my own and it was not a good feeling.

Toni strolled into the kitchen, opened the cabinet and grabbed a couple of shot glasses. I watched as she opened the freezer and pulled the massive bottle of Belvedere from it.

My head was still swimming from all the drinking we had done the night before, and she wanted more? Darlene had rattled off a bunch of crap in my ear and nothing she said made me happy.

"Look here, Darlene, Saturday! I mean it, and I don't want no excuses. You need to bring my kids and bring them Saturday or I'm gonna have to come and get them myself!" I pressed the END button and turned my attention to Toni.

"Girl, my head is pounding. I don't know about yours," she said as she offered me one of the shot glasses she'd filled up.

"What's this for?"

"Get rid of the hangover. I'm struggling over here," Toni said. Before I could ask another question, she took the shot glass to the head, then refilled her own.

"This is supposed to be the good stuff; not sure why we're hung over," she said.

I swallowed my shot. It burned going down, and made my eyes water. The crap Darlene said still swam around in my head. If she thought I was gonna sit back and let her take my kids, she had another thing coming.

"You okay over there?" Toni asked.

"Yeah, just tripping off Darlene."

Toni started to refill my shot glass. I was not sure if I needed another shot.

As we were about to take some more of the Belvedere, there was a knock at the door.

"You expecting company?" I asked Toni.

"No, I don't like surprises," she said.

"Go put on some clothes. I'll get it," I told her.

I got up and headed for the door while Toni rushed back to her room.

"Who's there?" I asked.

"Open the door!" someone yelled.

Immediately, I scanned the room, looking for something I could use as a weapon if needed. Suddenly, Toni rushed out of the room like the place was on fire.

She pulled the door open and I was stunned by the vision in front of us.

"Oh my God!" Toni cried excitedly.

I was speechless.

He stood there and looked at me blinking as if he was trying to adjust his eyes.

"Junie?" I managed.

"Mama," he mumbled.

My baby looked like a grown-ass man! He was dressed in a suit that was tailored to fit his frame. The suit, the tight haircut, and his facial hair lined up with extra precision made him look like my baby playing a bomb-ass game of dress-up.

"Boy, you better get over here and act like you glad to see your mama," I cried.

He fell into my arms and I held him for a long time. He was so big I could hardly believe this was my oldest child. I looked at him real good. It made me do a quick mental check about some serious shit I needed to get right.

EBONI

I peeked into my kids' room to make sure they were still asleep.

"Girl, I was so pissed," I said into the phone.

"So what happened?" Ulonda asked.

"When I saw him over there signing stuff for people, I already knew what time it was. It's like he turns on the charm and everybody is lining up to eat out the palm of his hands."

"What are you gonna do about him?"

"I really don't know. Think about it. When I call the police, they find a reason to let him go. It's like I have to wait until the fool does something stupid before anybody will check his simple behind."

"Did you get what we talked about last time?" Ulonda asked.

"Yeah, I had to order some from this military surplus store, so I'm waiting for it to come in."

"Okay, good. You really should've taken those officers' badge numbers. If that shit wasn't a huge violation, I don't know what was."

"Wait, that's my other line," I said to Ulonda. I pulled the phone from my ear to see who was calling. I didn't recognize the number but answered anyway.

"Hello?"

"Bitch, you're gonna pay!" a voice said.

I ended that call and clicked back to Ulonda.

"That's him playing on the phone again," I told her.

"When is this gonna be over? What is going on with the two of you?" Ulonda asked.

Out of habit, I walked over to the window and looked out the blinds. I needed to make sure he wasn't trying to come and kick down the front door.

"I'm gonna call my attorney tomorrow. I don't know why he won't get it over with; instead, his lawyer keeps trying to delay the hearing."

"Are you nervous?" Ulonda asked.

I moved away from the window.

"I don't know if I'd say I'm nervous, but some of these stories I see on TV make me feel like I'm not sure what's gonna happen in court. That's why I'm gonna call my attorney tomorrow. I'm tired of this mess."

"Good luck, and make sure you call and let me know what's going on," Ulonda said.

After talking to her on the phone for nearly an hour, I walked around the house and checked the locks.

With the kids asleep, there wasn't much for me to do. The house was so big that, at times, I felt completely alone and a little scared.

I eased into the massive cushions on the sofa. These were the times I hated most. Left alone with my thoughts and memories, I started to ask myself how things fell apart between Shawnathon and me.

"You workin' the hell outta that dress, Eb," Shawnathon said.

"You like it, babe?" I asked.

When he looked at me like I was a thick, juicy T-bone and he was a hungry Rottweiler, I knew I had made the right choice. The metallic bandage dress looked perfect on my body. It showed off all of my curves and knowing he liked it made me beam with pride.

"Girl, you tryin' to make us late, walking around looking like that," he joked.

We were getting dressed for a party at one of his teammates' houses. Shawnathon looked dapper in his three-piece suit. Where were paparazzi when you needed them?

"C'mere, girl." Shawnathon looked like he was about to jump my bones right there.

"Shawnathon, quit. We're gonna be late. You're gonna mess up my hair and makeup," I whined.

He grabbed me by the waist and buried his face into my bosom.

"Quit playin'," I squealed. I was enjoying every minute of the attention.

"Girl, what am I gonna do with you?" he asked.

"Love me," I said.

Shawnathon plastered kisses all over my face and neck as he loosened his grip around my waist.

"Stop! We're gonna be late; let's go," I cried.

"Aw, girl, you know you want all this good stuff. Quit playing hard to get," he teased.

I feigned frustration. "Shawnathon, if you mess up my makeup, we're really gonna be late," I threatened.

He kept playing, and I kept laughing.

As I struggled to get away from him, he pulled me closer until our faces were inches apart. When our eyes met, I felt my heart racing in my chest.

"You know you the bomb, right?" he said softly.

I felt special being in his arms. My favorite was hugging up with him when we were fully clothed. When we kissed, pyrotechnics literally went off. I knew from the moment we first met at a jazz festival in Cancun that we'd hit it off.

After the kiss, I pulled back and looked into his eyes.

"If we don't leave now, we're not gonna make it," I said.

"Is that a promise?" he teased.

"Come on, silly; we need to go!"

When he finally let me go, I rushed to the mirror to check my reflection. After touching up my makeup and fussing with my hair, we were finally ready to go.

Being on Shawnathon McGee's arm was like winning the Miss America title. Everywhere we went, people gawked. I saw envy in the eyes of other women and lust in the eyes of men. We were a power couple and I wanted the bliss I felt with him to last forever.

"Shawnathon McGee, over here!"

"Shawnathon! Shawnathon!"

I loved being out with him in public. Everyone was always vying for his attention, most of them stumbling all over themselves to get him to notice. Being with Shawnathon was a high for me.

Boom!

Boom!

Boom!

I bolted upright and gasped for air. I had fallen asleep. Panic gripped my heart and squeezed as I looked around, trying to catch my bearings.

I was on the sofa. It was dark inside, and the noise came again.

"Oh God!"

I glanced toward the hall, hoping the kids wouldn't wake up.

"Someone's at the door," I muttered as I got up from the sofa and shook off the sleepiness.

"Coming!" I yelled. My eyes searched the room for a clock, but it was so dark I couldn't focus on the one in the living room. I wanted to get to the door before the loud knock came again.

"Who is it?" I yelled.

"It's David," the voice answered.

I froze where I stood. Alarm quickly settled in.

"Who?"

"Um, my name is David," he repeated.

Fear washed over me as I looked around in the dark. My cell was on the coffee table. I reached for it, then returned to the door.

"Who is it?" I asked again.

"Ah, you don't know me. My name is David."

That's when I glanced down at the cell phone and saw 1:59 illuminating in the darkness. It was two in the morning!

"Who are you again?"

"Look, why don't you open the door? My name is David. Shawnathon told me it was cool for me to come through," he said.

"It is two in the morning! I don't know who the hell you are, but get away from my front door!"

I eased up on my toes to look through the peephole. I was so angry, I wanted to open the door and bitch-slap David, then do the same to Shawnathon. David was a big, husky-looking guy. His starched jeans were sagging and he wore a doo-rag around his head. He stood at my door glancing in both directions like he was looking for someone.

"Ah, Ma, whassup? Why you gotta be getting all hostile and shit?"

I jumped back when it sounded like he tried to turn the door knob.

"I've called the police!" I screamed.

"What kind of businesswoman are you? Shit, I got paper. Shawnathon said it was cool," he said.

"Get the hell away from my front door and I swear, if you come back here again," I said.

The noises from sirens in the distance couldn't have sounded at a better time.

Through the peephole I saw David scramble away from my front door.

I hadn't dialed 9-1-1 yet because I was still trying to wrap my mind around the fact that Shawnathon's simple behind would send a perfect stranger to my door.

Damn! Right when I thought Shawnathon's low-down butt couldn't surprise me, he proved me wrong.

SERENA

I liked everything I looked at on her website. The information about Gloria Allred, the celebrity attorney who fought for women and minorities, actually had me excited and hyped.

"You think she'd be interested in my case?" I asked my neighbor and good friend, Loren Harris.

"Girl, I don't see why she wouldn't be," Loren said.

Loren had been here for the last hour. Even though I usually tried to stay clear of female friends, me and her got along pretty good.

I moved my eyes away from the computer screen for a sec and leaned back in my chair. All kinds of thoughts raced through my head.

"Can you imagine the look on that fool's face when he sees me standing next to Gloria Allred during our press conference?"

Loren jumped up from her chair.

"Damn, girl! You better be dressed to the nines! I mean, think about it, anytime you see Gloria, she cleaner than the board of health, baby!"

"Umph, umph humph, two bad bitches! Girl, what if CNN picks this up?" I was excited as all get-out.

"I could see you on *The View* with this girl. I mean, think about it! You know Sherri is a mama, so is Elizabeth's crazy behind! Girl, this is right up their alley!"

The excitement in Loren's eyes was gassing me up.

"*The View*?" I asked. "You know they always giving away a bunch of free stuff!"

She rushed closer to me.

"Their free stuff would be just the beginning. Think about it. You are talking about a problem that millions of women experience every single day. Your deadbeat won't pay for his kid. Girl, I see all kinds of paper opportunities."

"Money? What? You mean when he pays?" I asked. I wanted to be very clear about what she meant.

She kneeled down in front of me. "Serena, his money is chump change, girl. I'm saying you could travel around the country talking to other women. You could go to sororities, churches, hell, anywhere you find women with kids," she said. "They'd be willing to pay big for your personal story, especially with your background, how you know the ins and outs of the system!"

Loren held up her hand and allowed her thumb to rub across the tips of her other fingers; she did the universal symbol for money.

"Girl, we could clean up!"

The thought never crossed my mind.

"I *could* do that, huh?"

"Shit yeah!" Loren said.

"So what do we do? How do I get in touch with these sororities and churches that would be willing to pay?"

"You need someone who will be like a middle man, or woman," Loren quickly corrected. The smile on her face told me she had an idea of who *that* middle woman might be.

I got up and started to walk around the room. My juices had really started to flow. I liked the idea of getting paid to go and talk to people. Money had been tight lately, so getting paid to run my mouth? That was gonna be like a no-brainer for me. Hell, they'd have to shut me up.

I turned to face Loren.

"So you can get people to pay me to talk to them?" I wanted to make sure I understood what she was saying.

"When I used to live in the shelter, they'd put on these classes. And I remember them bringing in regular, ordinary people to talk to us," she said.

"Regular? Ordinary?" I was too outdone.

She picked up on my attitude real quick.

"You know what I'm saying," Loren tried to defend.

I understood what she said, but I needed to make sure she understood what I was saying, too.

"There's nothing *regular* or *ordinary* about me," I said.

Loren rolled her eyes.

My hands flew to my hips. Once I twisted my neck, she should've known I was hot.

"If we're gonna work together, you need to get it straight. I ain't trying to work with nobody who thinks I'm some *plain*, *ordinary* chick," I told her.

"You're reading too much into that," she protested. She even got up and came toward me. "Serena, what I'm trying to say is, most times when you think of a speaker, it's usually a celebrity or maybe an educator, but you, as a single mom who's not famous, a lot of people can relate to you because they can probably see themselves in you."

I looked at her for a long time before I said another word.

"They'd be looking at you and thinking, she's just like me, a young, single mother who's struggling to try to get her deadbeat to pay!"

Even though I didn't want to show it just yet, I was real excited about everything she had said. The thought of me traveling the country, the world, talking to other women about shit that came second-nature for me, had me jumping for joy on the inside.

"So if I said yes right now, what's the first thing you would do? You know, if I agree to let you be my middle woman," I said.

"Girl, I'd get a list of shelters, sororities, and megachurches together," Loren said.

"Megachurches?"

"Yeah, we need to be talking to people who got money. I know I told you about the shelters, and we can reach out to some of them too, but I wanna go for the big-money clients."

"Oooh, clients. I love the sound of that."

"We can do this," Loren said.

The way she looked me dead in the eyes and insisted that we could do this made me believe it.

"Okay, well, let's look at Gloria's site some more. You still think we should try to reach out to her?" I asked.

We rushed back to the computer. Gloria's page was really sharp and polished.

"We need to get you a website, too," Loren said.

"A website?"

"When you're a speaker, you need stuff like that; business cards, a YouTube channel, all of that kind of stuff," Loren said. "You know what? I need to get a notepad so we can start brainstorming now."

I waited for Loren to grab a pen and notepad. When she flipped through it and found a blank page, I started talking.

"First things first, I want that bastard to pay! I want his money. Then I want to expose him as the fraud he is!"

My intentions were to see if Loren had a problem with that. When she didn't flinch, I knew we'd be able to work together.

PARKER

As I sat across from my attorney, I snuck glances at Roxy's face. I wanted to come to this meeting alone, but she insisted on being here.

I eased my hand onto her leg and massaged firmly. She was holding our son.

"You okay?" I asked. She seemed real tense, like she was struggling not to talk to me. I knew she had a lot on her mind.

"I wish they would make this fast," she said in a hushed voice. She also kept looking over her shoulder toward the door. "What's taking him so long?"

"He's wrapping up another meeting or something. He'll be here soon," I said.

That was part of the reason I wanted to come alone. I had waited years for my right to fight this thing. I know she probably felt like this had ended years ago when the court determined I *hadn't* fathered a child by Lachez Baker.

Lachez Baker was some random woman who hooked up with my best friend's ex, Serena Carson, to attack me because she felt like I had slighted her. It was one of the most difficult times in our lives. I understood why Roxy would want to forget, but for me, a whole 'nother chapter was just beginning.

From the moment my private investigator found Lachez and I confronted her about the false child support order she had against me, I knew I was in the clear. But it took a lot longer for the court to make it legal. Back then, the state of Texas had no recourse for something like that. I didn't get my money back and no one cared about the time I had spent in jail. We paid close to $50,000 before the nightmare was over.

Two years, that's how long it took! It took two years for the court to declare me innocent of the delinquent child support charge. Then it took another year for my lawyer to get the wording correct and get my record expunged. The entire situation was still a real bad memory for us. In the end we had to borrow against our retirement to pull our lives back together. It had been one hellish, uphill struggle.

The door creaked open and William Smith, or Bill as I called him, walked in. I could tell my misery had been good to him. I wondered who his tailor was and how much that suit had set him back. I stood as he walked all the way into his massive office.

"Parker!" He greeted me excitedly with a tight handshake. We hugged and I patted his back a couple of times. Before he turned his attention to Roxy and the baby, he said, "It's been a while, my friend; it's been a while." Then, he turned to my wife.

"Oh, Roxy, he's beautiful," Bill gushed. He inched closer and looked down at our boy. My son, Parker Jr., was sleeping.

"Thank you, Bill," she said, completely stoic.

Usually, when people uttered a single word about the baby, Roxy's entire face would light up like a Christmas tree. This time, however, her expression remained solemn.

"You ready to do this?" Bill asked. He couldn't hide his excitement, even if he tried. As he walked around to the back of his massive desk, I tried to calm my emotions.

"Is this something we have to do?" Roxy asked before I could react or respond to Bill's question.

My head whipped in her direction, but she was focused on Bill and never even flinched.

"I think we've been through enough. We're happy now. We finally have our child. It's over, and Parker's organization is doing well. Why would we want to dig up all those painful memories?" Her words poured out like liquid flowing powerfully from a faucet.

As Roxy talked, Bill's eyes kept shifting to me. I could only imagine what he was thinking.

He was probably like, *what did she think we'd been working on all these years?* It sounded as if she'd been rehearsing this tirade. I let her get it out. I sat quietly and didn't utter a sound.

"We're in a good place now. I don't see the point in digging this up again."

"Well, I can understand why this would be upsetting. That was a difficult time for us all," he said. I knew what he meant, but Roxy's face twisted into a scowl.

I thought she was going to drop the baby. I saw the worms coming out the can before he even had a clue.

"*Us*?" she deadpanned. It was as if the man had insulted her, her mama, and the baby!

Before Bill could take his words back or even fix them, Roxy exploded like a blown gasket. "You don't even know the half of it! Our marriage, our livelihoods, our lives, everything was in jeopardy. We didn't know if we were coming or going! We went broke! Our friends, neighbors, and even our relatives questioned whether my husband had any morals at all! No, no one understands the pain, humiliation, and downright degradation we went through," she huffed.

I was glad when her voice started cracking under the weight of the heavy emotions.

Bill nodded appropriately and allowed her to get it all out too.

Then he quietly said, "I understand Roxy, but shouldn't somebody have to pay for all that you've been through? Is it right that the two of you had to struggle to re-establish yourselves? Shouldn't someone be held accountable?"

I couldn't have asked it better myself. Finally, Roxy turned to me, her eyes were filled with water, and her nostrils flared. She said, "So, now you want revenge?"

Her words dripped with sarcasm, as if revenge would've been a shameful thing to want.

"It's not about revenge. It's about saying to the county, and the state, that what they did to me, to us, was wrong and we want them to pay!"

The expression on her face was a mixture between cynicism and frustration. She sighed and shook her head.

"We'll never see a dime of any money, Parker," she insisted.

"It's not about the money; it's about much more. But Roxy, I need to know I have your support with this thing. I can't be out there fighting for other men, fighting for vindication, and fighting at home," I said.

Roxy looked away as the baby began to stir, but I could tell she was simply trying to swallow back tears. I knew this wasn't gonna be easy for her, but she needed to understand this was *bigger* than her.

LACHEZ

I held my man-child so tightly my grip probably threatened to crack his spine. He looked real good, felt fantastic and smelled even better. My baby had been takin' real good care of himself, and even though I was away for some of his crucial years, I could see he hadn't missed a single step.

It wasn't until she cleared her throat that I realized someone was with him. I opened my eyes at the sound and saw an older woman standing off to the side. Who the hell was she, his counselor, probation officer or something?

We broke our embrace but I held on to his fingers. I didn't want to ever turn him loose. I locked eyes with my oldest and it was like love all over again. I remembered the day the doctors put the little mocha-colored bundle into my arms. Junie had melted my heart from that moment on.

He turned his head when she made another sound.

"Oh, uh, mom, this is Pricilla Douser." He grinned.

Pricilla stepped up like she was the first runner-up at the Miss Universe pageant. It had to be Miss Universe because her old ass couldn't qualify for Miss America.

I looked down at her bony little hand as it hung toward me in the air.

"Ms. Lachez, you don't know how excited I am to meet you." She smiled all giddy like. She knew damn well she was way too old to be calling me Ms., but I'd deal with that later.

My eyes danced from Junie's simple-looking smile to her old-looking face. Were those crow's feet at the corners of her eyes? She was about five feet five inches and had a medium build. Her jewelry was more than what was necessary for a mid-afternoon meeting, and her clothes screamed money.

Her hair looked real good, like when you can tell white people spend a considerable amount of time in the salon. I didn't want to say anything, but my mind was working overtime trying to understand not just *what* she was doing here, but *why* she would be excited about meeting me.

I flashed her a weak smile and was relieved when Toni hollered for us to come inside and shut her front door.

"Ms. Toni, I've heard so much about you, too," she said as she stepped across the threshold and completely into the living room. She needed to kill that Ms. stuff with her old geriatric behind!

My heart shattered when I realized that Junie had dropped my hand but still held on to hers as she walked in. What the hell?

"I only wish I could have the type of friendship you two women share. You know when Junie shares stories about your adventures, I'm like all women should go through life with a friend like the two of you are to each other."

I could read Toni's mind before she even said a word.

"So, Junie, you been talking about us, huh?" She glanced at my son, who didn't dare look in my direction.

I may have been absent from his life momentarily, but a mother's words were never far away. He should've known that putting folks all up in my business was not *the* business at all! I'd have to get in that ass later for that!

"And knowing what all you've had to go through to raise your kids as a single mom." This stranger rubbed me the wrong way with every word she spoke. "I just have such admiration for you," she said.

It was subtle, but the look that passed between Junie and her spoke volumes. Because the moment her eyes connected with his, it was like she checked herself and stopped speaking damn near midsentence.

Suddenly, a heat wave washed over me. I began to feel light-headed and thought I might need to hold on to something to help support my weight.

"Ma, I got something for you," Junie said, sounding every bit like the twelve-year-old I remembered.

My son and I shared a special bond. Before I went away, we made things happen when they needed to. I had trained my boy in the art of survival by any means necessary. I understood how hard it was for a black man and I didn't want my boys scraping and struggling like I had to.

Now I'd be the first to admit some of my methods may not have been the most conventional, but my kids ain't never had to worry about a missed meal, the lights and gas ain't never been turned off, and all of this was done without me having to punch anybody's time clock.

"Did you bring it?" he whispered to this woman who was so close to my child that it began to make me uncomfortable. But I didn't wanna play my hand just yet. I peeped the show as it unfolded.

"Oh, yes, I have it right here," she said as she fumbled through a large designer tote bag.

If I had to say something about her, I could say that she obviously had some taste. My mind was working overtime trying to remember the price tag I saw on that new Kate Spade tote bag.

This woman was a mess, whoever she was.

"I know it's in here," she huffed.

The room was so quiet I could hear someone breathing. We sat silent, all eyes on this older chick, as she franticly searched through her bag like she was struggling to find what she needed.

"I put it in there before we left, so I know it's in here," she mumbled.

I wanted to ask what *it* was. When Junie eased closer to the woman and placed his hand on her forearm, I was a bit baffled.

But again, instantly, her demeanor changed.

"Calm down, I know you're nervous, but I told you, my moms is cool," he said.

If I hadn't seen this with my own two eyes, you wouldn't be able to tell me that my once frail, thin boy had this kind of effect on a grown ass woman! What kind of wickedness had gone down in my absence? It was like he suddenly became the *woman whisperer* or something.

Right before our eyes, the woman took a deep breath, closed her eyes, and muttered a few words to herself. Toni and I exchanged knowing glances. I knew my girl would have a whole lot to say once this foolishness was over.

"It's in there. Just calm down and take your time," he encouraged.

Again, she exhaled, her eyes snapped open and she started going through the contents of her bag, this time calmer.

Smile lines suddenly appeared at the sides of her mouth when her features turned from distressed to relief.

"You're right, babe, it's right here." She smiled at my child.

The next move she made nearly cost her her life. It wasn't the thick, fat envelope she pulled from her bag of tricks, but the very adult, very X-rated, open-mouth kiss she plastered against my child's mouth that made me see colors.

"Whoa! What the hell is wrong with you?" I screamed at her before I could help myself. "You kissin' a child like that!"

Now all eyes were on me.

EBONI

I was tired of living in fear! If there was a creak in the middle of the night, I'd jump, sometimes out of a dead sleep. If the house settled, I'd grab for the phone. Every little sound was a sign to me that Shawnathon was trying to get me.

I was also mad at myself because I didn't take down the officers' badge numbers. How could they not have enforced the protective order just because it had expired days earlier? So all he had to do was wait the order out, then kill me!

If only someone would arrest his punk ass, I wouldn't have to live in fear. I couldn't wait for our court date to come because I was sick of him and all his stupid scare tactics. Shawnathon thought I'd run and hide, and he'd get to live his life like he was the perfect man that every woman wanted.

Days after that freak showed up at my front door, I was back in my lawyer's office.

"I will see if we can expedite things. If this is how he's going to behave, I don't see any reason we should provide any kind of courtesy," she said as she banged the keys on her computer's keyboard.

I pulled my hands up to my face and rubbed my eyes.

"Oh, sweetie, I'm sorry you're going through this. But I can assure you, we are gonna make him pay! There's no question about it."

"I'm running out of options here. We need to do something fast. Do you think the note will hold up in court? And will it matter that he waited so long to bring it out?"

My attorney, Nia Perkins-Ross, was more than confident about what she'd be able to do for the kids and me. She even agreed to take the case with no money up front. I was sure Shawnathon's name played a major role in that decision, but I didn't care.

I could tell she was in deep thought by the way her lower lids tightened and she contemplated the answer to my question. That made me worry, of course.

"It was a stupid, drunken prank. I don't even remember signing the dumb thing," I said.

When Nia looked up at me and said, "Tell me how it went again," I wanted to burst out crying on the spot. But I held my composure, exhaled real hard, and then went back in time.

"When we first met, everything was perfect! With his money, good looks, and his charismatic personality, women used to literally fling themselves at him. I remember feeling real special because I was the chosen one!"

"You like it here?" Shawnathon asked as he snuggled up close to me on the blanket we shared.

I loved it. It was a perfect spring evening, no humidity with a gentle breeze. We were at a throwback concert at the Cynthia Woods Mitchell Pavilion, an outdoor amphitheater in one of Houston's wealthiest suburbs.

The theater itself was nestled next to the lush, piney woods forest in the Woodlands. We were on the hillside and there was not a single lawn chair in sight, which meant we had a clear view of the stage.

I could've sworn every female eye was on us on our blanket. After all, Shawnathon McGee was considered one of Houston's most eligible bachelors and *I* had snagged him!

"This is real nice," I said. We were sipping on wine and had been eating snacks from the picnic basket we'd packed for the outing.

"I can't believe you've never been here," he said.

"I know, right?" I took a bite of the Frenchy's drumstick and savored the taste. Frenchy's Chicken was a Houston institution, and Shawnathon said he wanted everything to be perfect, so we stopped there before going out to the concert.

We started our day at brunch where I had bottomless Mimosas, then we went to the Galleria for some shopping. He was generous and only asked that I try on everything before he bought it.

Once the concert wrapped up, we melted into the crowd leaving the pavilion. We were literally sandwiched into throngs of people slowly walking out. That meant everyone was in earshot of our conversation.

"I got us a room at the Woodlands Waterway Marriott," he said.

"Oooh weee, can I tag along?" this big-breasted, bottle-bleached blonde asked loud enough for me to hear.

I cut my eyes at her audacity, and her friends giggled. They looked like a pack of sluts in their denim cut-offs, and itty-bitty tank and tube tops and hooker heels.

It was hard but I ignored them. Shawnathon had the nerve to chuckle, like that was amusing. I was used to women boldly propositioning him—they showed no shame! Mentally, I double-dog dared him to say something, but I guess he knew better.

We kept moving along and by the time I maneuvered us away from those skanks, three more were waiting right near the parking lot. They were black, but just as shameless.

"I told you that was Shawnathon McGee," I heard one of them whisper loudly to her friend.

I all but started speed-walking at that point, trying to put much distance between us and them. Right when we made it to Shawnathon's Escalade, one of them had the nerve to call out to him.

"Umm, excuse me, Shawnathon?" she sang.

He kept walking. He walked me to the passenger side, opened my door, and I climbed inside. As I buckled up, I turned and glanced over my shoulder.

That's when I saw him signing one of the women's breasts while her friends looked on giggling! The other one was taking pictures with her phone!

Oh, I was hot.

I was about to hop out of the truck and snatch him up by his collar, but he gave her back her Sharpie and finally got in the truck.

"These females are a trip," he said.

"Yeah, tell me about it," I muttered. I didn't want to come off insecure. I looked good and could hold my own against any of the skanks we'd encountered, but still, what was up with some respect!

When Shawnathon looked over his shoulder as he backed out of the parking spot, I screamed.

"Oh God! You nearly hit her!"

"Who?"

That's when we saw her. Some chick who was breathing hard like she'd run a marathon to catch up to his car. But when she grabbed onto the back door's handle while screaming my man's name, I was really through!

I rolled my eyes at the desperation.

By the time we finally made it to the hotel, we were both exhausted.

"Let's grab some drinks at the bar," he suggested.

I was okay with that until I saw the suite. The view from our room was absolutely to die for. The hotel sat right on the waterfront, and the colorful lights from restaurants and shops that lined the walkway illuminated the night.

It was by far the nicest room I'd ever seen in my life. It was more than enough for the two of us, but it had a bar, a sitting area, and a separate bedroom.

"Why you wanna go downstairs? We can stay up here and get sloppy drunk together, in private," I suggested as seductively as I could.

"Oh yeah, that's cool, babe, but I told a couple of my teammates we'd meet them down at the bar for some drinks. How about we have a couple down there, then come up when you're ready?"

I really didn't want to go, but afraid of disappointing or upsetting him, I agreed anyway.

"Only two drinks, you promise?" I asked.

After showering, we changed and made our way downstairs.

Nearly three hours later, I had to hold Shawnathon up, literally, as we stumbled off the elevator. Each time I inhaled, I felt like I was gonna throw up. We drank way too much and, of course, everyone else picked up the tab.

Being with Shawnathon was an incredible rush. We got the star treatment everywhere, and people were always throwing free stuff and services his way.

We hadn't entered the room good, and I rushed to the bathroom just in time. I threw up so much it felt like my guts were coming out of my nose. The entire bathroom reeked of stale liquor and hot vomit.

When I made my way back to the living room, Shawnathon was still in the spot where I left him. He was on the floor, leaned up against the sofa, snoring.

I was glad he was asleep so he didn't have to see or hear me when I had to call Earl. I walked over and shook him gently.

"Huh? Wha…whasup?" His eyes snapped open.

"You okay, baby?" I asked.

Suddenly, he jumped up, grabbed me by my waist and started kissing me. I was glad I'd had enough sense to rinse out my mouth and brush my teeth.

"C'mon, let's have a drink," he stuttered.

"Babe, you're drunk," I said.

"Nooo, I'm horny," he said.

I giggled. We kissed.

"You taste like liquor," I told him after I pulled back.

"I wanna taste you; c'mon, take off your clothes," he said.

I laughed at his antics. He pulled the shirt over his head and pulled off his wife-beater. His eight-pack was blinding. His tats were glistening and looking at him turned me on. I started taking off my own clothes, when suddenly his index finger flashed upward.

"Hold up. I don't want no kids, do you?"

"Umm, not right now," I said. It was an awkward moment, but I guess he wasn't *that* drunk.

Suddenly, he dug into his pocket and pulled out a used bar napkin instead of a condom.

I was confused. But I stood there in my bra and panties as he looked around the room.

"What are you looking for?" I asked.

"We need a pen. We're gonna make a deal," he said.

Blinking rapidly as I watched him, I wondered if he was serious. Shawnathon found a pen, then he scribbled something on the napkin and shoved it toward me right before he started sucking on my neck and unfastening my bra.

"Hold on, you want me to sign this, don't you?" I asked. The note read: *I Eboni no that Shawnathon don't want kids! I don't, either!*

After fumbling with the clasp on my bra, he backed up long enough for me to use his chest as a flat surface. I scribbled my name and gave him back the napkin and pen.

Shawnathon stuffed the pen and napkin in his pocket and stepped out of his pants.

Nia's ringing phone ended my trip down Memory Lane.

"I need to take this," she said.

I sat with so many memories and thoughts flowing through my mind. Finally, Nia hung up the phone, and focused on me.

"So what did you think you were signing?" she asked.

SERENA

I had started recording his TV appearances. I was proud and excited about all of the plans Loren had come up with for my new career. We decided to gather some information before moving ahead with plans to contact Gloria. For a person like her, we needed to have everything just right.

My phone rang and I grabbed it. Now, I was excited as all get-out any time Loren called.

"Hey, lady, what's going on?"

"Wanted to see if you could meet tomorrow evening. I'm thinking we can go to happy hour. I want to go over some stuff about your pregnancy, kind of establish what happened when you got divorced, you know, stuff like that," she said.

Honestly, I didn't feel completely comfortable about putting my business out there like that. Loren and I were cool, no doubt about that at all, but she had asked for quite a bit.

Before I could stay on subject with our conversation, I thought about all I had gone through. I can admit that I was wrong. Perhaps I didn't go about things the right way, but who among us was perfect? I sure didn't know anyone who hadn't done a couple of foul things.

James and I would've still been married today if only he didn't feel the need to go and stick everything with a hole. I admit now that I did marry him with revenge in mind. It wasn't like I'd set out to be with him, but he happened to fit into my plan. Then, as time went on, I forgot all about the reason I married him, and really wanted to make it work. We had our share of problems, but I didn't think those problems were enough for him to go out and cheat on me the way he did.

I remember the day the tramp showed up at my front door. I was hosting a jewelry party, or getting ready to when I looked around the room and smiled to myself.

Finally, it was my turn to host the jewelry party, and that meant I'd get an additional 10 percent of everything that sold. Things were moving along smoothly. There were seven ladies, including my so-called sometimey friend, Roxanne. I had only invited her after we bumped into each other at the Root of You day spa. While having our mud-pack facials in what was supposed to be a private session, we overheard a conversation about this great and easy way to make fast money. I wasn't big on costume jewelry at first, but this particular line had nice pieces, so I figured I'd give it a try.

Later that evening, when I told James the news about my new side job, he shrugged and said he didn't see why I wanted to be part of what he considered to be nothing more than selling Tupperware. I wasn't crazy. I realized James was starting to lose interest in quite a few things when it came to me, or us, but I didn't pay it no mind.

This wasn't a fancy dinner party or anything close; I had an array of finger foods and Mimosas. There was enough food there to fill everyone who was present.

"I hope you ladies are hungry," I announced as I stood near the doorway. "We can start eating now and we'll talk about the pieces when it's time for dessert."

The ladies looked around and agreed.

"Serena, you really pulled this together fast and nice," Alexandria from down the street said. "And I need to know where you got these eggrolls."

"Remind me later and I'll tell you," I said. The ladies mingled as they moved around the tables looking at the different pieces of jewelry.

I wondered if all of this small talk about insignificant things was necessary to sell jewelry. Before Alexandria could ask another question, Roxanne appeared by my side.

"You expecting someone else?" she asked.

"No, I don't think so. Why do you ask?"

"Everyone's here but someone's at the door. You know what? You stay here, and I'll go see who it is," she offered.

Roxanne walked toward the door, which was visible from the sitting room where we were gathered for the party.

"Good afternoon," I heard Roxanne say as she opened the door.

"I need to see Serena Carson," a voice barked.

Something about the way she sounded when she said my name made me stop and look toward the front door. I hoped the others didn't hear the desperation in the woman's voice. Her tone alone told me I needed to brace myself for some drama.

"Ah, can I tell her your—?"

"Look, I just need to see Serena, and I need to see her now!" the woman screamed. She had cut Roxanne off.

Before I could make it to the front door, the other women had stopped what they were doing and turned their attention to the loud-talking that was happening at the front door.

I rushed to Roxanne's side. "Um, can I help you with something?" I asked. I served up a bit more attitude than she gave.

"Yes," the woman answered.

She stood at my front door with one arm across her body, clasping the other arm by the side. I ran my eyes over the woman, from head-to-toe, then back up again. She was thin, but curvy, a size six if I had to guess. Her long, wavy hair was synthetic, but not the cheap stuff. Her eyes were red and puffy.

"You're Serena Carson, right?"

"Well, who wants to know?" I asked.

I already knew the heifer didn't have any good news. And I certainly didn't need anything to ruin all my hard work.

"Well, you ain't gotta answer that—it's not like I haven't seen your picture before. Anyways, I hate to tell you this way, but your husband ain't nothing but a lying, dirty dog. And if you don't believe me, um well, I brought these pictures with me." She held out the pictures as if I wanted to see her proof.

That's what led to my nasty divorce. From that day forward, I never trusted my ex-husband and God couldn't make my words soft enough. It got to the point where I was miserable, so I could only imagine what life under the same roof with me was like for him, but I didn't care.

Back then, my main goal was waking up to make his life a living hell. I made him move out of our house and tried my best to squeeze every nickel I could from him. When it came to child support, I had him by the balls.

But the joke was on me. My daughter has sickle cell disease, and both parents must carry a trait for the child to have the blood disorder. I am a carrier, but my ex was not. I was blindsided when a blood test at his job proved that our daughter wasn't his. I didn't expect him to be out getting no damn blood tests! Who would've thought a random act like that would've turned my world upside down like it did?

"So we're good for tomorrow then?" Loren's voice asked.

I'd forgotten we were on the phone. She rambled on about all of the things we needed to do.

"Hey, tomorrow's fine. I need to grab the door," I said into the phone.

When I got up to pull the door open, JahRyan stood with a bouquet of flowers hiding his face.

"Hey, baby," he greeted. He moved the flowers from his face.

"Oh, flowers. Well, you must've finally come to your senses and realized I ain't one to be played with," I said. When I reached for the vase, he yanked it back.

I pressed my lips together and gave him the evil eye.

"Now see how you wanna act? Here I come bearing gifts, tryin' to make things right, and you already starting off on the wrong damn foot!"

I threw my hand on my hip and waited for him to finish.

"If you don't come on in here and cut the BS, I'm closing my damn door and you know I won't get back up to open it again."

When I noticed the corners of his mouth turn downward, I secretly wanted to snatch my words back.

"Girl, why you gotta be so doggone evil all the time?" he asked.

I wanted to ask him how much longer he planned to be posturing at my front door, but I held my tongue. The little voice in my head told me he did bring flowers.

Instead of standing there with him, I turned and walked into the house. A few seconds later, I heard the door close, so I knew he'd decided to come inside.

PARKER

The blaring sound of a ringing phone jolted me out of my sleep. I must've been dreaming really hard because I woke up in a saturated T-shirt. It was plastered against my skin.

Roxy was still snoring when I reached for the offending phone and grumbled into the mouth piece.

"Yeah?"

"I need to talk to Parker, Parker Redman," a voice said.

"Yeah, this is Parker. Who is this?" I tried to focus on the digital clock positioned across the room, but the numbers were blurry.

There was loud music in the caller's background. But it didn't sound like he was at a bar or party. It sounded as if he simply had the music up very loud.

"Who is this?" I yawned and scratched my balls.

"Man, I'm about to do her," he said.

That woke me up! These calls were nothing unusual. They came at all hours of the morning, afternoon, and night. They were the reason I decided to keep a house phone versus switching us both to cell phones only.

As I sat upright in my bed, I reverted into counselor mode, and I made the transition quickly.

"Yeah, I know how you feel. The laws don't work fast enough, and you feel like you're all alone with no one looking out for you and your rights," I said.

"Shit, man! You feel me!" he screamed.

"Damn right I do, buddy!" I said as I swung my feet over to the side of the bed and onto the cold wood floor. I tried to lean over to my nightstand so I could see the caller ID and find out who was on the edge and on the other line, but I couldn't make it out.

"But here's the thing. You could hurt her, could probably put some serious pain on her, and when that's done and over with, ain't a damn thing changed," I said.

"Huh, bet I'd feel better," he said calmly.

"Yeah, you might, maybe for a hot second or two. But the truth of the matter is you'll be causing yourself far more pain than you can imagine."

"Shhiiiiittt, you don't know what I've been through with this bitch!"

Slap!

Suddenly, I heard a woman's voice scream out, then I heard whimpering sounds in his background.

"Now you tell me how the hell we gon' be married for four years, three kids and only one of 'em mine? What kind of foul shit is that?" he yelled.

"Partner, you know, if don't nobody else know how you feel, you know I know, right?"

"Yeah, Parker, that's why I'm calling you. You see, I received my letter today," he said.

As he spoke, I tried my best to catch his voice. He spoke to me like we knew each other well, but his voice didn't sound familiar.

"Lemme guess," I said, trying to gently nudge Roxy awake. "Was that letter confirming what I think?"

"Oh man, that's been done happened. Shit, I found out what this trick was doing before the tests confirmed it. Naw, playboy, this letter was the one telling me that I wasn't entitled to no damn refund!"

His voice was angry, but I could tell he was desperate. I knew all of the emotions that he'd probably gone through and how he probably fought the good fight for as long as he could.

"Aw man, yeah, ain't that a kick in the ass!"

"See, that's what the hell I'm talking about! I knew you'd understand. Now, don't get me wrong. I think you've done a lot for us fathers! Hell, I'd hate to see where we'd be if you hadn't gone through all you went through. You know, the funny thing is, I remember sitting back and watching your story on TV back in the day," he said. "Seriously, I know you probably hear this shit every day, but this is real talk! I remember sitting there thinking poor bastard! I can tell you the exact words I said, too," he yelled.

"What's that?"

"I said, 'I wish a bitch would!'"

"You know we can't control everything, but I'm a stronger man after going through that madness," I said.

He was silent.

I reached over, grabbed Roxy's shoulder and squeezed as tightly as I could. She stirred, but she simply turned to the other side and didn't move again.

"You see, Parker, that's where you're wrong. We can control some of this crap. The state may not be willing to do anything, a judge's hands may be tied, but there's something to be said for taking matters into your own damn hands!"

"Well, now what do you mean by that?" I asked.

"I'ma do her, Parker," he said.

He said it casually, as if he was telling me how to get from point A to point B.

"That's what I *don't* want you to do," I said. I was careful not to raise my voice or speak with too much emotion. As a matter of fact, I had been very casual during our entire conversation.

"I'm not like you, man. Ain't no way I can turn the other cheek. I mean, don't get me wrong, I feel like you've done a lot of good work for us men, you know, but sometimes, some cases, some situations, well, the best way to solve 'em is by a good old-fashioned ass whuppin'!"

This time, instead of gripping and trying to shake Roxy, I pinched her.

Her eyes snapped open and when they did, I said, "Listen, why don't you give me your address? Let me come over and talk to you in person. I don't want you to do anything crazy. You don't wanna go to jail, man."

Roxy had been through this enough times to know what she needed to do.

"You'd come over here?" he asked. The bewilderment in his voice bought me some time.

"You damn straight I would. Lemme bring some brews, let's talk about this," I said.

Silence.

I could still hear a woman whimpering in the background. As I grabbed a pair of sweats, a T-shirt and a pullover sweatshirt, Roxy put the iPad on her lap. Usually, it was on my side of the bed, but she used it before she went to bed.

"You still there?" I asked.

When he didn't answer right away, I became alarmed, but I couldn't react that way.

"Well, listen, I'm getting dressed now. It's funny, earlier tonight I wanted to go hang out, but my buddy is out of town on business. If you would've called me earlier, hell, I could've avoided an argument with the ole ball and chain," I said.

"What's wrong with them? These damn women, why can't they just act right?"

"Listen, buddy, if I knew the answer to that one, we'd both be billionaires." I chuckled.

When he did the same, I felt better.

"Okay, I'm dressed and ready. What's that address again?" I asked.

As I kept him on the phone, Roxy pulled up my contact list and grabbed her cell.

"Yes, he's on the line now, says he's about to go over there. No, haven't gotten an address yet," I heard her say.

"Okay, okay, let me make sure I got the address right," I said into the phone.

I repeated the address aloud slowly and slipped on my tennis shoes.

"So you really coming through?" he asked.

"I said I would, didn't I?"

"Well, yeah. Okay, cool, but you gotta stay on the phone with me 'cause the law has already tried to get in, and I told 'em if they come within five feet of this door again, I'm not only blasting her brains all over the wall, but it's gon' be suicide-by-cop before I'm done," he said.

I swallowed hard.

LACHEZ

It had been nearly a week since my baby was here with that child molester. He ain't talked to me since that day, but he should've known me better than to think that was gonna stop me from speaking my mind.

"You almost ready?" Toni asked.

"I will be in a few," I yelled back. I looked at my reflection in the mirror. I wasn't about to argue about it anymore, but I had told Toni that I was getting tired of wearing the skank outfits all the time.

I didn't even think people still wore these kinds of outfits unless they were on the pages of *Hustler* magazine. I adjusted the straps on my garter belt and turned to look at my butt cheeks in the mirror.

"You should rip a couple of holes in your fishnets," Toni said. She startled me.

"Don't be sneaking up on me," I said.

"Ain't nobody sneaking up you. I'm wondering what's taking you so damn long," she said.

Toni leaned up against the door frame. I grabbed my half-trench and pulled it on over the hideous outfit.

"Now explain to me how this is different than what we got busted for before?" she asked.

I rolled my eyes at her.

She looked down at what she was wearing as if the thought never crossed her mind.

"You don't think this will work?"

"No, you need to be showing some leg," I said. "Leggings are not gonna cut it," I told her.

"Okay, well, he's supposed to call your number when he gets through baggage claim and gets his car service," I said.

"Oooh, car service? Sounds important," she said.

"No, sounds like money! I told you I got this," I said. "Forget those chump-change clowns we were messing with before. I'm dealing strictly with businessmen this time around," I told her.

"Okay, so what's up with our dude? I'm ready to get this party started. You got the pills, I hope," she said.

I was messing with the clock radio next to the bed, but turned at her question.

"I'm no amateur," I said.

"I feel you, then do you, girlfriend; do you," Toni joked.

We stopped laughing when her cell rang.

"This is him," she said.

"Hello?" she answered.

I watched as she gave the caller directions to the hotel and our room number.

"Great, she'll be waiting and call me on this cell if you have any problems," Toni said. Instead of hanging up, she frowned.

"No, no, I was just saying in case you get there and you don't like her or something like that. Trust me, it's all good. I just wanted you to know you can call if you have questions, or if you have an issue; that's all."

She nodded a couple of times, then hung up.

Toni stood. After giving the room another once-over, she grabbed her bag and started for the door.

"In about an hour," she said as she left the room.

"Be ready when I call," I told her.

About fifteen minutes after Toni left, there was a knock at the door. I grabbed perfume from my purse and sprayed a little. I replenished my gloss, then stood at the door and looked out the peephole.

I saw a tall white man dressed in a business suit. I pulled the door open and smiled.

"You must be Richard," I said. "I'm Heidi."

Richard smiled. His teeth were perfectly straight and bright.

"Yes, that's me," he said. I stood there as his eyes took in my outfit. I could tell he was pleased.

"Please, come in, come in. I have drinks ready," I sang sweetly.

"Oh, okay," Richard said.

He had sandy blond hair, which had been freshly cut. His dark suit was not off the rack, and his crisp white shirt beneath the navy suit made him look like the typical executive.

I stretched my right hand out for him to shake and smiled when I noticed the tan mark around his bare ring finger. I was right when I told Toni that this plan was definitely foolproof.

EBONI

"So what did your lawyer say?" Ulonda asked. "Is the note on the used napkin gonna stand up in court or what?" She chuckled as she asked.

I closed the front door behind her, but not before I scanned the driveway and bushes near the lawn. I wanted to make sure my crazy stalker wasn't lurking in any dark corners.

We were having a girl's night lock-in. Her son was with his father, Dalton, and since I wasn't in the mood to go out, she came over with girly DVDs, pizza, wings, and drinks in tow. I needed the company since I'd been in a slump after my meeting with Nia.

"Ooh, that smells so good. I'm starving," I said. "Oh, the masseuses will be here in exactly one hour," I told her.

"Good, we'll be nice and stuffed, and tipsy by then," she joked.

"You promise?" I asked. "I need some liquor to help numb the madness in my head."

Ulonda walked in and got everything organized. The kids were asleep so we were virtually alone. She brought me a plate and a drink. At first it was so quiet because we were eating instead of talking.

After a couple of wings and slices, I was ready to chit-chat. With my feet kicked up on the coffee table, I started to spill it about the stupid note I had signed.

"Nia says it may pose a problem if he still has it," I said while chewing.

Ulonda's eyebrows jumped up to her hairline. "You've gotta be kidding me," she said.

"I wish I was." I shook my head. "She says a judge could try to say that it's a legally binding contract."

"But it's a used bar napkin," Ulonda yelled. "It's probably all stained and hard to read."

"I know, but she says we should prepare for the worst. Not only is it a used bar napkin, but I was drunk. We were both drunk when we signed it."

"I can't believe that punk is trying to say he shouldn't have to support his offspring because you two signed a contract! He's acting like you guys were in an attorney's office! Now that's some real soap opera type of drama right there," Ulonda said.

"Girl, I get sick, just thinking about it! What a loser! So you don't wanna pay for your own flesh and blood and you and your lawyer are gonna use a piece of paper signed in a drunken stint as your defense?"

"I hear what Nia's saying, and I know she's got the law degree and all, but all I'm saying is I wanna see the judge who's gonna sign off on this one. I mean, really?"

"Well, Nia is looking up cases where she can point to precedence, but right now, she's saying she fully expects them to present the napkin in court next week."

Ulonda's eyebrows bunched together.

"Next week?"

"Yes, I told her we needed to expedite this mess. I also told her how the damn police became starstruck when they showed up at my house, after he violated the protective order. Remember that?"

"Do I?" Ulonda sipped her cocktail. "I don't see why that mess even surprises you anymore. When these guys dribble a ball or catch one, you might as well say they've got a free pass to act the ass," she said.

"Hey, that rhymes," I pointed out.

"Yeah, we should become rappers," Ulonda said sarcastically.

She rolled her eyes. Ulonda was taking a shot at her own baby's daddy. He was a Houston rapper, Dalton, aka D-devastator, who wasn't really doing too much of anything. Once she asked for child support, he suddenly wasn't balling out of control like he first led everyone to believe. But at least he would take his boy and spend time with him.

"Once I get paid from Shawnathon, we can do whatever you like. Seriously, we should come up with a business plan or something. You know I ain't trying to punch nobody's time clock, so I've really been thinking about this a lot lately," I said.

"You may be on to something. Maybe we should. I'm sick and tired of my tired-ass job. Who knew we'd end up like this when we set out to find us some ballers? But seriously, though, what would we do?" Ulonda asked.

"Well, we can open a string of day spas," I suggested.

Ulonda nearly choked on her drink. She coughed a few times and cleared her throat. She used a napkin to clean up the liquid that splashed around when she nearly spit up.

"Damn, how much money you think you're gonna get outta him?"

"Girl, do you know how much money Shawnathon makes? He just signed a new contract and if I'm not mistaken, I wanna say he got something like a two million dollar bonus!"

Ulonda whistled.

"Damn, you sure hitched your wagon to the right one," she said.

"Females can hate all they want, but I ain't got time to be punching nobody's time clock, and I damn sure ain't got time for no broke nucca!" I raised my right hand. "Gimme some," I said.

"I'll say Amen to that!" Ulonda said as she slapped palms with me. "I don't know what the hell I was thinking with D's dumb, broke ass!"

"Wait, hold up, now, that was not your fault! Who knew he was nothing but a *wanna-be* rapper? The fool was pushing an eighty thousand-dollar car, iced from head-to-toe, always laced in the finest designer clothes. I would've thought he was balling, too."

We ate in silence as we watched the antics on the movie *Bridesmaids*.

"We should do our own movie about sorry ass baby daddies, like a celebrity documentary," Ulonda said.

"For real, we'd probably have tons of women lining up to tell their stories."

"A used bar napkin," Ulonda said as if she still couldn't believe it.

She had no idea how much that stupid napkin haunted me. I daydreamed about it, had nightmares about it, had even thought about sneaking into his place to see if I could find it.

"Do you know how stupid I felt when Nia first called and asked about the contract I signed?"

"I was wondering how he dropped that bomb on you," Ulonda said.

"Oh, he hid behind his attorney. The attorney was the one who called Nia, then Nia called me!"

"What did you think when she called you with that mess?"

"I was confused." I frowned. "I was like, I didn't sign no contract saying I didn't want any damn kids! Nia was like, are you sure because this attorney seems really confident about it? Says it's your signature and Shawnathon's, and the contract is between the two of you." It hurt to think about it, much less talk about it. "Then finally, it hit me like a wrecking ball. I still couldn't believe it," I said.

"When did Nia realize it was a napkin?"

"At first she kept talking about this contract. How could I forget signing such a document? Why didn't I get legal advice before entering into any contract? When did I sign it? The questions were never ending," I said. "Finally, I explained it was a frigging napkin from the hotel bar!"

"Yeah, he took this to a new low," Ulonda said.

"Girl, it's been crazy. He's had people calling me on the phone, telling me all kinds of crazy shit," I said.

"What are you guys gonna do?"

I smiled. "Oh trust, I'm gonna get the last laugh because we are taking his ass all the way to the cleaners!"

"I know that's right," Ulonda said.

"You just wait and see." I sipped my drink.

SERENA

"You got me a meeting with who?" I asked Loren. We were on the phone, but I was in bed next to JahRyan so I didn't want to put too much of my business out there. "I thought we were going to try to get Gloria herself," I said.

"She's not interested," Loren said. "But don't worry about that. I've got plenty of interest in this case," Loren tried to add really quickly.

I eased upright in the bed. "Whoa, hold up a sec! What do you mean, she wasn't interested? I'm trying to give her a hot ass story about a man who calls himself a champion for fathers, fights for men who have child support issues, and she's not interested? Um, that doesn't even sound right to me!"

"I told you, I got this. You should let me handle this—that way you can start working on your speeches," Loren said. "Besides, from what I could tell, several places have already started trying to vet you."

"Vet me? What does that mean?"

"You know, calling your references, checking your resumé, making sure you have the experience you claim and that you know how the system works."

"All this and Gloria still isn't interested?" I asked.

"Let's not worry about her. We'll be fine without her."

"I hear what you're saying, but hear what I'm saying. I know

I'm not crazy! I know damn well people would want to know that Parker Redman is nothing but a fraud; a snake oil salesman!"

JahRyan slowly pulled himself up next to me in the bed. He folded his muscular arms across his chest. But he didn't say anything at first.

"Loren, you told me you could make this thing work; now you're telling me Gloria Allred ain't interested in my story? Umph!"

"Let me make some more calls, but we already have one meeting set up. I say we go to this local lady, talk with her, and wait to see if Gloria changes her mind."

"Well, I'll have to think about that meeting. When is it again?"

"Tomorrow afternoon, Serena. Look, if you're serious about this, we need to get the ball rolling. I'll keep trying with Gloria, but if she's not interested, we need to move on."

"I'll call you in the morning," I told her, then hung up the phone.

I barely put the phone on the nightstand before JahRyan started up with me.

"Remember a while back when I found that piece of mail from that fertility clinic and I asked why you was on their mailing list? Well, I assumed you was one of those women who did it on your own. You never told me *that* dude was your baby daddy," he said. It sounded like he had an attitude.

I slowly turned my head to face him so I could see if the expression on his face matched the words coming out the side of his damn neck.

"I'm sorry. I didn't know I needed to tell you who fathered my child," I snarled.

"That man does real good work," JahRyan said.

I felt the slight rise of my eyebrows and my jaw dropping. Was he for real?

"He helped a buddy of mine, and I remember all that man went through back in the day," he continued.

My neck was twisting before he even finished.

"I remember watching his case on TV when a couple of women tried to rob dude," JahRyan said. "I remember talking about it every week in the barbershop. Brothas was hot over all that bullshit he was going through," he said.

"He didn't go through anything he didn't deserve," I said as I swung my feet onto the floor. My back was to him now.

When he touched my shoulder, I whipped around to look at him in the face.

"I need to understand what you're trying to say here," JahRyan said.

I stood and looked down at him. "You don't know the half of it with that bum. Just because you see him on TV and you think he's doing all this good for the community, you have no idea!"

"What I do know is dude was a victim. Some crazy chick pulled his name out the sky and tried to hustle him. I also know if I was in his shoes, somebody woulda been hurt."

"Is that so?" I asked.

"Serena, I don't understand. Why are you getting all bent outta shape over this?"

"Ain't nobody getting bent any kind of way. I'm just saying, you shouldn't be speaking on something when you don't know the whole story. I can't stand when people start jocking someone and they ain't got no damn clue!" I padded off to the bathroom and slammed the door shut on him and his tired ass conversation.

I didn't mean to have him all up in my business. That's why I was careful not to say too much in his presence. I didn't even appreciate being in the middle of an argument behind Parker's stupid behind.

After using the bathroom and washing my hands, I said a silent prayer, hoping JahRyan would be dressed and gone, or headed out the door.

When I walked back into my bedroom and he was still lounging around in bed, I had to struggle to bite my tongue. I walked over to the dresser and pulled out a drawer. Silently, I rummaged through it like I was searching for something.

At first, he didn't say anything and that led me to believe the issue had been squashed. Boy, was I wrong!

"Just so I'm straight," he began. "So your problem with Parker is that he tries to help other people, or you don't agree with how he handled that situation with his other baby mama?"

Slowly, I turned around and looked him right in the eyes.

"What other baby mama?" I asked.

His eyes grew wide and I watched as recognition settled into his features. His head tilted to the side ever so slightly.

"Are you trying to tell me that was you? But there was a white girl, and these chicks were stealing from this brotha!" he shouted. His nostrils flared and I thought I noticed his fists clench once he crossed his arms.

"See, that's what I'm talking about. You don't have a clue. Nobody was trying to steal from him!"

When that fool shook his head like he was about to tell *me* the truth, I was too through. How was *he* gonna tell *me* when not only was I there, but the entire idea was mine! I hand-selected Lachez. I was the mastermind behind Parker's misery and I'd do it all over again if I could.

"Serena, you don't wanna have this conversation with me. I remember this brotha's case like it was my own! He was arrested on his way home from the hospital with his wife. He didn't have any kids at the time, but was tossed in jail for nonpayment of delinquent child support! I was this close to starting a fundraiser to help with his legal fees," he said.

"What kind of punk-ass mess is that?" I asked.

He looked like he was confused.

"You gon' help raise money for a complete stranger? Someone whose story you don't even know?" I asked.

He looked up at me without blinking. I noticed an eyelash flicker but it was clear he was trying to stare me down. Did he think I was going to back off?

"I knew enough; I knew that shit could've happened to anybody. I can't believe you did some foul shit like that," he said. When he got up and walked to the bathroom, I felt strange.

He didn't walk out on me!

When he came back into the room, he didn't say anything. He grabbed his clothes, got dressed, and tossed me a look of sheer disgust as he walked out of the room.

"Hey! Where are you going?" I asked.

"I don't know you," he said. Then he left.

"What an ass! Leave! I don't give a damn!" I yelled.

But he was already gone.

PARKER

The sun was coming up by the time I got to the apartment complex on Club Creek Drive in southwest Houston. Two police cruisers were parked out front. As I walked up the walkway, the guy was still talking to me on the phone.

"I'm glad you decided to come over and talk with me. I know if anybody knows what I'm going through, it's you," he said into my ear through the phone.

"Yeah, we're in one of those unique fraternities," I said.

"Besides, what's your name? We've been on the phone all this time, and listen, my battery is about to go dead," I said.

"Where you at, man?" he said. For the first time since we'd been on the phone, he sounded unstable.

"I'm at your apartment complex. I'm walking up right now," I said.

"Oh, okay," he said.

"Where is she?" I asked.

"The bitch is right here," he huffed.

I heard his slap and the sound of her scream. I squeezed my eyes shut. I thought if I kept him talking, he would be less likely to harm her. When I made eye contact with the detective I worked with, I dismissed him with the wave of my hand. I knew he'd try to talk me out of going in, but I knew what I had to.

Steps away from the front door, Detective Bruce Johnson appeared.

He was a medium-sized man with a belly that hung over his belt. I often wondered if he'd be able to chase down a suspect. But we worked really well together. I pressed mute on my phone.

"Steven DePauws is armed. Not sure you going in is a good idea," he said.

"He called me. There's a woman in there and he wants to talk. You don't recommend I throw in the towel now, do you?"

"I want you to be careful. These guys are becoming more dangerous," Johnson said.

"Keep your cell on your hip," I told him. He eased back into the shadows and I knocked on the front door. When the door swung open, Steven looked around outside before he greeted me.

"Man, Parker, I don't believe you're really here," he said. He stepped aside to let me in.

The place was essentially empty. He had the very basics. His TV was balanced on top of several old blue milk crates. He had a ratty little couch and an old wooden chair. There were no pictures on the walls or anywhere in the room. The windows were covered with wooden blinds and I could still smell the faint traces of paint.

I pulled the six-pack of beer up where he could see it and smiled.

"Sometimes we all need somebody who can relate. I'm not sure who you've been counting on throughout all of this, but you're not alone any longer, my brother."

"Damn, you got the good stuff, too." He smiled and reached for one of the green bottles of beer.

Steven was about five feet eleven inches. He was thin, which surprised me somewhat. The entire time we'd been on the phone, his voice gave me the impression that he was a big, husky man. I tried to play it cool.

"Where is she?" I asked.

"Oh, got her ass tied up in the kitchen," he said.

I nodded. I tried not to be too obvious as I searched the room with my eyes. The apartment was small, and I could hear a woman's voice whimpering in the distance.

"Where are the kids?"

"Oh, I'm sure they with her mama, you know. I had to leave the house, so I came here," he said.

He offered me the remote, but I shook my head.

"No, whatever you put it on is cool with me," I told him.

He tossed the bottle cap opener to me with no warning and I caught it.

"Nice, good reflexes," he said.

By the time I opened my bottle, he had already swallowed nearly half of his.

"I don't know how you did it. You don't know how badly I wanna kill that bitch," he said casually.

"Well, listen, man, that's not gonna do nothing but cause a whole new series of problems. You should let her go," I said.

He frowned, and then he began to shake his head vigorously. He took another long gulp from his bottle.

"Before I called you, I had already made up my mind," he said. "Any woman who intentionally tricks a man into thinking he fathered her kids when she knew damn well he didn't, don't deserve to walk this earth!" he exclaimed. "Shit, for those kind, we should bring back the firing squads."

"I'm not sure about that, but you know, that's the reason I make my number readily available to all men. I've been there, dawg. I mean, *I've been there.* There's nothing like being locked inside a cold, dark, dank cell and being alone with your thoughts. Man, at my darkest hour, I started thinking maybe I had done it, maybe I had left some poor kid with no means of support. I was on the verge of losing my mind!"

"See, that's what I'm saying, man! This ain't the kind of thing we can expect people to understand. Who's been there? Who knows how gut-wrenching that is?" He jumped up from the couch.

"C'mon, lemme show you this conniving bitch." He motioned me toward the kitchen with his arm. "Now she wanna be crying, like she's the victim now!"

I followed him to the doorway of the kitchen and that's when I saw her. Where Steven was a small and petite man, she was much bigger. She was wearing a nightshirt and nothing else. He had her sitting on a chair with a piece of duct tape hanging across one side of her mouth. Her arms were tied behind her back. And each leg was bound at the ankles to legs of the chair.

Her eyes pleaded with me. They were full with tears that threatened to fall at any minute.

"Yeah, let her go, man. This won't end good. I know what you've been through, but you said yourself, you're already facing jail time. The money is gone, and we should fight this in court, not like this," I said.

He stood, staring at her. The fury in his eyes was evident. His features contorted like he was suddenly possessed and I stepped in right before he lunged at her.

"You ruined my life, you stupid bit..."

"This is not the answer," I said to him.

Steven looked at me like he was trying to decide whether he could take me. Spittle gathered at the corners of his mouth, and his nostrils were flaring. His eyebrows were so jumbled they looked like they'd been drawn on his forehead.

"Let's end this now; the kids, they need a mother. Let the courts deal with her," I said.

"But you said yourself, they ain't gonna do shit; nothing but make me pay!"

I shook my head.

"Here, I'm gonna untie her hands and let her get out of here. You and me, we can ride this thing out together. When the police come in, I'll talk to them with you," I said.

For the first time since I arrived, he looked at me with hope in his eyes.

"I'm probably in a whole lot of shit behind her, huh?"

"It's not too late to turn back," I said. "Let me untie her. She can go out there and show everyone that you have compassion. It's not too late."

Steven sighed really hard and loud.

"She shouldn't be able to get away with this shit, man! It oughta be against the damn law!"

"You know I'm with you on that one, buddy; as a matter of fact, I'm about to embark on a journey now that will hopefully make the state and the county pay for all I went through," I said.

His eyes lit up. He smiled.

"No shit?"

"Yeah, just got word from my attorney. We've been waiting on this for years now," I said.

Steven looked at me, nodding his head. He eased back and leaned against the doorframe.

"So you goin' after 'em, huh?"

"Yeah, man, they won't let me do anything to Serena and Lachez, so I'm going after the other *them*, the very lawmakers and laws that made what they did possible."

"Damn, man! I'm happy for you! That's the best news I've heard in a long while. If I was you, I'd sue those two bitches, too. Can't you go after them in small claims or something?"

"I think you may be on to something, Steven. I'm gonna have my lawyer look into that. Why should they get off scot-free?"

LACHEZ

Richard and me were on drink number two when he looked at me, licked his lips, then said, "Why don't you come sit over here?" He tapped his lap and smiled. "Close to me."

With my drink in hand, I got up and sashayed over to his side of the table.

"I was wondering what took you so long to ask," I said.

He laughed. His blue eyes were mesmerizing.

I straddled his leg and made sure to grind down on it really hard.

When he threw back the rest of his drink and grabbed me by the waist, I knew it was time to get this party started.

"Hey, you like black girls?" I asked as I nibbled on his earlobe. He smelled good and expensive.

He pulled back and smiled wickedly.

"I like all kinds of girls," he said, and then smothered his face into my breasts.

I giggled.

He had lost the jacket and tie, but he was still wearing his crisp, white shirt, although several buttons were undone.

"Well, how'd you like it if I invited my friend to come play with us?"

His bright eyes lit up even more. I could see a mixture of hunger and lust in them as they widened.

"You mean she'll come and do me and you?" he asked.

"She'll come and we can do whatever will make you happy," I said.

"Is she pretty like you?"

"Oh, yeah, she's totally hot," I told him. "Wait, lemme see if she's willing to come out and play," I teased.

When I got up from his leg, he slapped me on the ass. I wiggled it for him after he did. Before I grabbed my cell, I turned back to him and said, "I need to go to the ladies room. Say where you are."

He wasn't paying much attention to me as he picked up his own phone and started thumbing through the touch screen. I grabbed my glass and went to the bathroom. Once inside, I turned the water on and switched the empty glass for the full one behind the shower curtain. After sitting for a while, the liquid looked clear. I washed my hands and left the bathroom.

When I came back into the room, I placed the glass on the table. Richard still hadn't looked up from his phone.

"Are you still calling your friend?" he asked.

I grabbed the bottle of Patron and refilled his old glass. When both were full, I slid the glass from the bathroom closer to him and kept his old one for myself.

"Oh, yeah." I jumped up.

I walked away from him so he couldn't hear Toni's voice when I called. I was glad to see that he had taken a sip of the drink. When he frowned and looked at the glass, my heart skipped a beat.

Toni's cell was ringing in my ear, but I wanted to focus on him.

When I realized the frown was for what was on his phone and not the drink, I was relieved.

"What's up? We ready to do this?" Toni said as she answered the phone.

"Umm, hey, Trixie," I sang. I winked at Richard.

He smiled at me.

"So, I'm on a date with this really hot guy. He's a total hunk," I said into the phone. "And um, he loves black girls. When I told him about my best friend, well, naturally he wanted me to ask you to come join us." I giggled.

Richard was off the phone and his eyes were glued to me.

"So about thirty minutes?" Toni asked.

"Yeah, I think he'll like you," I said into the phone.

"Is he drunk yet?"

"Trixie, he's not freaky like that." I pulled the phone to my breast and feigned laughter.

"What did she say?" Richard asked. He was hungry.

"No, not yet," I said into the phone.

"Did you give him the drink yet?" she asked.

"Yeah, about ten minutes," I said.

"Hmmm, so if you gave it to him ten minutes ago, is he drinking slow?"

"Yeah, sort of," I answered.

"What's she saying? Tell her I'm willing to pay," Richard said. When I heard him slur his words slightly, that sealed the deal.

"C'mon, Trixie, he says he's willing to pay. So can you get here in about thirty minutes?" I asked.

"I think he'll be ready before then," she said.

"Well, I'm gonna enjoy another drink with him while we'll wait for you," I said.

"I'll be there in fifteen. Keep his ass up and alert," Toni said.

Just as I was about to hang up, she called my name.

"Yeah?"

"Would you fuck him?" she asked.

I glanced over at Richard's fine ass. He wasn't really my type or my speed, but he had money and that made him appealing.

"Yeah, I guess I would," I told her.

"Umph, okay, well, don't do anything until I get there. I'll be there in ten minutes," she said.

I was excited when after I hung up the phone, Richard held his glass up toward me.

"Let's toast," he said.

I grabbed my own glass and smiled.

"To what?" I asked.

"Let's toast to new friends and good times." He smiled.

He really was a gorgeous man. He had chiseled features with a well-defined jawline. He was like movie-star fine, and I meant it when I said I'd fuck him. As we raised our glasses and sipped, I decided I *would* fuck him.

Toni would have to understand. We could still handle the business, but I saw no reason why we couldn't have a little fun at the same time.

If ten minutes had passed before I heard a knock at the door, time must've been moving by the speed of light. But that was okay with me. Obviously, Toni also wanted to have a little fun with this one before it was lights out.

Even Richard's drunk ass noticed. "Is that your friend already?" he asked.

"Yeah, she was close by when we called." I smiled.

When I noticed his glass was empty again, I motioned for him to give it to me.

"I hope all this liquor doesn't impact, well, you know," I said, and winked at him.

"Oh darlin', liquor makes my cock harder than steel," he said.

That comment piqued my interest, even if he was putting a little extra into it.

"Then drink up, daddy, drink up," I joked as I poured more liquor into his glass.

Toni knocked again and I rushed to get the door.

She came waltzing in like this was a date, for real. I started to say something to her, but figured there was no point. She hadn't broken any laws.

"Hi, sexy," I greeted.

"Hi," she said and kissed me on the lips.

Richard nearly choked on his drink.

Toni turned to him. "Hi, I'm Trixie, but my friends call me Sexy. You must be Richard."

We both noticed how he stumbled as he rose from his chair. Toni and I exchanged knowing glances. I saw the smirk on her face and knew exactly what was running through her mind.

"I am. Thanks for joining us," Richard said, like a true gentleman.

"Where's my drink?" Toni asked.

I frowned a little, but extended my glass toward her.

Richard rubbed his forehead with the palm of his hand.

"Whew," he exclaimed, as he stumbled back down onto his chair.

"You okay over there, daddy?" I said. I looked around Toni to see him.

"Oh yeah, yeah, let's get this party started," he said right before he slumped over in his chair.

EBONI

Bright and early Saturday morning, I dropped the twins off at my mom's. I needed some *me* time and I was hoping she'd keep them all weekend. I was sick and tired of being stressed out over my meeting with Nia.

If she couldn't get that stupid note tossed, I would find a way to sue him on my own if I had to. Lately, when thoughts of Shawnathon overwhelmed me, I'd go wishing. Today, I planned on doing just that.

"Wishing" was what I called window-shopping for the list of things I'd buy with my newfound wealth once I got paid from Shawnathon. I didn't care what he and his stupid new woman had planned to do, she could marry him if she wanted, but she needed to understand that me and his kids were here to stay.

I had thought about us being a blended family quite a bit lately. I felt like once he realized he had to pay, I might actually change the way I feel about him.

Ulonda and I were supposed to hang later, but before then, I had plans of my own. I planned to visit the Bentley dealership off 59, the Southwest Freeway.

A baby-blue Bentley with personalized plates, navy interior with blue, tinted windows was at the top of my wish list. Sure, I had planned to buy my mom a new place, but I wanted some jewelry from Tiffany's, a Gucci bag for each season, and a set of Louis Vuitton luggage.

My cell rang right as I was about to crank up my old Camry.

The private number that flashed on my caller ID made me think twice, but in the end, I decided to answer anyway.

"Hello?"

"Is this Eboni?"

"Who wants to know?" I asked with much attitude.

"This is Elisa," she said and I nearly dropped my phone. What was Shawnathon's girlfriend doing calling me?

Silence.

"You there?" she asked.

"Um, yeah, but why are you calling me?" I asked.

"Listen, I want to know if you can meet me so we can talk," she said.

Thoughts of her luring me into a trap so Shawnathon could shoot me or kidnap and torture me danced through my mind. She was up to something.

"Ah, Shawnathon doesn't know I'm calling," she quickly added.

"So why wouldn't he know? I mean, I don't get why you're calling me," I said to her.

She took a deep breath, like she had something to be tired about, or like I might even care that she was.

"We can meet in a public place, if you're worried. I wanna talk, woman to woman," she said.

"If I agreed to this meeting, and I'm not saying that I will, but if I do, where would this meeting take place and when?"

"How about in two hours, and you pick the spot? If you decide to meet with me, I can call you back in two hours. At that time you can tell me where we'll meet and we go from there," she said.

I was tempted for several reasons. First off, since she had hooked up with Shawnathon, he had all but lost his mind. The kids were nearly two and he had no connection to them whatsoever. For that I partially blamed her. Even though he said he didn't want kids upfront, I could've changed his mind. But once she came along, it was a done deal. There was no point in even trying.

Shawnathon and I broke up for good when I was adamant that I wouldn't get an abortion. But after I'd had the babies, he started to soften up a bit. For a minute there, he'd slip me some cash and it looked like he was gonna pay. Then they hooked up. That was when the money dried up like a Texas drought, and I instantly became enemy number one. I probably hated her *more* than I hated him.

"So, what do you say?"

"Call me back in two hours," I said.

I got off the freeway at the Fountains and pulled into Pappadeaux's parking lot. I feverishly dialed Ulonda's number.

"Please pick up. Please pick up," I muttered as the phone rang in my ear.

When I got her voicemail, I was pissed.

Right when I was about to call her again, my phone rang and it was Ulonda.

"Hey, gurrrl," she sang.

"Girl!" I sighed.

"What's wrong?"

"You will never guess who called me asking for a meeting!"

"Shawnathon!" she screamed.

"Girl, no!"

I shared the details of Elisa's phone call with Ulonda, who was stunned.

When I finally finished, she asked, "What are you gonna do?"

"You think I should meet with her?"

"Might as well. Why not see what the hell she wants? If nothing else, she might be able to give you some information Nia can use," Ulonda said.

She had a good point.

"Will you come with me?"

"Did you think I'd let you go alone?" She giggled.

"Girl, what time and where?" she asked.

More than an hour after I got off the phone with Ulonda, she and I sat waiting for Elisa to call back. I had already told Elisa that I would meet with her. I also told her that I wanted to meet right away.

She said she needed to get dressed and would call back in thirty minutes.

"Well, once you get dressed, get on 59 and head south. We can meet at a restaurant in the Fountains," I said.

"Okay, which one?" she asked.

"When you get there, call me back and I'll let you know. I don't need you bringing Shawnathon," I said.

"Eboni, I told you. This is between me and you. He knows nothing about this meeting," she said.

As we sat in my car, Ulonda asked me to go over the first phone call again. I had already told her twice, but we sat there the whole time trying to dissect what Elisa could've possibly wanted.

"What if he put her up to this?" Ulonda asked.

"She said he don't know we're meeting," I said.

Ulonda gave me one of those *yeah…right* looks. I shrugged my shoulders.

"I can't do nothing but hear her out," I said.

"Yeah, but I don't like this one bit," Ulonda said.

She really had me thinking the worst. What if Shawnathon really did tell her to call me and set up a meeting so he could pounce?

I glanced around the parking lot. Now, all of a sudden, I became worried about the way we sat there. I was thinking all kinds of crazy thoughts, and I didn't even have my mace with me.

When my phone rang, I jumped. I had to laugh about it after the third ring.

"It's her," I said to Ulonda.

"Okay, ask her where she is, and then let's go meet her there. If someone is with her, we'll know."

That was smart. Unfortunately, when I finally decided to answer, the phone stopped ringing.

"She'll call back," Ulonda said.

Before she could finish her prediction, the phone rang again.

I allowed it to ring three times before I answered.

"Hello?"

"Hey, Eboni. I'm here at the Fountains," she said.

"Where exactly are you?"

"I'm in front of Sam's Boat. I'm in a gold car," she said.

"Okay, are you alone?"

"Yes. I told you, no one knows about this," she repeated.

"I'll be there in five minutes," I said, then hung up.

I turned to Ulonda. "What do you think?" I asked.

She shrugged her shoulders at first. Then she turned and looked out the window. "I say we go over there and see what's what," she said.

It took three minutes to drive around the corner and locate the gold car. When I pulled up alongside the gold 2013 Special Edition Range Rover, I felt more than a ping of jealousy. My 2009 Camry may as well have been fifteen years old.

"Daaauuummm," Ulonda exclaimed.

Suddenly, I wasn't sure this was a good idea.

The minute she spotted us, she waved. I wasn't sure what to do, but because I wanted a better look at her whip, I jumped out of my car first.

"You wanna just go in here?" she asked.

I looked at Sam's Boat and figured what the hell. She rolled up her window, and Ulonda and I stood and waited for her to get out. The glimpse I got of the interior was more than anything I could've expected, and then some.

Not only did her Range Rover have a custom paint job, but the interior was a butterscotch color and I had to admit, she looked good in it, too. Her honey-blonde complexion and hair color seemed to fit perfectly. She and her car had the nerve to be color coordinated! I rolled my eyes at the thought.

But when she eased out of the driver's seat and I took a better look at her, I was so sick that I thought for sure I was gonna throw up!

SERENA

This wasn't the way I pictured it, but I guess I had to shit or get off the pot. I wasn't trying to be Debbie Downer, but Loren hadn't really delivered on a damn thing she promised.

I couldn't focus on what the woman next to me had said because I couldn't stop thinking about the fact that she wasn't Gloria Allred.

If there was a silver lining, I guess it would be that just about every single TV, radio station and newspaper in Houston showed up for the press conference. I didn't get a chance to be nervous because this chick, my attorney, Deena Johnson, had been running her mouth for close to forever. I wanted to remind her that this was about me and not her!

What in the hell had I gotten my hair, nails, and everything else done for, if all I was gonna do was stand quietly next to her? I wore a bright-red wrap shirt and a pair of navy tailored slacks. It was an outfit I had seen on Gloria, so there was no doubt that I was dressed the part, but still, I was nothing more than a prop.

It was music to my ears when a reporter said, "Can we talk to Serena?"

That's when Deena finally turned to me and glanced as if she wasn't sure about giving up the spotlight.

"Yes, my name is Serena and I wanna tell the world and anybody else who will listen that Parker Redman is nothing but a hypocrite!" I said.

"Why is he a hypocrite?" another reporter asked.

"Parker Redman is the father of my child. To this day, while he runs around acting like a go-between with police, showing up to court with other deadbeats and jet-setting all across the country, he ain't paid one red-hot cent for his own flesh and blood," I said.

They must've really liked that because they started scribbling on their little notepads.

"What does he say when you talk to him?" someone else asked.

"I haven't talked to him in years. Did you hear me say he don't do anything for his daughter?" I shook my head.

I don't know if it was the fact that all these people were asking me all these questions or the fact that I was the center of attention, but suddenly my eyes began to moisten.

"You have no idea how hard it is to be a single parent in this economy," I said.

"What would you say to Parker if he was watching right now?" a female reporter from Channel 11 asked.

I turned to her camera, looked directly into it and began, "I'd say, Parker, you need to do right by your own flesh and blood. I'd say, Parker Redman, this is your Judgment Day! Your child needs you, and what happened between us has nothing to do with her. She's innocent and didn't ask to be brought into this world!"

Deena stepped up and eased herself in front of the microphone.

"We'd like to thank you all for coming out this afternoon. Again, we will be filing suit against Mr. Redman, but it is our hope that we will be able to fix this and end his daughter's suffering."

It seemed like her announcement did nothing but get them all riled up. Suddenly, they yelled and screamed questions toward the podium at the same time. Deena steered me away and whispered in my ear.

"You did a fantastic job," she said.

Her driver was waiting inside the black Town Car. I felt like a movie star as we pushed our way through the throngs of people. They yelled questions about Parker, his organization, and our daughter.

Once we were safely inside the car, Deena turned to me and said, "Now let's see how long it takes him to reach out."

"What if he doesn't?" I asked.

"Oh, he will—trust me. I've done dozens of these. He'll reach out and he'll probably be ready to settle. The bad publicity is far more detrimental to him and his business," she said.

I didn't respond. I hated Parker even more today than I did more than five years ago when I set out to exact my revenge against him. He had this air about himself. He acted like he was God's gift to women and the best thing to walk this earth.

Back at her office, we walked off the elevator to an unexpected audience. The moment the doors opened, everyone stood clapping and cheering. I was confused, but I didn't say anything.

"How'd we look?" Deena asked.

I wanted to question why she thought wearing that bright yellow suit, considering how big she was, would be a good choice, but I held my tongue. The truth was, from the moment Loren arranged the meeting with us, I couldn't stop scrutinizing the woman.

She wasn't too big, but she wasn't Gloria. For instance, anytime I saw Gloria on TV, the woman was sharp! From her hair to her makeup and her clothes, she was on point.

Deena must've spent the bulk of her money on her fancy office because she damn sure didn't spend it on her clothes.

A few minutes after we'd arrived and settled into her office, her receptionist buzzed.

"Loren is here. Should I send her in?"

"Yes, we're just getting started."

Loren walked in, smiling like a Cheshire cat.

"Didn't I tell you she was tha bomb!" She grinned at me.

I wanted to ask if she was for real.

"How'd it look?" Deena asked Loren.

"That yellow really popped on screen," Loren said. "I'm excited. The good thing is that most of the stations will run it again later tonight, then probably on the early morning shows, too."

"You okay, Serena?"

"Yeah, I'm good. I wanna get this over with. I want to make sure Parker won't get off easy," I said.

Loren and Deena looked at each other.

"Get off easy?" Deena asked. "Oh, honey, we're well past that phase."

"Let's talk about what's next. I have you booked at two churches this weekend," Loren said. She was good for jumping into business mode when I wasn't in the mood. It wasn't that I didn't want to talk about Parker and my experience; it was just that to date, most of the places Loren had booked me were nothing close to the megachurches she had promised.

A couple of times, when I went to congregations, the members were so old that a couple nodded off during my talk.

Anytime I tried to reason with her or even raise concerns, she'd simply say we had to start somewhere. Then she'd start telling me these stories about how many computers Steve Jobs designed before he perfected the Apple computer and other products we know today.

"Deena." Her receptionist's voice filled the room. We all looked toward the phone.

"Yes?"

"Attorney William Smith is on the line. Says he represents Parker Redman," the woman said.

Deena grinned at Loren and me.

"Tell him I'm in a meeting and take a message," she said.

My eyes nearly exploded.

"Yes, ma'am," the receptionist said before clicking off the line.

"What the hell did you do that for?" I asked.

"Serena, I've been doing this for more years than I care to admit." She leaned in closer as if she was about to share a secret. "Rule number one, you never take the first call, never!"

"Yeah, never," Loren had the nerve to repeat like a trained parrot.

I eased back in my seat. All I could think was whether that was something Gloria would've done.

"So, what we want to do is give them a reason to come to us hungry. If we hold out long enough, by the time we come together, he'll be willing to give us everything, including the kitchen sink," Deena said.

"Besides, we want the media stories to settle in and run their course," Loren said.

"If we tried, we couldn't get better publicity, and for free, too?" She chuckled.

I heard what they were saying, and I did believe in strategy, but I also wanted them to understand that, for me, this was not a game. I didn't have a plan B, so I had to take my best shot, and I absolutely had to win.

PARKER

The standoff with Steven lasted longer than I expected, but when it ended, I was relieved because no one was hurt. His ex-wife was a little bruised in the face, but she was alive and seemed grateful as she was brought out on a stretcher. Steven didn't want to hurt her. If he had wanted to, he wouldn't have reached out to me. Even as the police handcuffed him and led him off to the cruiser, he talked to me like we were old friends.

"You go after 'em, Parker. Go with all guns loaded and blasting, man!" he said.

I didn't condone what he had done to his ex-wife, but I understood his frustration. Even better than his frustration, I understood his anger. After spending most of my night with him in his apartment, I didn't have any energy left to go fight the good fight.

"You coming in for questioning, right?" Detective Johnson had said as I tried to walk to my car. I wanted to tell him I had a business I needed to run, but I couldn't.

"Yeah, but you guys got me for about an hour. After that, I can't promise what's bound to come out of my mouth. I'm dog tired," I said.

"An hour—I'll make it happen within that time," he said. "You've got my word."

As I followed Detective Johnson to the station, I thought about

Steven. He was like so many other men who stumbled into DFF. By the time they found me, they were usually at their breaking point. How could you tell a man the kids he helped raise weren't his, and then expect him to smile and turn the other cheek?

Steven was going to face a series of charges, but I had to look at the bright side of things. If he wanted to, he could've killed his ex-wife and himself. I decided he simply wanted to put some fear in her. It wasn't right, but it ended the best way possible, with her free to go back to her kids and him in custody.

At the station, I answered the questions they asked. I didn't have much information, but I told them what I could. I told them how I took the phone call and agreed to meet with Steven when I realized he had a hostage. I described the apartment once I got there and the condition his ex-wife was in before I convinced Steven to let me untie her.

When he was finished, Johnson asked me to read over his report.

"It look okay to you?" he asked.

"Yeah, I think that pretty much covers it all," I said. I yawned.

"Hey, man, you can go. Thank you for your help. You know this could've had a completely different ending, right?"

"I'm glad we were able to bring it to a peaceful close," I said.

"Not *we*," Johnson corrected.

I smiled faintly, then stood.

"I'll let you know about his court date," Johnson said as he let me out a side door.

Before I even turned down my street, I knew Roxy would be burning mad. She wanted no part of what she called my *vigilante work*. There wasn't much I could do, but my only other hope was that she'd take it easy on me tonight.

The house was dark when I pulled up, but I knew they were at home and probably asleep.

When I turned the lock and stepped quietly into the house, I was startled to see Roxy sitting there. The only light in the house came from the TV.

"I told you to leave this mess buried where right it was," she said without greeting me. "In the past, but could you listen?"

She shook her head, answering her own question. That told me the level of anger she was experiencing.

"He could've killed her, Roxy. I had no idea I'd be gone all that long. You know I've got tons to do at the office. You think I wanted to spend my entire day talking a madman off the ledge?" I asked.

She frowned, but never pulled her eyes off the screen.

"I'm not talking about that, Parker," she said. "I already knew you'd be there a week if that's what it took! I'm talking about the shit I wanted you to leave alone, but you refused!"

I was nearly past her and headed for our bedroom, but her words stopped me. My pulse was racing.

"Then what are you talking about?" I asked.

"Didn't you watch TV while you were holed up with that crazy man?"

"No, actually he kept it on *SportsCenter* the entire time I was there," I said.

"Wow! So you don't know, do you? You have no fucking clue!"

"Roxy, I'm tired. The riddles won't get solved tonight. Either you can tell me what you're talking about or you can sit here in the dark and keep doing what you were doing before I came in."

"I tried to call you," she said. "When you didn't answer, I called Bill. He put a call through to her lawyer, but nothing happened."

"You care to tell me who and what you're talking about?" I asked.

"Serena. She's been all over the news today and tonight. She and her attorney held a news conference. She says you're Semaj's father and she wants you to pay child support," Roxy reported emotionless.

My legs wobbled. She may as well have taken a baseball bat and swung it with all her might into my midsection. It felt like the wind had been knocked completely out of me.

"She said what?" I screamed.

"I told you! I told you! I told you to leave the shit alone, but you wouldn't listen! You just wouldn't listen to me! Well, I damn sure hope you're happy now, Parker!"

Roxy got up and pushed past me and down the hall to our bedroom. She slammed the door so hard that the entire frame seemed to rattle.

I felt weak. I wasn't sure if I was tired from the drama of the day, or this foolishness rearing its ugly head all over again. It had to be about the lawsuit. That's what I told myself, until I realized Bill and I hadn't leaked that information yet.

Instead of going after Roxy, I eased into the chair she'd just vacated and took a deep breath. The truth of the matter to me was that Serena was trying to pin this on me because she was probably sick and tired of being alone with her bitter, evil ass.

I wasn't worried about myself because I knew damn well I hadn't touched the skank. What concerned me was the possible impact her negative publicity would have on the organization and the work we were doing to help other men.

So Serena had finally struck. I only thought about her on days when I was at speaking engagements. When I gave my personal testimony, she was of course included. I rarely even spoke her name otherwise. Sure, recently it had come up, but that was only because Bill and I had talked about the lawsuits we planned to file next week.

If I didn't know anything, I knew two things. The first was that I would sleep on the couch because Roxy was probably *hot grits* mad, and second, I knew damn well I hadn't screwed Serena's evil behind.

LACHEZ

"Damn, you think you got enough shit in that basket?" I asked Toni.

She pushed an overflowing shopping cart and I was right behind her with mine.

"Make sure you get enough cleaning products so we won't run out for a minute," Toni said.

We'd been on a serious shopping spree and I had to admit it was fun. We were only buying food, cleaning supplies, and other things from the twenty-four-hour Walmart. If I had it my way, Gucci would've been open twenty-four hours, but it wasn't, so we had to take what we could get.

We headed straight to Walmart the minute we left Richard asleep in the hotel room.

We'd shopped for nearly three hours.

When we'd stuffed both shopping carts to their limits, we moved toward the checkout lines.

"Make sure you go over there to the older woman," I suggested to Toni.

I followed her and navigated my basket in the direction of the older clerk.

"You think she's gonna ask us for ID?" Toni asked.

"Nah, as long as *I* whip out the card, trust, they won't even give you a second look," I said.

And I was correct.

"Oh, this is all together," I told the woman after she rang up everything in my basket. Toni was working fast to empty her stuff onto the conveyer belt.

"Wow, you two have been busy, huh?" she asked.

By the time she finished ringing up Toni's stuff, I knew she had to be tired because I definitely was.

When the woman looked at me and said, "Okay, that will be eight hundred and ninety seven dollars," I whipped out the credit card and gave it to her.

She took the card, looked at it, and said, "May I see your ID, please?"

"Oh, it's my husband's card." I dug into my purse like I was searching for the ID. "Trixie, I don't have my ID," I yelled, panic-stricken.

Toni tried to fit the many bags into the baskets.

"Did you get it off the sofa table? Remember, you paid for the pizza earlier," she said.

I slapped my forehead with the palm of my hand, and sighed.

"I'm so sorry. Let me guess—we're gonna have to put all of this stuff back?" I asked.

"Well," she sighed, then looked at the baskets and all of the stuff. "I guess I can let it pass this time, but technically, you're supposed to show ID for credit transactions."

"I understand," I told her. "But it was a simple mistake, and I can assure you, this is my husband Richard's credit card. We've been married for eleven years," I lied.

We pushed our carts out to the parking lot where we loaded everything into the car and drove home all smiles.

The day after we left Richard in the hotel room, Toni and I were still in celebration mode.

"Didn't I tell you to trust me?" I asked.

"Girl, you should've seen yourself in Walmart last night," Toni said.

I laughed. "I didn't have to see myself. I saw you," I said.

"And who travels with five thousand dollars in cash?" she asked.

"The same businessman who is missing his Rolex this morning," I said.

This was our second *come-up* this week, and I told Toni I didn't want to get too greedy. But I could see it in Trixie's, aka Sexy's, eyes, she knew we were on to a great thing, and so did I.

"I keep telling you, Toni, these guys are different. I am careful about who I select for us."

As we put all of our food, supplies, and everything else away, I started thinking about Junie and the other kids. I was going on week number two of freedom, and Darlene was still full of excuses about why she couldn't bring my kids to see me.

"How are you so sure?" she asked.

"Toni, these guys are married, number one. Number two, they are executives, which usually means morality clauses in their contracts. Number three, they're far too embarrassed to call the police and admit they were willing to pay for…eh-hem," I said.

"I guess you have a point there, but if there was anyone who wouldn't have to pay for eh-hem, it would've been Richard's fine ass," she said.

We laughed at that one.

Toni stopped what she was doing and turned to me.

"Was it really necessary for you to try and get it up when you knew the man was out cold?"

"Girl, I was only trying to make sure." I chuckled. "I wanted that man something terrible! You showed up way too fast that time."

"He's not even your type." Toni wrinkled her nose.

"Yeah, but sometimes, there's nothing wrong with trying something different," I said.

"We should take his card to the Galleria," she suggested.

I wagged a finger in the air.

"Now, now, now, let's not get greedy. That's how you get caught. Besides, by the time the sun comes up, he will have had the card canceled, and we'd be walking into a trap if we tried to use it again."

"Yeah, good point there," she said.

"You think he'll remember us?" I asked.

"Let's see, Heidi." Toni smirked, using my alias.

"Looks like you're finally catching on." I winked at her.

I felt like I'd finished a full shift on my feet by the time we were done stuffing the pantry, refrigerator, and our freezer.

"Well, girl, I'm about to crash. I'm wiped out," I said.

"Okay, in the morning then," Toni said.

I left her in the kitchen and dragged my tired ass off to bed with thoughts of my son swimming in my head.

It felt like I'd just laid my head on the pillow when the strong aroma of bacon started tingling in my nostrils. It literally woke me up. I didn't realize how hungry I was until my stomach growled loudly.

Toni was fixing breakfast.

I rushed out of bed and followed the heavenly scent.

"What are you doing with yourself today?" Toni asked as I finished the feast she had prepared.

"Finding that bitch Pricilla so I can try and talk some sense into my son," I said. "She's way too old for him, Toni!"

Toni pressed her lips together as if she was trying to stop herself from saying something.

Honestly, I didn't give a damn what she had to say about this. Pricilla was too old for Junie and that was that!

"How you gonna get in touch with them?" she asked.

I didn't really want to talk about it because I still hadn't figured everything out; I only knew I was hell-bent on making it happen.

EBONI

I didn't know whose mouth hung wider, mine or Ulonda's. I knew for sure my eyes were the size of saucers. Elisa was pregnant! I wondered if she knew the way her man was running behind me all over town.

As I watched her closely, I felt like she had only called a meeting so she could rub my nose in it. Elisa hated me and the kids with a passion, even though we were around before she met Shawnathon.

The kids weren't born yet, but she knew that he and I had been together and could've possibly worked it out. I hated her ass.

As I looked at her, I felt like she was putting way too much in it. There was no need for her to be walking around like that with that small baby bump.

"Thanks for meeting me," she said as she made her way toward us. "Hi, I'm Elisa," she said to Ulonda.

"I'm Ulonda," Ulonda said.

"Nice to meet you, Yolanda," Elisa said.

"No, it's U-londa," Ulonda corrected.

"So what did you want to talk about?" I asked her.

"I was thinking we could go inside and sit down. Are you in a hurry?"

"Not really," I said. "But I have stuff to do," I added. After I said it, I realized it didn't make sense, but I didn't care. The curiosity was killing me.

We walked up to the bar and asked if we could be seated outside.

When Elisa reached for the menu, I placed my hand on it. Suddenly, she looked up at me with a frown etched into her pretty features.

"Elisa, this is not tea time. What do you want?" I asked.

Her eyes darted to Ulonda, then back to me.

"I thought we were meeting alone. I didn't expect you to bring a friend," she said.

"I had no idea what you wanted. I still don't know. No way in hell I was coming to meet you by myself," I told her.

"Okay, well, I wanted to see how you would feel about something."

I had no idea why she was stalling, but she was working my last nerve.

"You don't have to decide right this minute," she said, "but this thing with you and Shawnathon is really taking its toll."

I wondered if she expected me to feel sorry for her or them. She was the one driving around in her new custom-painted Range Rover, and coordinating her hair and clothes.

"So..." She dug into her caramel-colored leather Gucci bag. It was nice, too. "I was wondering if you'd be willing to accept a sort of peace offering," she stammered.

My eyebrows rose slightly.

She trembled as she held the check out to me. I looked down at it, then looked up at her and clamped my hand over my open mouth.

My eyes connected with the check. I allowed the zeros to register in my head for a minute before I spoke. Ulonda kneed me under the table. When I found my voice, I asked the first thing that popped into my head.

"You're offering me two hundred thousand dollars? For what?"

"Here's the thing," Elisa said.

"You guys been waited on yet?" a waiter appeared and asked.

"No, can we have a moment? I'll call you when we're ready," Ulonda said.

"Shawnathon and I are trying to start off the right way," she continued.

I wanted to tell her she should've thought about that before she got knocked up, but I held my tongue.

"So next Saturday, a bunch of our closest friends are going to Vegas and Shawnathon and I are getting married. So, I wanted to, like I said, present you with this peace offering, if you'll drop your suit against my um, Shawnathon." Her head hung low.

My index finger popped up. "Lemme get this straight. You wanna pay me off so you and that idiot can ride off into the sunset and forget about me and my kids like we don't even exist?" I asked.

"Eboni, I thought I could come and talk to you, woman to woman. I didn't want any drama. I'm trying to make this right. I mean, everybody knows you and Shawnathon were nothing but a hookup," she said.

Ulonda popped up from the chair. "Meeting over!" she announced. She looked at me. "Come on, let's go. Let's get outta here," she said.

I got up, too. It was probably illegal to hit a pregnant woman, but she had some nerve. I snatched the check she tried to give me and ripped it to pieces.

"You can tell Shawnathon I said, 'Nice try,'" I said as I tossed the confetti in her face, followed Ulonda, and headed back outside so we could leave. "Oh, and good luck in Vegas," I said over my shoulder.

In the parking lot, I considered keying her ride, but thought better of it. I couldn't believe her. Did they think I'd settle for a measly two hundred grand? I was sick of them and their so-called contracts! Who did they think I was, some special kind of fool?

As we turned to get on 59, I looked at Ulonda and said, "Can you believe that mess? She really thought I was gonna agree to that?"

"Well, if they figure you just in it for the money, they probably figured you'd accept anything they threw your way," Ulonda said.

"Why would I settle for two hundred thousand when I could get more than that every single month!"

Ulonda's head whipped in my direction.

"You think you'll get that much from him?" she asked.

"I keep telling you, he's worth bank, girl." I shook my head. "Nia's gonna take him, turn him upside down, and shake until we get every penny he's got. Girl, I got two kids for him, not one, but two!" I held up my fingers. "That's gotta be worth way more than two hundred grand," I said.

I exited the freeway and stopped at an intersection.

"You know what? I'm gonna fix both of them," I said to Ulonda.

She looked at me. The light turned green. I took off and said, "How about we're going to Vegas? I think I hear wedding bells," I sang.

"Ooh wee, girl, don't even play like that," she said excitedly.

"I'm not hardly playing. I'll scrape up my change, and if you willing to take the money plane, we can make this happen," I said. The money plane carried cash to Las Vegas. So all we had to do was drive to Louisiana, and we could fly out on that plane at a discounted price.

"Umph, well, if we put our change together, I think we can make that trip happen." Ulonda said.

"Yes, I think it's time I give Elisa and Shawnathon a taste of their own medicine!"

SERENA

"You better be glad I don't know where you live, bitch!"

"Uuuggh." I slammed the phone down, pissed at the coward who was on the other end. My phone hadn't stopped ringing. Since the press conference yesterday, I had already received tons of crank calls and several death threats. Something in my gut told me Parker and the other deadbeats he supported were behind it. I didn't have the proof, but I knew it.

As I sat in my kitchen and waited for Loren to come discuss strategy with me, I began to get pissed.

"Why are they calling me? What did I do wrong? He's the jackass! He's the one not paying child support!" I screamed.

Twelve-year-old Semaj snaked her neck around the door.

"Mom, are you okay?" she asked.

"Yeah, honey, I'm fine. Go get my cigarettes, please," I said.

She disappeared. A little while later, she reappeared in the doorway.

"Mom, you really shouldn't smoke. Not only is nicotine addictive, but it's bad for everyone around you," she warned.

I eyed my child in a way that she understood. She presented my pack of cigarettes and lighter, then took her narrow behind out of my sight.

If I only did what was good for me, she wouldn't be here today. I chuckled at the thought as I shook a cigarette out of the box.

Smoking was a nasty habit, but for me, men turned out to be even worse. I wanted Parker the moment I laid eyes on him. I knew he was different. He looked like he was polished and important. The other guys, they were dressed like they might be ready to watch the game. He wasn't the only man in a suit that night, but he was the best-looking one.

"Who's that?" I asked Abbie, one of my coworkers. It wasn't that we were tight. I asked her because she was a regular at Saltgrass, the steakhouse. We were there for an office-sponsored happy hour event.

"Hmmm, I don't know, never seen him in here before," Abbie said.

As the evening wore on, I kept a close eye on this tall, dark stranger. His shoulders were broad. It wasn't that he was drop-dead gorgeous or anything like that, but he was very polished. I kept thinking if I could snag a man like that, maybe I'd finally make it on to Easy Street.

He laughed, drank and seemed to enjoy himself with his group. I watched him closely for nearly two hours before I finally made my move. The moment I noticed him walk toward the restrooms, I waited for what I felt was a good amount of time, and then I got up.

"I'll be back," I said to my coworkers, who barely responded.

Right as Parker walked out of the bathroom, I bumped into him as hard as I could.

"Oww," I yelled.

One look into my eyes and I knew I had him. He stumbled and pulled me up before I fell.

"Damn, I'm sorry. I didn't even see you," he admitted.

"Are you okay?" he asked.

"Barely," I said.

He seemed taken aback by my response.

"I'm sorry, what's wrong? Did I hurt you?"

"Yeah, but I'm sure it's nothing a drink can't fix." I smiled.

The worried expression faded from his face and he broke into a genuine smile.

"If you promise not to turn me in, I think I can handle that drink," he said.

We looked so good together, but I could tell he was probably way outside my league. I was accustomed to reformed bad boys or the kind of brothas who only had something to offer if I was going half. Parker was different—he was classy.

At the bar we shared a little small talk. He told me his name, where he worked, what kind of degree he had, and I listened.

I worked for the state at the time, but my job was nothing to brag about. You didn't need a degree for my position or anything like that. So mostly I sat in awe and imagined myself as Parker's woman.

Two weeks after our initial meeting, I held my breath as I waited for him to answer the phone.

"Parker speaking," he said.

I had never heard a man answer the phone like that before. I wanted to give him some that first night, but a couple of the guys he'd been with pulled him away. This time it was gonna happen for sure.

He was reluctant at first. He was vague about whether he had plans until I offered to cook for him. I silently kicked myself because I should've called him sooner. Instead, I tried to figure out what was the acceptable amount of time to wait after getting his number. I didn't want to risk giving him my number in case he wouldn't call.

I didn't date like that, but I figured the kind of women he was used to did that kind of stuff.

If it could've gone wrong, it did that night. First, I got lost as I drove around in search of Parker's place. I had to call him for directions something like three times. Finally, he told me to stay put and he came and met me.

I followed him into the gated subdivision and along the winding, tree-lined streets until we pulled into to his driveway.

Parker's house was meticulous. I'd never seen light-gray carpet before. His taste was classic and on the high end. Suddenly, I was mad at myself. I should not have offered to cook for him. His kitchen looked like one of those that should've been featured in *Architectural Digest*. His things looked too perfect to touch. Whose appliances blended in with the cabinets? And his cabinets had smoked-glass windows! The flooring throughout his house was gray and blue-colored cement that led to gray carpeted areas.

Although I was completely feeling him, I didn't get a good vibe from him. When I realized he was watching the History Channel, and really digging it, I wanted to run. Maybe he was one of those boring men who behaved far older than they actually were.

"What you watching?" I asked.

"Oh, this documentary on the Kennedys," he said.

Yawn!

I hurriedly finished the shrimp and pasta dish I had prepared and got to drinking. There was absolutely no chemistry between us. He asked questions about my job, but it felt like the questions were forced so he could help fill the quiet.

After a few drinks, I tried to ease up next to him on the sofa. That's when it dawned on me, he hadn't made a single attempt or move on me the whole time I had been there. Unfortunately for me, liquor impaired my judgment so much that I still saw Parker as a challenge.

"You want a refill?" I asked.

He nodded, but I could tell he was either close to being drunk or sleepy. I didn't drink anymore. Parker barely hung on.

"You want me to call you a cab?" he asked and I was crushed.

I wanted to say, "No, I'd like to sit on your face," but I didn't. What little liquid courage I had—quickly dissolved.

"No, I'm fine. I wasn't ready to go yet," I told him.

"I don't mean to be rude, but it's been a long day for me," he said. He stumbled a bit as he got up from the sofa.

Oh God! Was he asking me to leave?

"I'll be right back," he said.

Nearly twenty minutes passed and he still hadn't made it back into the living room.

"Parker?" I called after him.

No response.

I thought all kinds of things. Unsure of what to do, I decided to go and make sure he was okay. I walked into his bedroom and was nearly blown away. It wasn't the sight of him laid out on top of his king-sized poster bed, but the fact that his bedroom was even more impressive than the others.

"Look, baby, I'm sorry," he said.

My ears perked up. I walked over to the bed and eased next to him. I began to rub his legs.

"Oh, that feels good," he said. He was good and drunk.

"Why don't you take them off? I won't bite," I said.

There was no way for him to know then how he had shattered my heart into a million pieces. How could he *not* want me?

"I wouldn't be any good to you tonight," he said.

Excuses.

"I won't do anything you don't want me to do," I whispered.

He chuckled a little.

"You'd better go home. Thanks for dinner—I needed the company."

I heard his words, but my body didn't want to listen. There had to be a place for me in his life. He was impaired, so I moved in.

Once I helped him get out of those pants, I didn't even bother with the sexy boxer briefs he wore. I reached into them and grabbed his muscle. Parker may have been out of it, but not everything was down for the count.

I maneuvered my body until I was hovering over him, and I went to work. Although he was limp, he filled my mouth. I didn't understand why he didn't want me, but I was determined. Once he was hard enough, I slipped on a condom I found in his nightstand drawer.

Soft moans escaped his lips. After a while, he tried to hold my head in place, and that's when I knew I had him.

"Girl, what you sitting here doing, daydreaming?" Loren's question pulled me back to the kitchen.

"I didn't even hear you come in. I was waiting on you," I said.

"Umph, looks to me like you were in another world. Look, that cigarette is just sitting there burning to its butt." She pointed at the line of ash in the tray.

"Let's get to work," I said. "What do you have for me?"

PARKER

Interview requests had poured in from all over the country. It was just my luck that Serena and her crazy press conference went viral. It seemed like that was all she wrote.

My office staff was frustrated and shooting off complaints left and right. I couldn't blame them. Tongues were wagging overtime after her accusations.

"We even had a couple of people call to say they didn't need Parker at court," the receptionist said.

"Listen, guys," I started. "I can't apologize enough for this. I plan to fight these claims from her to the fullest extent of the law. I think she heard about the lawsuit and decided she'd strike first."

All eyes remained on me as I spoke, but I could tell they were frustrated. It was hard talking to our clients with this rumor hanging over my head.

"I want to reassure each of you that her claims are false. Let's stick together and fight this thing head-on." I felt like an idiot talking to them, considering all that was going on.

If they showed pieces from her interview one more time, I was planning to call in and complain myself.

"Remember Don't Force Fatherhood is bigger than all of us," I said.

I was more than a little apprehensive when the phone rang again.

"Bill is on line two," the receptionist said.

I breathed a huge sigh of relief. I couldn't remember the last time I was so happy to hear from my attorney.

"Bill," I greeted cheerfully. "Please tell me you've got some good news. Things are falling apart around here," I said.

"Yeah, buddy, I watched her news conference. Luckily for you, her attorney, Deena, and I know each other well. I've already reached out to her, and I'm waiting on a call back," he said.

I got up and closed my office door. I didn't need the staff hearing my concerns.

"Well, you remember what Roxy was like the last time we were in your office, right? Imagine that being a hundred times worse. I haven't felt this ostracized since I was released from jail after wiping out our savings to pay for a kid that wasn't mine!"

"I wouldn't want to be in your shoes right now," Bill said.

"The crazy thing is—why would a lawyer even take her case? She just walks into an office and says I fathered her child? This is after she was married to my best friend and lied about him being the father?"

"Who knows what she said to Deena? Remember Serena Carson is very resourceful, and she doesn't do anything without planning and thinking carefully."

"Yeah, it's a pity people like her can't use their intelligence for good versus evil," I said.

"But let me ask you this," Bill said.

"Anything," I said.

"*Could* you be the kid's father?"

"Not unless pigs have started to fly," I said with great certainty. "It would have had to be the Immaculate Conception." I laughed.

"Good. Good. That's what I needed to know. When can you come down? I've got the papers ready for the suit. In light of this, however, I wanted to see how you'd feel about adding her name to the list," Bill suggested.

"What would I be suing her for? Here's why I asked. How can I sue Serena but not Kelly or Lachez?" I asked. "I don't want to make any errors or mistakes with this. We've got to come out the gate swinging hard and accurately."

"Yes, I agree. And while that would be tricky, it's not impossible. Here's what I mean. Because Lachez and Kelly agreed to cooperate, we could say that was immunity for them," Bill explained. "Also, let's not forget, Lachez did go to jail," Bill reminded me.

"Yeah, she did, but she didn't go to jail for what she did to me. I want to be clear about what we're gonna do and how we're gonna do it. I don't want this suit thrown out because it lacks a viable target."

"Parker, believe me when I tell you, no one can accuse you of a frivolous lawsuit after what you've been through."

"Do we have to file today?" I asked. I heard what he was saying, but I had so much to consider.

"We don't *have* to do anything. You're in the driver's seat here, buddy. I do what you tell me. If you've changed your mind, I sit tight," he said.

"I haven't changed my mind, not by a long shot, but I guess what I am saying is, I need to figure out the pros and cons of adding Serena to the suit. I want this to be taken seriously, but then again, because she stepped out before us, I don't want this to look like I'm being vindictive," I said.

"So in other words, you want her added, but Roxy might pitch a bitch over it is what you're really telling me."

I laughed. After all these years, I guess Bill was able to read me better than I could read myself some times.

"Gotta keep the little lady happy," I joked.

"Yeah, buddy, I understand. So why don't we do this? Today is Thursday. So that you can think about it, fix things at home, let's say Wednesday is our *do* day. When Wednesday rolls around, either we *do* it, or we don't. The choice is yours."

"Fair enough," I said.

I sat alone in my office long after the call with Bill. So much of this didn't make any sense. Why after all these years? Why was Serena doing this and what was she really up to?

I picked up the phone and called James.

"Parker, dawg, what's good?"

"Hey, man, I can't even call it," I said.

"Shhiiit, you sounding pretty good to me," he said.

"It's been a minute," I admitted, feeling instantly guilty about not being in touch as much as I should've been.

"How are things at DFF?" he asked.

"We're still fighting the good fight," I said.

"I read about you in *Texas Monthly*, and I saw a story about you talking some dude down in a SWAT standoff, man. What's really going on in the Bayou City?"

"If you've heard all that, I'm stunned you ain't heard the latest with your ex," I said.

"I probably ain't heard it because I try to avoid anything having to do with her," he said. "What's Serena the Sicko doing now, still using her bare hands to snatch brothas' hearts from their chests?"

"You know some things never change," I said. "This time, it looks like I'm back on her radar."

"No shit? I'm almost scared to ask, but what now?" James asked.

"Dude, she held a news conference yesterday to call me out for being a hypocrite, says I should be ashamed going around the country trying to help other deadbeats when I'm the biggest one of all," I said. I felt awkward relaying this to James because he had lived for many years thinking Semaj was his daughter.

Even after the dust cleared and we thought things were settled, he kept trying to have a relationship with Semaj, but Serena wouldn't have it. She told him he couldn't play if he didn't want to pay! I stood by and watched as that woman literally destroyed my boy.

He wouldn't admit it, but to this day, I believe that's why he decided to move to Austin. Sure, I believe his job offered him a promotion, but I think what really made it more attractive was the fact that it would put distance between him and Serena.

"She says I'm Semaj's father," I said.

It felt like an eternity as I waited for his response or reaction.

LACHEZ

I knew it wouldn't be easy getting into this office building, but I also knew the skin-tight, bright-red, leather mini dress and stacked heels with matching fishnet stockings wouldn't hurt. And the way I sashayed would definitely help.

"Oh, Lawd!" a woman cried. "My baby! My baby is gone! She was right here!"

The minute security focused on a ruckus near the information desk, thanks to Toni, I walked by like I had a purpose and joined the crowd of men dressed in dark, expensive-looking suits. I stood out like a sore thumb, but that's what I needed in this situation.

It had been smooth sailing until I stepped off the elevator on the twenty-first floor. The problem came outside the executive suites where an older woman, with a butch haircut, wearing a headset and a menacing scowl on her face, eyed me up and down.

"Can I help you," she said more than asked.

It was obvious my outfit was lost on her.

People shuffled back and forth down the long, carpeted halls to the left and right of me. Sure, I may have seemed out of place, but I was on a mission.

"I have an appointment with Mr. Douser," I said.

"Your name?"

"Honey, that's not important," I said. "Actually, it's not as much an appointment as it is me having to deliver some very timely, but most unpleasant news."

One of her bushy eyebrows went up.

"Ma'am?"

"I just got back from the doctor, and well, you know what, the more I'm thinking about it, maybe *you* should tell him. You probably know him a whole helluva lot better than me anyway," I said.

Her eyes grew wide.

"Can you tell him that the doctor says that the oral form of HPV, you know, genital warts..."

She cut me off by raising a *stop right there* hand while she used the other to press a button.

"Mr. Douser is on a call, but right this way, to the left, then your first right," she said.

I pranced down the hall and into the most spectacular office I'd ever seen.

She was right. He was there on the phone. When our eyes met, he frowned a bit. He had the oddest hazel eyes I'd ever seen. One looked green and the other looked brown. He placed his hand over the mouthpiece of his phone.

"Excuse me, ma'am, who are you?" The salt-and-pepper-haired white man looked at me as if he couldn't believe my audacity.

"I'm here to talk to you about your daughter," I said with a straight face.

His frown deepened. I could tell what he was probably thinking, but I didn't give a damn. Yeah, he was probably wondering how someone like me had even come in contact with his rigid, high-society daughter in the first damn place.

"I'm gonna have to wrap this up. I'll be in touch about that proposal," he said and ended the call.

"My daughter—what's this about?" He looked confused.

Barron Douser was a bigwig in the oil and gas industry. Don't ask me exactly what he did for a living because I couldn't tell you. But what I did discover was enough to make me lie my way right into his fabulous, glass-enclosed office.

He was a mainstay on the *Forbes* list, and his office, which was in one of the high-rise buildings in Houston's Galleria area, gave hints about his wealth. Never before had I stepped into an office that had no walls!

Every place I stood in his massive office gave me a spectacular view of the Houston skyline. He wasn't bad-looking, either. Or at least he wouldn't have been if he wasn't frowning and looking down his perfectly-tanned nose at me.

"Is my daughter in some kind of trouble?" he asked.

"Mr. Douser, it's worse," I said.

"Let me call." He snatched the receiver off his phone.

"No, don't call anyone. This is kinda sensitive, if you know what I mean," I said.

He looked at me as if he was unsure. This spoke volumes. It made me feel like I was on to something with Pricilla. Slowly, Barron reached over and dropped the phone back where it belonged.

"I am a very busy man. I don't understand why you're here, and you need to get to the point of this visit before I call security," he said. "Who let you in here?"

"You can call security all you want, but I'm actually here trying to do us both a favor."

"I'll be the judge of that," he said.

"Mr. Douser, your daughter is about to make a grave mistake," I said.

"Oh?"

His reaction and expressions told me this wouldn't be the first time Pricilla had disappointed him. He leaned back in his massive leather chair and laced his hands behind his head.

"What has Pricilla gotten herself into now? Let me guess, fifty grand?" he asked.

Now it was my turn to frown. I knew he wasn't offering me money. Was he?

"Fifty grand?" I repeated slowly.

"Listen here, I've been through this before. Although I can't recall a character quite as colorful as you, but it's always something with Pricilla. So get to the point, and tell me how much it's gonna cost me now so I can get back to handling my business," he said.

"Barron, you listen to me! I don't know what you're used to with your daughter, but her marrying my son is what I'm here to talk about. Now I'm thinking a man with your means could help prevent a mistake before it happens."

"Your son? How old are you?" he asked in disbelief.

"Now Barron," I said, "you don't ask a lady her age!"

"I'm confused. So you're not working with Pricilla?" he asked.

"Working *with* her? I want her to disappear," I said. "Uh, I mean out of my son's life, of course. I think she's too old for him. But his nose is wide open, and he won't hear a word I'm trying to say."

"Well, how old is the young man?" Barron asked.

"He'll be eighteen in a few weeks," I said.

"Eighteen?" he repeated. But absent from his voice was the anger, disgust, and shock I needed.

"Yes, as in still a child! Now I understand your daughter is a grown woman, but quite surely there's something you can do to prevent her from marrying a child."

Barron shook his head.

"Pricilla marches to a different drum. I can't imagine she'd find happiness with a eighteen-year-old man, but there's nothing I can do. Can you find your way out?" he asked.

He was finished. After all I had gone through not just to find him, but to make it up into his office, that was all he could say?

Before I even moved, he turned his attention to something on his desk.

"So you're not gonna try to help? You're just gonna let this happen?"

He looked up at me.

"Pricilla is an adult. Your son, although young, is also legally an adult. I don't have time to waste," he said.

For the first time since I came up with this plan, I felt defeated. Although he was still talking to me, I could tell Barron had already dismissed me and was on to his next task.

"How old is your daughter?" I asked.

"She's thirty-six," he said.

"Thirty-six-years old! I don't get it. What could she possibly see in a kid?"

"Perhaps you should ask her, but you can't do it here. Now, unless there's something else, I really need to focus my attention elsewhere," he said.

Defeated, I turned to leave. I didn't understand what my child saw in a woman old enough to be his mother. Barron had been my last hope. As I walked out of his office, I thought about what, if anything, I could do to make Junie see the mistake he was about to make.

I had been worried sick since the visit last week, but after meeting with Barron, I felt like I was headed for even more heartbreak.

EBONI

I pumped my arms into the air, flung my head back, then snaked my body seductively as I shook the sweat from my waist-length weave. I wanted to go hard in Sin City.

The loud music pulsated and worked like an aphrodisiac. With the Belvedere in my system, I was literally on top of the world. Or at least that's how I felt, considering I was in the middle of the makeshift dance floor at Blush Boutique, the sleek and sexy club tucked into a corner inside the Wynn Las Vegas.

There had to be at least 200 people all crammed onto the dance floor area, and that was not counting those seated at the tables and chairs that were lined up the middle of the club. The dance floor was nothing but a small bit of space between the two rows of side-by-side sofas and couches, but it worked.

Right above our heads on the dance floor, tons of color-changing lanterns shone light down and made our skin glow in shades of purple, yellow, blue and red hues. So there was a purple babe to my left and a yellow hottie to my right. We had a VIP area over to the side near the patio, but we hadn't been there much since we hit the club.

I didn't know why everyone else was here, but Ulonda, her cousin Judi, who tagged along because she hooked us up during the trip, and I were celebrating. We hadn't been in Vegas for a good three hours, but we couldn't tell. We hadn't left the dance floor since we hit it.

Bodies were packed in the club like sardines, so there was really only enough room to party by ourselves. Sure, there was the occasional rub-up next to some sexy stranger, or even the random ass-grab from some guy who took advantage of the close proximity on the floor, but all in all, we were having a good time.

When I opened my eyes, to my surprise, Ulonda was doing the Beyoncé booty shake right next to me, which only got me hyped. Ulonda pulled her shoulder-length curly locks to one side and used her hand to fan her oval-shaped face. It was hot for sure.

Our eyes met, and her face broke into a wide grin that would've lit up the room had these lights not been doing their own parade. Ulonda stepped closer to me, then turned so that her butt came in contact with my midsection.

As I lost myself in the music, I thought back to the good, fun days. I remembered when I used to think Shawnathon McGee was the answer to my single-girl, sick of being broke prayers, but he wasn't. Turned out, the perfect man was nothing more than a sorry-ass deadbeat who knew nothing about being a *real* man.

But soon, Shawnathon, his new trophy, and all the drama they had brought into my life would be a thing of the past, and I couldn't wait.

The music changed and we switched, jamming to 50 Cent.

I closed my eyes and listened to the lyrics. I thought that's what the hell I should've done—found me a loaded rapper, maybe that's what I'd get next. No more ball boys, that was for damn sure! But then thoughts of Ulonda's fake-ass-rapping baby daddy popped into my head and killed that thought.

All of a sudden, cold hands grab my shoulder, and I snapped my eyes open. It was Judi, holding up the sequin evening wrist-bag, and beckoning me with her index finger.

"What?" I mouthed and shrugged.

She used her other hand to signal a phone and pointed to the bag, I nodded and smiled. Maybe our hookup had finally come through. Judi motioned toward the bathroom, and soon I was right behind her as she followed Ulonda through the maze of hot, sweaty bodies.

As we made our way into the bathroom, I rushed to the sink to try and cool off with a splash of cold water.

"I think our information has come through. Someone's been blowin' us up," Judi said as she dug for the phone.

"Hopefully, it's the ballers we met at the airport," Ulonda said.

We had already agreed, even though there were only two of them and three of us, we'd do some naughty things and really give them a time to remember. After all, we were in Sin City!

Judi dug for her phone and pressed a few buttons when she found it.

"Yes, this is Judi," she said. Judi worked at a popular Houston magazine. She had a column and wrote about any- and everything under the sun.

Her hookup got us the rooms once we hopped on the money plane to Vegas from Louisiana. With Judi's help, we hadn't even spent two hundred dollars.

I watched as Judi spoke into the phone.

"Yes, great! Thanks," she said.

She ended the call and turned to me.

"The wedding is Saturday evening at the Cancun Resort, located at 8335 Las Vegas Boulevard," Judi reported.

High-fives went all around. In order to get the deal on the flight, we had to leave on Thursday, so we still had a couple of days to put my plan into motion.

"The Cancun Resort, huh?"

"Yes, they rented out the entire resort from Friday to Sunday. Guests will be arriving tomorrow morning."

Damn, Judi was good.

Ulonda came over to me.

"So how much you planning to spend?" she asked.

"I figured we tell them twenty dollars an hour, and we get ten of them for three hours."

"So, six hundred?" she asked.

"Yeah. You think that's too much?"

Ulonda tilted her head sideways, as if she was pondering my question.

"Considering how much we've saved, I think that's actually a pretty good price for what you want to pull off," Ulonda said.

"Okay, so we have one day to go out and get our team together. Let's party tonight, then get up and get to work tomorrow," I said.

"Girl, I can't wait to see the look on their faces," Ulonda said.

"Can you believe his stupid ass is about to get hitched days before we're headed to court?"

"What an ass," Ulonda said.

I turned to Judi. "You got your media contacts on alert?" I asked.

"It wasn't hard to do when I tipped them off that Shawnathon McGee was planning a secret wedding. Trust, paparazzi will be in full effect!"

Knowing that the world would see me exact my revenge made me that much more excited. I couldn't wait to put him on blast!

SERENA

I felt like they were talking about someone else as they introduced me to the women at the center. It wasn't that my credentials were anywhere close to being impressive or anything like that, but I always got nervous when it was time for me to speak.

"So, with no further ado, please welcome Serena Carson with a hearty round of applause."

I swallowed dry and rose from my seat. I walked up to the podium as I clutched the index cards Loren had suggested. She said that writing out a speech was never a good idea. Let her tell it, reading an actual speech left too much room for mistakes. So, the plan was for me to jot down four key topics on the cards. Under each topic I'd put three points. Beneath each point, I had written words related to what I wanted to share.

The Young Women's Auxiliary Group at Sweetwater Powerhouse of God would be the second time I was using the new method. For a megachurch, I expected far more people, but I couldn't complain because their four hundred-dollar check had already cleared the bank.

"My story is one of pain, lies and finally, a broken system. I stand in front of you a victim of the system two-times-over. As a single mother, I expected the state to hold up its end of the bargain and help me make my children's fathers pay. Boy, was I sadly mistaken when I learned these men didn't have to do anything they didn't really want to do. Unless I kept leaning on the attorney general's office, they assumed I didn't need financial care for my children."

I talked about how Parker was on national TV programs, the local news, in magazines, and newspapers all over the country, yet he didn't have to pay child support. I amped up the part about how he acted like he didn't even know me. When I saw several women in the audience shaking their heads, I knew I had them.

At the end, I agreed to take a few questions. So, after speaking for about thirty minutes, I ended and urged them to keep up the fight.

"Don't let them get away with it. You didn't make those kids by yourselves, so you shouldn't have to go on welfare or food stamps to feed them," I said.

Loren jumped up and looked around the room. She held on to a cordless microphone that she flicked on and off.

"Are there any questions?" she asked.

A couple of hands shot toward the ceiling. I drank from my glass of water as Loren rushed to the first person with a question.

"What should I do if my ex keeps quitting his job to avoid paying?" a woman asked.

"That's a great question. Remember how I told you Parker did the same thing? If you can show a history of him quitting jobs to avoid payment, you can turn him in for that foolishness. If he's already fallen behind, he can be arrested!" I said. "If I were you, I'd look at his history over an eighteen-month period. It usually takes about six months to get an order executed. If he quits shortly after, you can make the argument that he's quitting to avoid paying. I'd get the attorney general on that right away. Good luck," I said.

"Next question?" Loren asked. She shuffled across the room.

A middle-aged woman stood.

"What information does the attorney general need to find a deadbeat?"

"Another great question," I said. "Honestly, when I speak to younger women, especially teens, I tell them if you're giving it up, know his last name, his social security number and his date of birth!"

The room exploded in laughter.

"No, I'm serious," I said when the laughter quieted down. "Be on top of your business! Before you call the AG's office, the most important information you can provide, aside from your baby's daddy's current address, is the name and address of his current employer. If you don't know the current employer, you should at least know the name and address of the last known employer."

I added, "Also, you should make sure you have the following information about him—names and addresses of relatives and friends, names of banks or creditors like a utility company, the names of organizations, unions or clubs that he may belong to, and let's not forget, places where he spends his free time."

I received a standing ovation.

As Loren and I were in the car, we debriefed. The speaking engagements weren't flowing in as quickly as I wanted, but when we were able to snag one, I tried my best to provide lots of good information. I also dogged Parker out as much as I could. It wasn't just because I hated him, but the women seemed to get more excited and more engaged when I portrayed him as a real dog who didn't try to reach out to his daughter.

"You did great," Loren said. "And that call came in after the news conference. We need to get the YouTube channel updated. I hope you are able to look at the bigger picture and see that we're on to something here," she said.

"Yeah, I know what you mean, and I do feel good after I finish talking to these women. Have we heard anything from Gloria's people yet?"

Loren's jaw tightened at the question. She didn't like it when I rode her about it, but I wanted to go all the way with it, and for that, I had to have a big-time, high-profile attorney.

"I know, I know, Deena is the Gloria Allred of the South, but I should be on *The Today Show* with this, or even *The View*," I said.

"Let's conquer our own backyard before we try to take on the rest of the world," Loren suggested. She wasn't nasty when she said it, but I felt like that allowed her to book me in these little hole-in-the-wall places and sell me a bunch of crap about the big picture.

"I'll admit, Sweetwater is a megachurch and I do want more of those, but what's up with Lakewood?" I asked. I knew her cousin used to be married to one of the bigwigs over there, but I didn't tell her that.

Her head whipped in my direction. I wasn't sure if she expected me to flinch, but I was dead serious. I knew where I wanted to take this, and I needed to know that she was on the same page; otherwise, she and I might need to part ways.

"Um, it's gonna take us a minute and far more speaking engagements before we make it to Lakewood," she said.

"I don't mean like tomorrow, but I need to know that it's at least somewhere on the list," I said.

"Lakewood is there, but we've got quite a ways to go before we can get in on that type of crowd," Loren insisted. "You know Oprah and Tyler were just there a few weeks ago," she said.

"See, that's what I'm talking about. Hey, maybe you should contact Oprah, or even Tyler. He could do a movie based on my struggle," I said.

If I had blinked, I would've missed it, but I was very observant. When I suggested Tyler do a movie about my struggle, I noticed a facial tic from Loren. That pissed me off.

"What? You don't think Tyler Perry could turn my story into a movie? What's so ridiculous about that?"

"I didn't say it was ridiculous. I'm just saying, everybody knows Tyler only does his own stories—that's all. Besides, you know what? Nothing—forget it," she said.

"No, what? What were you gonna say?"

"Well, I'm not trying to get you all worked up or anything, but you do know that you kinda stretch the truth quite a bit when you tell your story," she said delicately.

"Stretch the truth?" I hollered.

"Um, yeah, Serena. I mean the way you tell it, it's like Parker intentionally walked out on you and your kid. You make it seem like he knew he had fathered your child and then refused to pay or refused to have contact with Semaj!"

I couldn't believe my ears! This was what I didn't like about Loren. The minute I suggested ways we could make things better, she took it personal and got all defensive and started to attack me.

PARKER

I felt like I was trapped in the twilight zone for the second time in my life, and I didn't understand how I could be a target not once, but twice.

After my conversation with James yesterday, I stupidly came home and tried to talk to Roxy about what Bill and I were considering.

"You just don't get it, do you?" she screamed at me.

"What's the problem? What are you getting mad for?" I asked.

"You're allowing yourself to get dragged right back in! First, it was a lawsuit against the city and the state. Now you're telling me you need to bring Serena into this, but it's not about revenge! Yeah, right! You're full of shit, Parker, so do whatever the hell you want! I'm tired of this mess!" She stormed off again.

There had been more doors slammed in the last two weeks than in the past five years in this house. Trying to talk to Roxy was more difficult than figuring out who had really fathered Serena's daughter.

When a man had to think twice before entering his own damn house, things weren't good. I dragged myself out of the car and slowly made my way up the walkway to our house. Each step was heavier than the last as my mind thought of the many other places I could've gone.

It wasn't completely dark outside, but when I walked into the house, Roxy was sitting in the living room and the TV was off. The baby was in his swing.

"Hi, how are you?" I tried to greet her with enthusiasm, regardless of how I really felt.

She half looked at me and acted like it hurt her to mumble *hi* to me. Back when Roxy was trying to figure out if I was telling the truth or had been lying to her about fathering a child with Lachez, those encounters was common. We'd been through so much. She left me, but eventually came back. She tried to buy information about my past. I was so angry when I found out she had paid one of those on-line background check services. Of course it was a scam; they sold her a bunch of false crap about me and delivered it to the house when she wasn't there. I was beyond pissed at her, but still, somehow, we made it.

As I watched her, I wasn't sure we'd make it this time around.

"I've thought about it, and on Monday I'm gonna go see Bill so we can finalize everything for the lawsuit," I said.

She didn't respond. I waited a spell, and when she behaved as if I'd never spoken a word to her, I walked to the back. She and James really had me going crazy. As I started to undress, I thought about my phone call with James.

So much time passed between my announcement and his response that if I hadn't heard him breathing, I would've sworn he'd hung up or the line had gone dead.

"You still there, dawg?" I asked.

"Oh, yeah, yeah, I'm here, I wasn't expecting that. You caught me off guard with that one," he said.

"You think you're caught off guard, imagine me, or hell, better yet, imagine Roxy," I said.

James blew out a breath.

"Damn, you guys have already been through so much behind her lying ass," he said.

"I know, dawg, I know."

"What's up, whatchu' gonna do?"

"Well, I told you, Bill and I were planning to file suit, but I'm supposed to be rethinking whether to add her name to the suit. That might hold things up, and I don't want to do that. Besides, I don't want to give the impression that this is payback for her recent press conference."

"Yeah, but still it seems to me like she shouldn't be able to keep getting away with fucking up people's lives," James said.

"Well, I think I'm gonna tell Bill to move forward with the suit minus her name. Then I'm gonna insist on a paternity test. Once the results come back, I'll announce the results on TV. After the results clear me, I'll hold another press conference at the DFF offices where I'll announce plans to sue her for defamation of character and anything else Bill can slap her simple ass with."

"Now that sounds like a plan," James said. "And please, man, make sure you call me so I can be on hand to witness that one with my own two eyes. I don't want to read about it in the papers or see it on TV," he said.

We spent the rest of the conversation talking about a new case I was called about earlier that morning.

"Damn, wasn't he Rookie of the Year?" James asked.

"Yup, he was last year. I told him he should come in as soon as possible, but he's planning to get married over the weekend and said he'd come in next week."

"These broads are a trip," James said. "Can you imagine the kind of money that's at stake with him?"

"I can only imagine, but that's why I'm trying to tell him, he needs a buffer between him and the woman. He can't give into temptation and do anything stupid. Lashing out at her will only land him in jail!"

"You've come a long way, dawg," James said before we ended the call.

When the mirror in our bathroom fogged, I knew it was time

to step into the shower. With any luck, the heat would help ease some of the tension in my neck and shoulders. I wasn't looking forward to a weekend of sleeping with one eye open next to Roxy.

It wasn't that I feared she'd try to harm me. She'd never do that, but it seemed like anytime Roxy was mad at me, the entire house was on her side.

Our son was too young to choose sides, but it felt like he cuddled with her more, smiled at her more, and saved all of his gas-induced frowns for me.

I didn't like being at odds with my wife. I had no question that this battle would be more difficult that I could imagine, and the last thing I needed was for her to withhold support and other benefits that could make things easier.

When I stepped out of the shower, I was startled. She stood there like she was waiting to say something to me.

"Hey," I said. "Can I get that towel over there?"

She reached for it and gave it to me.

"I don't have to like this, but I don't want you to have to go through this alone. All I ask is that you leave it at the office. I don't want you to come home pissed about something else she's done or said in the press."

I dried off as she laid the ground rules. Occasionally, I nodded to let her know that I was listening.

"And I don't want to have to hear about anything for the first time on the news. If something happens, no matter how minor or how insignificant *you* think it is, I want you to call me first."

"Baby, are you mad at me?" I asked.

"No, why do you ask?"

"Well, the way you're talking to me, your finger is wagging in my face and you're getting louder," I pointed out.

"I'm sorry, Parker, but you know how I feel about Serena. She tried to ruin our marriage. She got into my head, had me doubting what we had, and convinced me to leave you and move in with her. She's very conniving," Roxy said. "I guess I'm a bit scared of what damage she might cause this time around."

I pulled her close to my naked body.

"We're gonna be fine. That was all in the past. Think about it," I said. "That was her very best shot! She came at us with everything she had in her arsenal. If we were able to survive all of that, this won't be a cakewalk, but baby, the worst is already behind us."

Her lips found mine and soon, she was naked, too.

LACHEZ

Music was blasting throughout our apartment as we got dressed. Toni and I were getting ready for work. I felt extra good because I had finally talked with Junie and he agreed to come over for dinner tomorrow. Initially, I wanted him to come alone, but he said if Pricilla wasn't invited, he wouldn't come, either. So I quickly changed my tune and reluctantly extended an invitation to her ass, too.

"You should wear that red dress you had on the day before yesterday," Toni said.

"Really?"

"Yeah, girl, you're unstoppable in that dress," Toni said. "Who's the lucky fella tonight?" she asked.

"Oh, just another one of my special picks." I giggled.

What I liked most about this was that we didn't do too many of them at any given time. There'd only been one other since Richard, and it went as smoothly as all the others.

"Lemme ask you something," Toni said as she fidgeted with her hair in the mirror next to me. "How did you come up with this hustle?"

"Well, remember back when we were doing it before?" I asked her.

"Do I ever! How could I possibly forget," she said.

"I know, right. Jail ain't nothing nice, so I know you won't forget, but basically, I ran through the entire operation from start to finish. While I was sitting up there with the rest of them behind bars, we dissected this thing. You see, the main problem with what we were doing back then is that we were relying too much on the party lines. We would meet the guys over the phone." I leaned in to apply my eyeliner. "The problem with that was we had no control over who showed up at the motels. The other main problem was most of the people we met were single. Forget the fact that they met us after calling a late-night party line—that's not illegal. The major issue was that they really didn't have anything to lose. So for them, getting robbed by two chicks in a motel room was a *real* crime. And because they had nothing to lose, going to the cops was no biggie, either!"

"I never looked at it like that," she said. "Also, who knew we'd snagged the son of a well-known pastor?"

"Don't remind me," I said.

"He didn't look like no man of the cloth to me," Toni said.

"Who you telling? Remember when we saw that bad-ass whip pull into the hotel's parking lot?"

"No, remember how we pulled *him* in?" She laughed.

We could laugh about it now, but years ago, there was nothing funny about how it had gone down. When that Escalade turned into the parking lot, we were still standing outside our door near the back of the building. The driver pulled up and parked close to our door. So naturally, we thought that was our date.

He got out of his car and we looked at him.

"Hey, daddy, looking for a good time tonight?" Toni asked. We would sometimes tease them like that. He smiled. That's what made me think he was the one we'd been waiting for.

"Jazzlyn put y'all up to this, huh?" He laughed.

"Yeah, she said you like to have fun, but I wanna know, can you handle us both?" Toni asked.

I wondered who the hell Jazzlyn was, but the way he looked, I really didn't care. He was chocolate, dressed to the nines, hair nicely lined, and his jewelry was on point.

I watched closely as he turned his cell phone off.

"Nice phone, is that the new iPhone?" I asked.

"Yeah, it is," he said.

"Damn, you look nice," I said.

I could see him undressing us with his hungry eyes. We were rocking sexy club gear, so his eyes lingered at everything that was exposed and on display.

"What y'all doing hanging out here?" he asked as he walked closer.

"We were waiting for you, daddy," I said.

He smiled.

"That's Big Daddy to you," he said.

"Oh shit, Trina, we got ourselves a live one tonight," Toni said to me. Trina was my alias back then.

"Oh, you don't know the half of it. Jazzlyn didn't warn y'all?" He stopped. "Shit, where is she anyway?"

I frowned, but Toni quickly spoke up.

"She's not coming, but she just called before you pulled up to make sure you was here, so your timing is perfect."

"It usually is," he bragged, sticking out his chest.

"Well, we can't get to know each other out here," I said. "We've got some drinks in the room? You ready to party, daddy…uh, I mean Big Daddy!"

I noticed that he took one last glance around the dark parking lot before he followed Toni into the hotel room. I was right behind them.

What we had no way of knowing then was that he was the son of the famous Pastor Ethan Ezekel Goodlove III, the founder and pastor of a Houston megachurch.

It wasn't until we were watching TV one day that we saw the story of how Damieon Goodlove was found in the room by the maid. He had lost his memory, but once he regained it and came clean about why he was at the hotel room, the hunt was on.

"So again, he was single, his father had investigators on our asses the minute he told what happened, and that's what led the police to our door," I recounted for her.

"Yeah, but he wasn't from the party line," she reminded me.

"No, but we didn't know that at the time. We thought he was there for the same reason we were. How were we supposed to know he was there to meet a different couple of chicks? Honestly, if he was just a regular Joe Schmo, it wouldn't have made the news," I said.

She looked at me.

"You ready to roll?"

"Yes, girl, let's do this!"

This time we raked in nearly $15,000. This particular executive was a jeweler. They always traveled with a ton of cash and precious gems. We left the gems, but we took a laptop. Toni wanted to grab his iPad, but I told her that was not a smart move.

"Don't you know they're able to track those things?"

"Yeah, but who's gonna track it? Trust when I tell you, he doesn't wanna explain to his wife or his board of directors why his company-issued iPad was found with two strange women," she said.

The next morning, we put away our stuff we got from Walmart and split our cash.

"So, when are they coming over and what you fixing?" Toni asked.

"Girl, I'm going to Pei Wei and grabbing a few dishes, and we're gonna sit here and eat like I sweated over a hot stove," I said.

"I ain't mad at you. I love Pei Wei. I am invited to dinner, right?" she asked.

"Invited? Who the hell else is gonna be here to help Junie pull me up off that old hag if she look at me wrong?"

Toni looked scared.

"Girl, I'm playin. I'm gonna act right tonight. My plan is to get back in my baby's good graces, then I'm gonna casually talk to him about his decision to be with a woman old enough to be his mama," I said. "You know, if I was old as her," I corrected with a wink.

"Uh, yeah, I knew exactly what you meant." Toni laughed.

Not even an hour after I got in from the restaurant, there was a knock at the door.

"Damn, they're here already?" I asked Toni.

"What time did you tell them?" she asked.

"I said eight, but it's barely seven," I said. I walked over to the door and said a silent prayer for help with my behavior before I pulled the door open.

I nearly fell out at what I saw.

EBONI

By the time Saturday rolled around, we had done Vegas! We partied Thursday and Friday nights like there was no tomorrow. But now, it was time to get busy and handle the real business that brought us to Sin City.

On our way back from Home Depot, I was hoping we had enough poster boards and the other supplies we needed. I turned to Judi.

"Did you get us some guys?" I asked.

"Yeah, you said you needed ten, right?"

"Yeah, but how are they gonna get there? We can't pick them up," I said.

"We have to pay for taxis to come and get them. I've already called for two minivans that should work fine," she said.

"I told you we could pull this off," Ulonda said to me.

When I first told her what I wanted to do, I thought she was gonna think I was crazy, but she didn't. As a matter of fact, she told me it was a fantastic idea, and she immediately rolled up her sleeves and started planning how we'd pull it off.

Once back at the hotel room, the work began immediately. It took close to three hours, but it was well worth it.

"Judi, your idea to buy these covers for the floors was brilliant. I don't think any paint seeped through."

We worked diligently. I already had the messages we needed to get across, so it was just a matter of making sure the letters were the perfect legible sizes.

Once we finished, the three of us stood back and looked at our handiwork, and I had to admit it was the bomb!

"You think that one's too much?" Ulonda asked, wrinkling her nose as she looked at it.

I looked at it closely, and considered her concern. But in the end, I decided since it was a true statement, it would be fine.

"Nah, I only made one of those, so that should be fine," I said.

I looked at the clock and said," Oooh, we'd better get going. Judi, it's time to call the taxi company," I said.

"On it," she said.

We pulled up outside the resort and waited for the taxis to arrive. When I saw them, I was so excited because everything really had fallen into place perfectly.

As the men jumped out of the vehicles, we got out and waved them over to the back of the SUV we were in.

"Who speaks English here?" I asked Judi as I stood in front of the guys.

"Most of them do, but this guy, Felix, he will communicate whatever information you give to the others."

"Okay, cool." I turned my attention to Felix. "So here's the job. I want your guys to fan out and hold these signs in front of and on the sides of this resort."

Felix looked around at the resort like he was trying to figure out where people should stand.

"Okay," he turned to me and nodded.

"We will be near at all times. The job is for three hours and it pays twenty dollars an hour, just like we agreed," I said.

"Okay." Felix nodded again.

"No one is afraid to be on TV or to be photographed, right?"

"Oh, they can hold signs in front of faces?"

"Yes! Exactly. They don't have to show their faces at all; it's the signs we want to see," I said excitedly.

Judi and Ulonda began to hand out the massive signs we had spray-painted back at the hotel room.

Shawnathon McGee is a Deadbeat

Shawnathon Pay Your Child Support

Shawnathon McGee Support Your Kids

Shawnathon McGee hates his Kids

Shawnathon McGee Feed Your Children

Shawnathon McGee STOP making babies

Shawnathon McGee should have to pay

Shawnathon McGee Your Kids are broke

Shawnathon McGee Shame on You

Shawnathon McGee's Penis is Tiny!

The signs looked so good that I beamed with pride. I took pictures with my phone, then turned to Felix and told him to keep his men on public property. I didn't want anyone to get arrested for trespassing.

Nothing could've prepared me for the sheer pandemonium that broke out when people began to converge on the streets around the Cancun Resort. The media showed up, and cameras were everywhere, which attracted even more people. Finally, I felt vindicated.

By the time the wedding party began, there was more action going on outside than inside. A few bold reporters walked up to the office and tried to get in to talk to Shawnathon.

When cop cars arrived, I got nervous, but both Judi and Ulonda assured me that we were not breaking any laws. I had never been more proud to be in a country where freedom of speech was appreciated. Soon, the cops sat in their vehicles and watched the circus unfold. So they, along with crowds of people, simply looked on as we exercised our right to free speech. Most importantly, we were not trespassing.

I thought I was gonna die when Shawnathon himself stormed

out the door and walked over to the car. I was ready for him. I pulled out my flip and started recording. He walked up to the car and smacked the window.

"What the fuck is wrong with you?" he yelled. "Why would you do some evil shit like this? Call them off!" he ordered.

"Pay your child support!" I said.

"I swear, I hate you! On my wedding day, Eboni?"

"Pay your child support," I insisted.

"My wife is in there fucking crying! Bawling out her eyes! You can hate me all you want, Eboni, but this?" He waved around at the guys who held up the signs. "This is some way outta order type of shit!"

At this point tourists began to snap their own pictures. Some even posed next to the guys while they held the signs.

"Damn! I'm beggin' you, stop this shit now!"

"Pay your child support," I said.

Shawnathon was pissed. He shook his head, but there was nothing he could do. Two guys came over and tried to drag him away from the car, but he jerked beyond their reach. He wouldn't go.

"What do you want? Seriously, tell me. Is it money you want? What's it gonna take for you to end this right now?"

"I want you to pay your child support!"

He exhaled.

"Let's go, man. Don't talk to her," someone said.

"Yeah, don't talk to me. Pay your child support."

"Man, this some foul shit right here," Shawnathon said. But I didn't feel sorry for him. Now he had an idea of what I had been going through for more than a year.

He smacked the window again and again.

When a couple of reporters rushed the car with their cameras and their microphones hanging off a long rod, I couldn't be more excited.

"Man, what's it gonna take? I just need them to go away," he said.

"Well, my attorney is standing by. If you call your attorney and tell him to call my attorney and do an instant transfer as a good-faith payment, I'd be happy to leave you guys alone. You know we're expected in court next week, and here you are getting hitched while my kids don't have food or clothes," I said.

I was very aware that cameras were rolling and recording, but that's exactly what I wanted. I was well prepared, and my plan had been completely thought out.

"All I want you to do is pay your child support."

"Call her up," he said.

His buddies started in on him.

"Man, don't cave!" someone said.

"Man, Elisa is sick over this. I don't need her getting any more worked up than she already is. This is supposed to be a happy time for us. This is a bunch of bull!" he declared.

SERENA

Now, I'd be the first to admit that I may have taken extreme steps to have a baby by Parker, but I'm not the only one doing things in her own way. So when Loren tried to make me feel like my situation was less than someone who got pregnant the traditional way but the relationship didn't work out, I wanted to slap the taste out of her mouth.

"I may have used a menstrual cup to get pregnant, but lots of people use unconventional methods. Actually, I got the idea from this show on TV. Did you know that there are women who meet strangers in hotel rooms to get their sperm so they can have a baby?"

"I didn't know that," Loren said. She looked less than impressed.

"Well, my daughter may not have been the product of a marriage, but she was conceived out of love—my love and need for a child. Parker doesn't ever have to claim my child, but I'm not gonna let anyone make her feel like she was an accident or that she wasn't wanted."

Loren didn't respond.

Needless to say, by the time we pulled up in front of my place, I had had just about all I could take of her. Even if she felt like what I did was wrong, she should've kept that to herself.

"I think you got the wrong idea about what I was saying," she tried to explain.

"I thought you were pretty straightforward," I said. I grabbed the door handle. "You basically said that I don't need to be going around making Parker out to be the bad guy because apparently, it's my fault that his deadbeat ass ain't paying for his daughter," I snarled.

"That is not what I said! I didn't say anything like that," she said.

"You didn't say those exact words, but what did you think you were saying? You're supposed to be in my corner. Here I've got this plan in motion, and you're acting like you don't know whose side you're on."

"Serena, don't go yet. Seriously, I don't want you to leave until we get this straight. Really, all I was saying to you is that I know the story behind you and Parker. Do I think that's the story you need to share with everyone else? Absolutely not! We're in this together. Why do you think I'm working my butt off to try and land you some better gigs?" She looked at me and it made me uncomfortable. I wanted to make my statement—then get out. I liked the dramatic exits much better. But I guess Loren wasn't having it.

"We work together so we need to make sure we are on the same page when we are in front of a crowd or an audience. Regardless of what I believe or what I may know, you don't have to worry about what I'd say if I was asked anything about you and Parker," she said.

Although I tried to hang on to the anger I felt for her, what she said was deep. It was no secret really. Most people couldn't remember what went down with Parker and me if they wanted to.

"Also, before you go, I wanted to tell you that Deena may want to have him thrown in jail again," she said.

That caught my attention.

The idea of Parker being locked up again was nothing short of a turn-on for me. If he was arrested, the world would know what I was said was right all along.

I turned to her.

"Could she really make that happen?" I asked. "I mean, with all the work he's been doing, he's very connected."

"I'm not sure, but we could find out. I can get her to meet with us first thing Monday morning. At that time we can ask all the questions about that possibility. Think about it. If he hasn't paid any support, how far in the hole is he?"

In all these years, I never thought about it like that. Parker hadn't paid a dime for Semaj.

"Okay, set it up," I said.

"Wait!" Loren yelled. "Before you go, we're cool, right?" she asked.

"Yes, we're cool," I said.

She finally allowed me to leave. When I walked into my house, I started thinking about how great it would feel if Parker was thrown back in jail. I knew it was probably highly unlikely, but I couldn't think of a better place for him. That punk! I wondered what would happen to his following then.

I stepped out of my shoes as the phone rang. Normally, I'd let it ring, but this time I answered.

"Hello?"

"Serena Carson, please?" a man's voice asked.

"This is she," I said.

"Are you the same Serena who held a press conference last week?" he asked.

"Who wants to know?"

He told me his name and said he was a reporter with the *Houston Press*, a weekly magazine. He also said he was doing a special on deadbeats and wondered if I'd answer a few questions.

"Sure," I said.

"I'm about to record the conversation," he said.

"Okay."

"Please state your name for me and spell it."

Once I did, he asked his first question.

"While jailing non-paying parents—the vast majority of them men—does lead to payment in many cases, critics say that it unfairly penalizes poor and unemployed parents who have no ability to pay, even though federal law stipulates that they must have *willfully* violated a court order before being incarcerated."

I waited a beat, then I said, "And your question was?"

"Oh, I'm sorry, I just want your thoughts on jailing those who fall behind on payments," he finally said.

"I find it very funny how these same men who claim to be poor and unemployed once the baby gets here were not so destitute when they were making the baby."

"But Ms. Carson, I've been to some of these hearings. You see a room full of indigent parents—most of them African-American—and you have a judge and attorney general, both of whom are white. The hearings often take only fifteen seconds. The judge asks, 'Do you have any money to pay?' The person pleads and the judge says, 'Okay, you're going to jail.' The threat of jailing delinquent parents is intended to coerce them to pay, but in rare cases, it can have tragic results."

"You wanna know what's tragic? A woman forced to go on welfare to feed and clothe her children because the father finds other things to do with his money," I said.

"So it doesn't bother you that many of these men are jailed without legal representation?"

"What does bother me are the millions of parents who get away with not paying child support."

"Ms. Carson, I think I have everything I need, is there anything else you'd like to add, something I didn't ask or anything at all you can think of?"

"People say jailing parents for not paying should be left for the most outrageous violators. I say, if you were jailing more, there'd be fewer outrageous violators."

"Well, Ms. Carson, thank you so much for your time."

"You're welcome," I said and hung up.

PARKER

My weekend turned out better than I expected, and for that I was glad. It was business as usual Monday morning as I waited for Bill to come by the office. Since I had an appointment with Shawnathon McGee, who delayed his honeymoon so we could talk, I wanted to be in the office early.

Coverage of the boycotted wedding had gone viral quickly. The national news programs, the tabloid TV shows, and online programs ran coverage of it continuously. A friend of his set up an emergency phone call and I tried my best to console him before he caved in to some of the take-no-prisoner, strong-arm tactics his ex had demanded.

When I first saw the news coverage, I thought it was one of those reality TV programs. I just knew it was an episode of *Basketball Wives*. I couldn't believe a woman would boycott a wedding with actual picketers. And the cameras soaked up the vicious insults painted on those posters for everyone to see.

I remembered thinking the McGee camp would have a serious public relations nightmare after this one.

"Joe Butler is here to see you; says he has an eight-thirty appointment," the receptionist said.

Butler was a thirty-six-year-old Iraqi war vet. Last year in November, a Harris County judge sent him to jail because he had violated a court order to pay child support.

I walked out of my office to meet him.

"Mr. Butler, come on in," I said.

He was a short, stocky guy with brown skin and dark, wavy hair. He wore jeans, and a Houston Texans t-shirt.

"Thanks for meeting with me, and call me Joe," he said.

His handshake was firm and strong.

Inside my office, I offered him a seat and listened as he shared his experience.

"I was stunned, man, when the judge adamantly criticized my argument. I tried to tell him, I said, 'Listen, up to the point that I lost my job, I made regular payments.' I told him, if he looked at my record he'd see that for more than a decade before I lost my job, I paid like I was supposed to." I could see the anger as he spoke. "Then while they checking me for payments, ain't nobody checking her for my visitation rights! But me telling him about my record..." He shook his head like he was becoming choked up.

"Let me guess, didn't matter, huh?"

"I felt like, with my payment history and the fact that I had just started working a new job, maybe I would be able to convince the judge to give me another month and a half to start making the payments again," he said. "But that didn't sit too well with him because he went ahead and decided to lock me up."

"We see this too often. Your case is not rare, unfortunately. Then guess what happens while you're sitting in jail—you lose the current job."

Joe shook his head.

"Man, I feel like somebody should be able to do something about this."

"Yeah, but the problem is all too often, they see this method as a way to increase payment rates. The logic behind the threat of jail is supposed to force parents to pay. But more times than not, it doesn't work out that way. Then there are those rare cases we never hear about, when tragedy strikes. Like the case of that New Hampshire father, Thomas Ball, he was a military vet.

"He died after dousing himself with gasoline and setting himself on fire in front of the county courthouse. The note he left behind said he did it to focus attention on what he considered unfair domestic violence laws and because he expected to go to jail at an upcoming hearing. He was only about $3,000 behind in delinquent child support. But the man fell behind after he had been out of work for two years."

"One of the reasons I wanted to meet with you today is to see what you know about this class-action lawsuit," Joe said. "I'm torn, but I figured if anybody would know what to do, it would be you."

"Of course, here at DFF we've been contacted. But I try to give my clients the facts and allow them to determine whether their case should stand alone or be lumped into a class-action situation," I said.

"So, you wouldn't join if you was me?"

"Nah, that's not what I'm saying. Me personally, I am filing suit alone. But my case is different from the average. So would I personally join a class-action suit?" I shook my head. "No way, it wouldn't be advantageous for me. I lost more than fifty thousand dollars in my case that was proven to be fraudulent—different situation. Would it be wise for you? Maybe, I'm not sure."

"Man, I thought those reports were exaggerated. So you spent time in jail *and* you had to pay?" he asked.

"Couldn't get out until I coughed up the cash," I said.

Joe leaned back in the chair and sighed hard. "I don't know what to do, man. I know in class-actions suits, it's really only the lawyers who make money, but a part of me feels like this is more than just about the money."

"I completely understand. Here's what I think you should do.

We have some referral attorneys; I suggest you talk to one of them about your personal case. See if there's any merit to you going at it alone. If there is, weigh the pros and cons of doing both. In the end, you've gotta do what's best for you."

"Yeah, okay, that sounds good," he said.

"Along the way, if you think of anything we can do here at DFF to help, man, don't hesitate to call."

Joe stood. He looked at me with heavy eyes.

"You're a good man, Parker. The work you do here at DFF is real important. I'm gonna take your advice and the referral." He smiled.

"No problem, let me walk you out and I'll get that information for you."

We shook hands before he followed me out to the reception area.

About thirty minutes after Joe left, Bill called.

"I've been delayed," he said.

"No problem. I'll be close to the office all day. Take your time," I told him.

The next call was from the receptionist.

"Shawnathon McGee is here for you," she said.

"Okay, thanks. I'll be right out."

LACHEZ

Drew Levin looked even better than he did years ago. His caramel-brown complexion was just as pretty as I remembered.

At the height of my drama, he and I had some words after I got him to help pay for an abortion when I wasn't really pregnant. I needed the $1,100 for other things, but we got over all that. It was all good before I took my fall.

In the end, when I told Drew what was going on with Parker and Kelly, he didn't haul ass like I thought he would. Honestly, I think we would've pulled through had Toni and I not gone down for that misunderstanding back in the day.

"Lachez Baker," he said. And damn if he didn't sound all sexy and delicious. He called me by my full government name, and it didn't even bother me.

"Drrreeeww," I sang.

"Is that any way to greet a long lost friend?" he asked. "Especially one who had premium benefits," he joked.

I threw my arms around his neck, wiggled my body up against his and held him close in a tight and long embrace. Once it broke up and we both reluctantly pulled away, I leaned against the doorframe and stared into his eyes. Oh, how I had missed me some Drew!

That's when it dawned on me, since I'd been home, I hadn't

given anyone the privilege of allowing me to take them to paradise.

Sure, while Toni and I worked, I flirted with the idea of breaking someone off a little, but we never really made it that far in the process. I hadn't been out a good month, and I figured I must've learned some real coping skills in the slammer, because I had functioned as if I didn't really miss sex at all. Lord knows I did, the sight of Drew simply reminded me of just how much.

"I didn't mean to drop by unannounced, but I wanted to drop off a little something for you. My homeboy works security down at this oil and gas company, and he swore he saw you strutting in there the other day," Drew said.

"Damn, how he know me?"

"Don't act like we didn't kick it something fierce back in the day." Drew smiled. "My homies knew what I was working with back then," he said. "It ain't too often a brotha lucks up on a bona-fide dimepiece like you, Lachez."

Drew all but undressed me with his eyes and all those old, lustful memories washed back over me like one of those unexpected rainstorms. I started getting weak.

"Is it Junie?" Toni yelled from a back room.

"No," I said. I stood and eyeballed Drew like he was a tender, juicy T-bone and I had suffered from famine for years.

"Oh, hey," Toni said as she walked into the front room.

"Hey, Toni," Drew said. If he pulled his gaze away from me, it didn't stray for long.

I licked my lips and soon he started sucking them. I grabbed his head and pulled him in closer so my hands could get reacquainted with his body properly.

"Eh-hem," Toni interrupted.

"Junie called and said they'd be late. I need to run out so I'll be back in about an hour," she said.

I grabbed Drew by the collar of his shirt and pulled him in as Toni squeezed past us on her way out the front door.

"You kids be good," she sang as she left.

The door hardly closed all the way before Drew was on me like steel being drawn to a magnetic force. He felt good, smelled good, and tasted even better. We kissed hard and long as my hands ran up under his shirt, over his muscled chest, and down his six-pack abs and into his pants.

I was excited to discover the huge bulge was still there. He had me going in a bad way.

"My son is on his way over," I whispered as I pulled back so I could see what I was doing. I tried to unbuckle his pants. Once I got them loose, I pulled them down over his hips and rubbed his crotch after getting on my knees.

"Looks like someone really *is* excited to see me." I smiled up at him. I tried to swallow him whole. As I used my mouth to work him over, my mind raced with thoughts of how much I missed having a man.

"Damn, Lachez," Drew moaned. "Work that shit, girl!"

His words were music to my ears. I missed the feel of a man's muscle when it expanded between my jaws. I couldn't remember what had grown more, him or my appetite. I didn't want him to come, so I resisted the urge to suck him dry. I eased back and got up so I could take off my clothes.

"Sit down on the sofa," I told him.

Moving wasn't an easy thing to do with his pants down and around his ankles, but he managed to maneuver himself over to the couch. He sat and dug a condom from his pocket. By the time he was shielded, I walked up and swung one leg over and straddled him. My descent was swift and pleasurable.

"Oh shit, how I missed you," he said.

Drew's rod felt like it was trying to come up and out through my throat. I couldn't find words as I grinded my hips and rode him slowly, methodically, and unmercifully.

He grabbed onto my hips and guided me the best he could, but I kept bucking like a wild bull. He felt magnificent. He was just the right amount of stiff and hardness that seemed to expand with my moisture.

"Damn, Lachez," he moaned.

I rubbed my breasts against his bare chest and that felt like heaven. Right when that blissful sensation started nipping at my senses, I threw one leg up on his shoulder. He grabbed my ass and pulled me in harder.

"Oh yes, Drew. Yes, baby, yes," I cried.

The orgasm was so hard and so long overdue I literally fell down on the job. But when I collapsed, Drew was nowhere near being done, and I was exhausted. I didn't have any more energy. But he understood because he flipped me over, eased his head between my legs and used his tongue to lap my already sensitive area. In no time flat, I was hungry once again.

"Put it in," I cried after a little while. "Please, put it in."

He moved his head and looked up at me.

"You want it again?" he asked.

"Yes, put it in," I said. But before he did, I said, "Lemme turn over so you can hit it from the back." I knew that was always the deal breaker. Within minutes that steel pipe felt like cotton.

Afterward, we lay there and lingered in the afterglow for a few moments, but then I nudged him. "Hey, we need to get cleaned up before Toni gets back. And my kid is coming over for dinner."

"Okay, cool," he said as a yawn nipped at his voice.

Drew and I cleaned up quickly, then visited for a little while. It didn't feel right inviting him to have dinner with us, so I told him we'd have to hook up later.

"Are we going for a repeat?" he asked.

"You damn straight we are," I said.

At the door, we kissed, smiled, and petted each other like horny teenagers.

"Oh, I brought something for you," he said.

"And I'm glad you did. I hope you bring it back later, too," I said and winked.

He laughed. "Oh fo' sho'! No doubt about that, but that's not what I was talking about. I know you've only been out for a hot minute and probably struggling to get back on your feet, so I wanted to break you off a few dollars, nothing major, but just some pocket change," he said.

"Damn, Drew, that's sweet. You know I appreciate you, right?"

He smiled at me. Drew placed a small roll of cash in my hand, and then brought that hand to his lips. He suckled my fingers and nearly made me wet myself again.

"Ya'll still at it out here?" Toni's voice rang out.

We giggled.

"You back already?" Drew asked.

He and I giggled again.

After Toni walked in, I kissed Drew goodbye and went inside. I leaned my body up against the closed door.

"Ah-ah, don't sit there, it might be wet," I warned Toni.

"Eewww." She rolled her eyes. "Not on the damn couch, Lachez!" she said.

I shrugged. "I didn't have to warn you. I coulda let you sit in it."

"Now that's some nasty shit. Next time, take that mess to the room." She scowled. "But seriously though, I'm glad you got you some. I was starting to get worried that you may have switched teams while in jail!"

"That ain't even funny, Toni! You already know what's up over here! I'm strictly dickly, even when there's a shortage, please believe that!" I testified.

EBONI

"Technically, we can't enforce the promise he made. His attorney can argue he was under duress," Nia said. I was hot.

"What do you mean? So he doesn't have to pay me?" I asked.

"He can, and he may, but legally, he's not obligated to do so," she said.

"So you think his lawyer will tell him to simply not pay, and I'm supposed to sit here and take it? After he promised?" I said.

"Eboni, we're in court in less than four days. I don't want to spend a lot of time on this. Our energy needs to be focused on getting the note thrown out. That's where the focus should remain. If we get the note tossed out, that's when we can start thinking about naming our price."

"I can't believe I let him sucker me again!" I was pissed.

"You shouldn't look at it that way. You said he picked up the tab for the protestors and gave you ladies money to go away, so technically, you did get something."

I thought about what she was saying. That day, if Shawnathon had a million in cash, I'd be a millionaire today. I made him pay each of the picketers one hundred dollars for their time. Then I made him pay Felix two hundred. In addition to that, he emptied his pockets and paid for Ulonda, Judi, and me to go on to the strip and gamble for the rest of the afternoon on him.

But still, none of that changed the promise he made to have his attorney wire the three hundred grand into my account. Nia tried to explain to me that I might never see that money!

"I'm tired of playing games with him. He better call and tell me he's deposited that money. He made a promise and if he goes back on his word, Nia, we need to be prepared to do something about it. I hear what you're saying about where our focus needs to lie, and I agree, but I don't think we should let him get away with saying stuff just to get out of a situation and buy himself more time."

Nia gave me an exasperated look and I wanted to tell her if she thought she was frustrated, she should walk in my damn shoes. I was the one who came up with the brilliant idea of how to shame Shawnathon into paying up, only to realize that I had called off my picketers for nothing. The punk was once again lying to me about his intentions!

I wanted to cry as I sat across from Nia. This was no big deal to her, but to me, it was much more. I had borrowed money to put the plan into motion. When he agreed to make that good-faith payment, which would've taken care of all of my debt, I thought I had made progress. That money was gonna come in before I got what the judge was sure to force him to give to me.

"Eboni, are you ready for court?" she asked softly.

I frowned. "I guess I'm as ready as I'll ever be," I told her.

"We need to focus on the big picture here. I'm sorry he told you he'd make that payment and I'm sorry that you're disappointed, but if we play our cards right, you can get that and then some—on the back end," she said.

Nia rose from her chair, signaling the meeting was over. I didn't get up right away, but I wasn't going to force her to tell me I had to go. I was devastated by this. I knew there was nothing she could do. I wanted to be mad at her for not answering over the weekend when I had Shawnathon literally by the balls. But what good would that do now?

I got up and sulked as I walked toward the door.

"If anything comes up before court, be sure to call me," she said.

That did it! I was almost there, nearly out of the door, and she had to go and say that.

I looked at her. "Nia, I tried to call you this *weekend* when Shawnathon was ready to pay up, but guess what? *You* didn't answer. You were supposed to be standing by and you didn't answer the phone. Who knows what would've happened if you had answered."

Nia looked me in the eyes. "Is that what this is about? You think that I cost you the three hundred thousand dollars he offered?"

She stood in a stance that made me uncomfortable. With one hand on her hip, she started to tell me the truth the way she saw it.

"Honey, I could've been waiting by the phone with pen and paper in hand, and Shawnathon would've pledged his three-hundred grand, but that doesn't mean you would've ever seen one red cent of that money! Hear me when I tell you, his lawyer would've had that order thrown out! You cannot essentially blackmail someone into paying you. That's extortion," she pressed.

"How was it extortion if it was his idea?"

"Eboni, he only made the offer so you would call off your picketers. Once a judge heard that part of the story, you could've faced charges. While I'm sure your mother would be happy to help you with your kids, she wouldn't want to have to do it because you're in jail for being greedy," said Nia.

The finality of her statement left me feeling bitter and angry with her. Even if she was right, I'd always feel as though I missed out on an extra payday because *she* didn't take it seriously.

"I'll see you on Thursday morning," I said and walked out without another word to her.

Ulonda's timing was impeccable. The moment I sat behind the wheel, she called.

"Hey, girl, what's up?"

"Uh, I expected some celebrating in the background; instead, you sound like you've been to court and the judge told you to pay Shawnathon instead of the other way around. What's up? And what the hell did Nia say to steal your joy?"

"I'm gonna need to get a job," I blurted out.

"Perish the thought!" Ulonda cried. "What the hell happened in that meeting?"

"Can you meet for lunch?" I asked. "It's too much to go into over the phone." I said.

"Yeah, where?"

"Let's go to our spot," I said, referring to Maggiano's.

"Um, try again," she said.

"Damn, I forgot, okay, where?"

"P.F. Chang's," she said.

"In River Oaks?"

"I'll be there in fifteen minutes," I told her.

Traffic wasn't bad, in mid-afternoon my drive down Kirby was quicker than normal, so I arrived at the restaurant in ten minutes. I'd have to wait on Ulonda, but I didn't mind. It gave me a chance to clear my head and try to come up with a plan.

A few minutes later, she arrived and we were being seated.

"Hey, honey, what's the matter? You don't look so good," she said. Ulonda gave me a hug.

"What if a judge sides with him? What if I've put all my eggs in this one basket and the bottom falls out? Who's gonna look out for me and my kids?"

Ulonda's eyebrows went up on her forehead.

"I don't like the way Nia didn't own up to the fact that we could've gotten paid from Shawnathon if she had only answered the phone," I said. "And it just got me to thinking—all this time I've been waiting on my court date. I've been holding out hope that some judge will look at our situation and demand that he makes this right, but what if their idea of what's right and mine are so far apart that I'm still left poor?"

"I never looked at it like that," she said. "What did she say about him not giving the money he promised?"

"She said any judge would've thrown it out, and I could've faced jail time for extortion."

Ulonda's eyes widened in shock and her mouth fell open.

"Extortion?" she deadpanned.

"Extortion, girl!"

"But he agreed. It's not like you said, 'Pay me or I'm gonna make these people stay out here.' He offered," she insisted.

"Apparently, that doesn't matter. She says the fact that he was paying me off to get rid of the threat is somehow seen as extortion."

"Dayum," Ulonda said.

We studied our menus in silence.

Once we settled on our order, I closed the menu, then said to her, "Basically, anything he would've promised me at that time can be argued as payoff because he was under duress."

"Well, sweetie, I know this isn't what you want to hear, but better being told in Nia's office than by a judge right before he throws the book at you." Her eyebrows went up. "So, what's the game plan?" she asked.

"For me, it's looking for work, then gearing up for court and life after court," I said. "And that's real."

"Eeewww...work. We weren't designed for jobs," she joked.

SERENA

From the moment I walked into Deena's office, I had a funny feeling. But nothing could've prepared me for what happened when she finally strolled into the office where I'd been waiting. Even Loren was caught a bit off guard, I think. Deena walked around to her desk and leaned over it. She got all up in my face, and that definitely rubbed me the wrong way.

"Are you *sure* Parker is your daughter's father?"

"I heard you the first time," I snarled. I didn't appreciate the way Deena was talking to me. I'm not sure what the hell she was on, but she needed to ask somebody.

She worked for *me*! It wasn't the other damn way around. Loren stood off to the side and stared out the window as that barracuda attacked me. I figured I'd deal with her later for her lack of support.

"How did you become pregnant by this man?" Deena asked. She behaved like I was some undisciplined three-year-old who she had to handle firmly.

"Where are these questions coming from?" I asked.

All of a sudden, Deena pulled open a drawer, snatched a large manila envelope and pulled some papers from it. She slammed it down on her desk in front of me.

I looked down at the papers, then up at her with much attitude.

"What's that supposed to be?" She thought she could talk to me any ol' kind of way and I was just supposed to fall into line?

"This is a counterclaim!" She hissed. "Please take a close look at it. You stole the man's sperm?"

Loren turned slowly and glared at me.

I jumped up from the chair. What was wrong with everybody? What difference does it make *how* I got pregnant? Why weren't they concerned with the fact that he wasn't paying child support?

"So you're telling me *he's* suing *us*?" I asked.

"There's so much more to this story. You can't go around throwing accusations at this man like he's scum and your story is so questionable," Deena said.

"Since when does any of that matter? Who cares what *my* story is? *He's* not paying child support!"

Loren walked over and, for a second, I thought she was coming to help defend me, but I should've known better. When she started to talk, I sat back down in the chair.

"The problem that poses is really that critics could say he has a right to defend himself. When you said you used the menstrual cup to get pregnant, I didn't know you didn't have actual intercourse with the man!" She shook her head. "That makes this seem like something completely different. Now it goes from this poor, single mom struggling to get support to a questionable character who targeted this man out of revenge, greed, or any other malicious goal."

I wasn't sure what they thought this little intervention was gonna do. If Deena didn't want to be my attorney all of a sudden, I'd get rid of her and Loren and find a way to get to Gloria Allred myself. That was who I wanted in the first place. It was now painfully obvious that my current team was made up of amateurs.

"So what are we gonna do?" I asked them.

They both looked at me like I was from outer space.

"You think we can still move forward with this?" Loren asked. She looked mortified.

"Why can't we?" I asked. "What's changed? It's still *his* child, he's still *not* paying. I don't understand the problem."

A buzz from her phone pulled our attention away from this conversation.

"Yes," Deena yelled with the phone on speaker.

"Someone called and said you should put the TV on thirteen," the caller said.

"Okay, thank you," Deena said. She grabbed a remote and turned the TV on.

We tuned in just in time to see the anchorwoman talking into the camera.

"I've heard of some pretty crazy paternity suits in my lifetime, but a recent case with a Houston man claiming that an ex-associate gave birth to a child by stealing his sperm puts everything I've ever seen Jerry Springer or Maury Povich to absolute shame. Thirty-six-year-old Parker Redman, Founder and President of the men's rights group, Don't Force Fatherhood, is launching a court battle claiming that a woman became impregnated by his sperm that she took to a Houston fertility clinic without his knowledge."

Video of Parker popped up and he said, "Actually, I couldn't believe it could be done. I was very, very devastated."

The anchorwoman came back on and continued the story. "The father's rights advocate, Redman, says he was shocked to find that this woman, Serena Carson, had become pregnant from his sperm. He says she then set out on an intricately detailed scheme to defraud him through child support payments. We've discovered she became pregnant at Success Fertility Services of Texas. In his lawsuit, Redman claims he was completely unaware of the situation until he received an anonymous letter suggesting that he check out that company and the previously mentioned woman."

Deena threw her hands up like she was beyond frustrated. I

rolled my eyes dramatically. I felt like a skilled attorney would know exactly what to do with this case. I didn't see why there was a problem.

"So what's the deal? Are we gonna do this or not? Who cares how I got pregnant," I said again.

"We've built our case on painting this man as a deadbeat. We've attacked his integrity; we've all but slandered his name, only now to learn that he may be the *actual victim.* Well, I'm gonna have to give it some thought to try and figure out what's the best way forward, if one exists," she had the nerve to say.

I was beyond mad. What made him think he was so much better than me? Why did everyone automatically rally around him?

"Just so we're clear," I said to Deena, "I'm supposed to go home and sit by the phone and wait on you to make up your mind about whether you still want to represent me?"

"I don't really want you to look at it like that," she said, but sighed.

"Hmm, I'll bet you don't," I said. I grabbed my purse, got up and stormed out. I didn't care whether Loren was behind me. As far as I was concerned, she walked me into this trap with no warning whatsoever.

PARKER

At first, I didn't agree with Bill's strategy. Why had we worked all these years for the right to sue everyone—only to hold off on filing?

But it didn't take long for me to realize he was correct! It felt as though the minute he pressed the send button on the email press release announcing the countersuit against Serena, my phone began to ring, and it hadn't stopped yet.

Once again, I was back in the middle of a media storm. Considering all of this, Bill's move was actually genius. I could still see him selling me on his brilliant idea.

"So here's what I suggest. We've won the right to sue the state, the county, and any other municipality we think shares blame in what happened. But in light of what Serena has done, we hold off on that lawsuit and countersue her!"

I was more than skeptical. I was even a little confused. Not that it was about money, but we knew for certain she wasn't worth a dime.

"What in the world would we sue her for?"

"What she's doing goes to the heart of your credibility. Despite the years you've dedicated your life and your mission toward helping countless fathers and other men, all the public will remember is that a woman is accusing *you* of being a deadbeat!"

"But..."

"Let me finish," Bill cut me off. "As a public figure who is often called upon in court, relied on by many, including desperate fathers and their lawyers, your reputation is *your* calling card. I'd venture to say that her accusation, left unchecked, would do more damage to the future of your organization than an actual financial judgment against you." He paused, but it was more for dramatic purposes. "We need to shift gears and focus squarely on letting the entire world know that Serena Carson's charge is not only untrue, but it's even more devastating based on her own personal history and her outrageous theft."

Bill would never be accused of going to battle without a strong game plan. He pulled papers from his briefcase.

"When we got that letter, I knew it was only the tip of the iceberg and I was correct. Considering her past, the fact that she stole your sperm, took it to this fertility center, it allows us to show that there's something terribly wrong with this woman."

"Wow," I said.

"I know it's quite a bit to take in, but trust me when I say that this is the best way to deal with her and this situation. It doesn't matter if we sue the state next month, in six months, or a year from now. But we simply cannot allow Serena to continue to taint a possible jury pool with thoughts and ideas that could lead to questions about *your* credibility."

I watched as the cameraman put his equipment away. That had been the fourth interview of the day. By the time we were finished, I knew Serena would kick herself for not trying to come to us quietly about this matter.

Things had been good at home lately, and I hoped that this would not be the turning point to take us backwards. When Bill came to the office, I called Roxy and told her what was going on. I didn't want any surprises and I wanted to make sure she was with me every step of the way.

"Hey, honey." She greeted me with a smile and I nearly ran back outside to make sure I was in the right house.

"You know the phone has been ringing off the hook, right?" she asked.

"Yeah, it was wild at the office too," I told her.

"Well, I want you to know, I'm behind you 100 percent! I think Bill is absolutely correct on this one. And I wanted to ask your thoughts about something," she said.

"If in fact we find out that Semaj is your daughter, we should fight Serena for custody. My heart goes out to that little girl and all she's been through. We can provide her with a more stable home environment," she said.

I pulled her close to me and held her tightly. Roxy didn't know how much her support meant to me. I owed Bill so much for his diligent work with this case. He was right—this could've gone in another direction, and everything Roxy and I had worked toward over the years could've been ruined.

"I'm the luckiest man alive," I told her. We kissed and the baby giggled in his highchair.

"Are you just now figuring that out?" she joked.

"I've known from day one, but sometimes things happen that make it more obvious each and every day," I said.

She smiled and it was good to see her looking happy again.

Later that night, I watched one of the many interviews I had done. The late news made me think about Shawnathon and I hoped he fared well in court the next day.

He was a nice young man. I couldn't imagine being so filthy rich that women would go to such lengths to have my baby. I laughed to myself at the irony in my thoughts. Here I was, nowhere near as rich and popular as Shawnathon, and I had a story that could rival his.

Some things really stood out when I spoke to him. I didn't understand how, with all that was going on, he hadn't requested a DNA test.

"Oh, I know the kids are mine," he said to me.

I had of course seen his kind before. He would've bet his own life on the paternity of his children, only to later be stunned.

"I'm not insulting you, but you can never be too sure about these things," I said.

"No, I feel you, after what you've been through, but on the real though, those kids are mine. Eboni and me, we were together. I got mad at her because she told me she wasn't really ready for kids yet. I know it was crazy, but I got her to sign something saying she knew I didn't want any kids. The minute she got pregnant, she started tripping. You know how they get, pushing the whole marriage thing."

I nodded as he told his story.

"I wasn't ready. There was something about her. It was like she didn't have anything going for herself and she was okay with that. I mean—I make enough money for me and a slew of wives, but damn, can't you try to be about something? We started having problems. That was another reason I didn't want kids with her, but after a while, I started to chill and figured it might not be all that bad, until she *really* started trippin'," he said.

"Well, I think the attorney is doing the right thing. He should push the agreement until a judge says it's not valid, then after that you can decide what you're gonna do. But if the kids are yours and you know for sure..."

"Yeah, I'm gonna pay, but man, it sucks! Women should respect a man's right to not have kids if he don't want 'em. We used protection but that shit didn't work. She shouldn't have lied and said she didn't want kids."

We agreed to check in after court; in the meantime, I'd get to work on a media plan for him.

LACHEZ

I couldn't believe my son, my own flesh and blood, stood me up. But that's exactly what had happened. Not only was he a no-show, but Darlene, who was supposed to bring the kids, didn't bother calling to say they weren't coming. To say I was in a bad mood would be an understatement.

When Toni knocked on my bedroom door, I barely wanted to answer, but of course, she knew I was in there.

"Are we working tonight or what?" she yelled.

"I'm moving a little slow. How much time I got?" I asked.

I was feeling pretty shitty. I knew that didn't mean our business needed to suffer, but I wasn't really up to going out.

When twenty minutes had passed, and I was still in the room, Toni started beating on the door even harder.

"C'mon! We need to get moving," she yelled.

I opened the door and she jumped back.

"Daaaauumm, what the hell happened to you? Why are your eyes so puffy? Girl, fix your hair and throw on some makeup. Ain't no way in hell we making any money with the way you looking," she said.

"Who we got tonight?" I asked.

"Nobody with you looking like that! What's wrong with you?"

"I'm not feeling like myself. I'm in a real funk and I can't seem to pull myself up and out," I said.

Toni stood with her hand on her hip.

"You need to get it together. We got money to make and you slacking. What's the problem? What's got you moping around?"

"I'll be ready in ten," I said as I tried to close the door. Toni slid her foot in the doorway and prevented me from closing the door.

"It's only gonna take ten minutes to fix those eyes?" Toni asked.

"Oh, I see you got jokes, huh? That's why I spend lots of money on my concealer," I said, and kicked her foot so she would move it.

Twenty minutes later, I was in the mirror pimping my new wig. I was going as a redhead tonight. When I walked out of the room, Toni started whistling.

"Damn! I stand corrected," she balked. "You clean up real nice, and I am loving those bad-ass, thigh-high boots!"

"Never doubt a pro," I said.

"You ain't lying; my mistake. So we're ready to do this then," she said.

"Yeah, might as well. I'm tired of sitting around getting mad at Junie and Darlene. Maybe I need to enjoy my newfound freedom and stop tripping off shit I can't control."

"That's what I've been saying all along," Toni said.

We pulled off yet another successful lick and I couldn't have been happier. Each time we left one of those executives passed out in a hotel room, I was glad that none of them called the police. But still, I couldn't fathom how we were able to pull this off with no problems.

"How much did we rake in tonight?" Toni asked on our way back from the store.

"From what I counted, it looks like we're just under five grand," I said.

EBONI

When I saw Elisa walking next to Shawnathon in court, I wondered what they were thinking. I couldn't understand why he thought bringing her to court was a good idea, but just like he had a posse, I had one, too.

Judi and Ulonda were with me. I started to bring the kids, but in the end, I figured leaving them with my mom was the best thing to do.

I felt good about today and was hoping the judge would rule in our favor. The proceedings went pretty fast. The courtroom was packed, but there weren't that many attorneys.

"What's the problem?" the judge asked Shawnathon's attorney.

"My client wants you to rule on the validity of the contract signed by both parties," his lawyer said.

"Mister Baas, where is the contract in question?" the judge asked.

"May I approach? Here it is, Your Honor." The attorney presented a sandwich-sized plastic freezer bag that contained the used bar napkin.

I held my breath as the judge first held the plastic bag up as if he was trying to check it out through the baggie. He opened it and carefully removed the napkin. He put it down, then looked around the courtroom.

"You've got to be kidding me," he said.

Both sides stood quietly and watched.

The judge held the napkin up between his index finger and thumb. "*This* is the *contract* in question? This old bar napkin that has some words scribbled on it? I can hardly decipher what it says," he said. "You gotta give me something to work with."

When the judge shook his head, placed the napkin on his desk and looked down, I started to get hope.

"Your Honor, my client entered into an agreement with Ms. Brown and she became pregnant..."

"I can tell you now," the judge cut him off. "I'm gonna throw this out. If there was an agreement written here, it looks like it was written by three-year-olds. Now, has your client been paying for the support of his minor children?" the judge asked.

"Well, Your Honor, he had been paying, but..."

"Had been? Mr. Baas, I'll take that as a *no*. Your client needs to come current by the close of business today or he will be held in contempt and sent to jail."

I was so excited. So far pretty good!

"Yes sir, Your Honor. What about the other issue? She's requesting an increase in payments and we'd like to submit that the amount she's requesting is..."

"One thing at a time. I won't rule on item number three if item number two hasn't been addressed. You're asking for far too much. Come current, then we can talk," the judge said. When he banged his gavel, I wanted to kiss Nia.

When I heard the word *next*, I struggled to contain my excitement. The judge was already done and had moved on to the next group!

Outside the courtroom, I danced and jumped for joy. High fives went all around. When Elisa and Shawnathon walked out, I laughed even harder. His lawyer tried to steer them in the opposite direction, but I was certain they still heard all of the hoopla.

Nia turned to me and said, "As I told you, that settlement

would've been a fraction of what we've received here today. I'm glad you finally allowed me to handle this situation the right way," she said.

Translation: You blamed me because you missed out on three hundred thousand dollars. Now we're getting seven times that amount and I want every dime of my 33 percent.

Nothing she said was going to ruin my moment. I felt completely vindicated. All that time I was stressed and worried about that stupid contract that I knew was not a real contract. I was glad a judge used common sense to tell Shawnathon and his legal dream team that they were wrong and he still had to pay!

"Let's get out of here and celebrate," Ulonda squealed. "It's on me! Let's go!"

We rushed toward the door. Nia said, "Come by the office tomorrow. I expect your first payment by Monday."

I was smiling so hard my cheekbones ached. As I followed Ulonda to her car, I pulled out my phone to call my mom and share the great news.

We ran across the street and I nearly stopped at the sight before us. He stopped talking when he realized I was walking up.

"I would've paid for my kids. You were out of order," Shawnathon said.

I looked around, trying to figure out what he had done with Elisa. It wasn't that I cared, but I really wanted her to be in on the gloating I planned to do.

"If you would've paid like you say you were going to, we would never have had to drag lawyers and courtrooms into this," I said.

"How are they anyway?" he asked.

His question caught me a little off guard. In the last few weeks, I had spent so much time running from Shawnathon that I forgot he could actually care about his kids.

"They're getting big," I said—still guarded.

"Yeah, I'll bet."

I glanced over his shoulder and didn't try to hide what I was doing.

"What's up?" he asked.

"Where's your new wife?"

"Oh, she went home. That morning sickness really makes her tired and sleepy," he said.

I was suddenly sorry I asked.

"So, what are y'all about to do?" he asked. Ulonda went to get the car after I assured her I was gonna be fine.

"Nothing much. Ulonda is treating me to a celebratory lunch," I said. "Why?"

"Just wondering, You gonna be home later tonight?" he asked.

"What's it to you? You wanna send another guy over?" I asked.

He grinned. "Man, I'm sorry, I kinda lost it there for a minute. I was way out," he said.

"That was low," I said.

"Yeah, it was, but man, you and the picketers." He shook his head. "Man, they're gonna be talking about me for years with that one! But seriously, if you let me come by, I wanna see the kids and I'll bring some money. You know I'm down for mines," he said.

"Why don't you call me? That way I can make sure they're up when you get ready to come through."

"Cool, it'll be after six," he said.

"Okay, I'll see you then," I said. I motioned to Ulonda that I was finished and she drove up. After I climbed into the car and buckled up, she started plummeting me with questions.

"What did he want? When is he paying you? Was he mad? Did you tell him to pay up? Where was Elisa? Do you trust him now?"

"He wants to see the kids and give me some money," I said.

"Whaaat?"

"Yes, girl, I'm so glad this nightmare is over. I'm gonna talk to him about Elisa. I know they're having their own baby, but I don't want my kids to suffer. I'm just glad he admitted he was being stupid, chasing me all over town and acting the fool," I said.

"I can't believe he's finally gonna pay up. You're lucky," she said.

But it was the *way* she said it. Ulonda and I were way cool, but I didn't want her to get jealous of me.

"So, I guess over lunch we need to start talking about this business plan of ours, right?"

"Yeah, girl, we can do that," she said.

But again, there was no enthusiasm in her voice at all. It was like I'd lose one problem only to pick up another. I sighed and the rest of the ride was silent.

SERENA

Things were spinning out of control a lot faster than I could handle. I felt so alone, betrayed even. Every time I looked up, Parker was either on TV, on the radio, or someone was talking about his case. How did he suddenly become the victim? Now I was the woman who had stolen a man's sperm for my own desperate motherhood quest!

A tiny part of me wished I had left things alone. This was a mess! It was like my press conference never happened. Where were my supporters? There was no one looking out for me. I hadn't heard from Loren since I left Deena's office. When the phone rang, I didn't even try to check caller ID. I no longer cared who was calling.

"Hello?"

"Serena Carson, please," a voice demanded.

"This is Serena," I said dryly.

"Yes, this is Tamera Sleets. I'm calling from Salem Missionary Baptist. You *were* scheduled to speak here next month. Well, our program has been put on hold, so I wanted to cancel with you as soon as possible," she said.

"Oh, yeah sure…right," I said. I didn't even try to hide my disbelief. But it seemed like she couldn't care less.

"Thank you, and God bless," she said and hung up before I could say anything else.

I couldn't really get upset because hers was the third cancellation so far and there were only four events scheduled.

My head whipped toward the sound of something smashing against my front door. If the TV or radio were on, I would've missed the sound altogether. I wasn't sure what was going on, but when I rushed to the window and glanced out, I saw two guys dressed in black with hoodies running away from my house and toward a car. The two jumped in and the car screeched off down the street.

It wasn't until I opened my front door that I saw the egg bath on my front door!

"Really? Grow up!" I screamed.

My neighbor looked at me and I frowned until she looked away.

"Now I have to clean up this mess! Uggh."

I walked inside and grabbed the phone. I was about to dial 9-1-1, but then I thought better of it. It wasn't like they'd send anyone over here to look after me. But if I was Parker Redman, I bet they'd have the entire force over here in a hurry.

I cursed as I went to the washroom and grabbed a bucket. I turned on the hot water while I searched for cleaning gloves. This foolishness was really getting out of hand. If people weren't calling to insult me and hang up, my neighbors were shooting daggers at me. I wanted people to mind their own damn business.

As I stood and scrubbed yolk stains from the crevices of my front door, I couldn't help but wonder if Parker had put his followers up to harassing me.

"Eeeww, Mom, what are you doing?" Semaj asked from behind.

"Oh, I'm cleaning the door," I said. I didn't think it was a good idea to tell her exactly what was going on. I had been careful to shield her from all that was going on.

"Cleaning the door? Why? And Mom, those shorts are too short," she balked.

"If you don't go inside and leave me alone," I warned jokingly.

"Thank God none of my friends are out here," she mumbled under her breath.

I watched my pre-teen daughter step over the bucket and walk into the house. I could only hope, for her sake, that this thing worked itself out.

Once I was finished cleaning up, I stood back to look at the door. I had been through so much, worked hard to keep this house, and to think people trashed it with no thoughts of me or my feelings really pissed me off.

I jumped, then turned when a car horn blurted behind me.

"Sperm-stealing bitch!"

If I hadn't ducked, the thirty-two-ounce cup they threw would've hit me in the head!

This was getting out of control. I rushed inside and grabbed the phone. Enough was enough and I refused to live like this.

"Yes, I need to talk to an officer about harassment," I said when someone answered the non-emergency line at the Houston Police Department.

"Ma'am, what seems to be the problem?" the person asked.

"I'm being harassed. People keep calling and hanging up, my house has been egged and someone just threw a bottle at my head," I said.

"Would you like to file a report?" the person asked.

"Um, I guess I would," I said.

"Okay, hold on and I'll have someone take your report."

"Over the phone?" I asked.

"Yes, ma'am," she said. "Hold on, please," she added.

I listened to elevator music and waited. After about three minutes, which felt much longer, another voice came back on.

"Ma'am, I'm Officer Kurtz," a man said. He rattled off his badge number and asked how he could help me.

I gave him the information and told him why I felt like I was being harassed and stalked.

"Do you have any idea of who might want to harm you?" he asked.

It wasn't the question, but the way he asked was as if he'd rather being doing anything other than talking to me about my problem. It was almost like he didn't think my problem was real.

"Um, actually I do," I said.

"Okay? And who is this person?" Was he being sarcastic?

"His name is Parker Redman," I said.

When he didn't respond right away, I realized this phone call may have been a mistake. Parker worked with the police. They probably knew him on a first-name basis.

"Hello?" I called out.

"Yes, ma'am," he said.

"I said that it's Parker Redman, the guy who runs DFF," I screamed.

"Okay, ma'am, what are you alleging?" he asked. The way he talked to me was really pissing me off. Ever since I mentioned Parker's name, his tone had changed dramatically. I was getting sick and tired of this foolishness.

"I'm not *alleging* anything. Look, it's no secret that you guys protect your own, and Parker may as well be one of y'all, but somebody needs to take this seriously," I yelled.

"Ma'am, I need you to calm down," he said.

"No, you don't know what I've been going trough! Ever since I told the world that Parker Redman is my daughter's father and he ain't paid one red cent to take care of her, my life has been a living hell, and he's over there on Easy Street," I yelled.

"What?" a stunned voice cried.

I closed my eyes. I didn't need to turn around to know my

daughter was behind me. I held the phone but my voice was gone. I had completely forgotten that she was in the house.

Reluctantly, I turned to see my child crying her eyes out.

"I thought James was my daddy! How could you be with both of them? That's why he left! That's why he abandoned us!"

"Semaj, wait," I yelled.

"I hate you!"

Before I could get up, she was out the door.

PARKER

There was no denying it. The letter B stood for Brilliant—because that was exactly what Bill was. His plan worked better than we'd expected. If we needed to pick a jury from the current population, I'd feel completely confident going into court.

Not only had every radio and TV station run with the story about Serena stealing my sperm, but magazines and newspapers jumped on board, too. This ran across my mind as I walked into the grocery store and saw the headlines on one of the local magazines. It brought a smile to my face.

"Houston man vows to fight after sperm stolen and used without his consent!"

"Excuse me," a deep baritone said.

I looked over my shoulder.

"Aren't you Parker Redman?" he asked.

"Yes, I am." I turned to face the stranger.

He extended his hand for a shake. I gladly accepted.

"I'm pulling for you, buddy! Give 'er hell for all of us!" he said.

"I appreciate it," I said.

"Me and my buddies, we're gonna come down to the center and volunteer. You tell us what you need done—we just wanna show our support," he said. "We've already signed up for premium membership with DFF."

"Hey, man, I really appreciate that," I said earnestly.

"Don't mention it," he said. He walked away. "This Saturday, it'll be four of us. We already talked about it," he added.

"Thank you," I told him.

"No, man, thank you. Keep up the good work!"

I pulled my list and went to buy what Roxy needed. I felt good knowing that things were turning out better than Bill and I expected. In addition to getting out ahead of Serena's so-called smear campaign, Bill also asked for an extension in court, so our court date was pushed back.

Again, I wasn't sure about the strategy, but apparently, he knew exactly what he was doing.

"When the tide turns, we want it to wash all the way onto shore," he said. "We want to hit her hard, then before she gets a chance to get up and catch her balance, we hit her again," he had said.

Now, I fully understood what he meant. I had no idea how she was dealing with this, but the plan was to hit her from every angle possible. She wanted to be in the spotlight, so that's where we were taking the fight, right to her front door.

Later that afternoon, I was huddled over my computer screen behind my locked office door when the receptionist called.

"Mr. McGee is here," she announced.

"Oh, I'll be right out," I said.

I walked out and was surprised to see the pleasant expression on Shawnathon's face.

We did the brotha greeting and handshake, and I invited him into my office.

"You look good, man. What's going on?" I asked.

"Yeah, I wanted to come and tell you personally. My agent and the team support the commercial for DFF," he said.

"Aww, man! That's great news! That's awesome!" I said.

Shawnathon and I had talked about him appearing in a commercial that we could run on cable and on the Internet promoting the services of DFF. I knew that he was usually paid for that type of work, but he told me to let him check with his people because he'd be able to do it pro-bono.

"Yeah, I'm excited. You were really in my corner—even though as it turns out, my situation worked itself out," he said.

"Yes, I was glad to hear that. Have the two of you settled on an amount yet?" I asked.

"Well, after court, I went over there, paid up and let her know that I was planning to take care of my shorties. I told her if she wouldn't have started trippin', we could've handled ours on our own."

"Well, buddy, I'm glad to hear that," I said.

"Yeah, I'm glad it's over. I hate court, lawyers, judges and all that craziness," Shawnathon said.

"So you two settled before the judge ruled?" I asked.

He frowned.

"Nah, it went to court. And next week it'll be official. But I wanted to kind of smooth things over before then," he said.

"Well, you know you'll have to take a DNA test since the judge ruled you have to pay," I explained.

"Yeah, it's all good. My lawyer explained it was just a technicality. We did the test already and she wasn't tripping either. I'm glad we're beyond that. I get to see my kids and we're working on being cool with each other," he said.

"Man, I always love to hear a happy ending," I said

Shawnathon and I talked a little more about my situation with Serena. He told me how the guys at the barbershop, the gym, and just about everywhere else were really on my side. It was only additional confirmation that Bill's idea was right on the money.

Serena and her lawyer thought they were going to ruin me and my business by beating me to the press, but it was obvious they didn't really understand the game.

We hadn't heard back from her lawyer since Bill countersued. The ball may have been in their court, but we definitely had home-field advantage.

I wrapped up with Shawnathon and finalized everything related to the shoot. As I locked up the office, Bill called.

"Hey, what's up?"

"I have great news," he said.

"What's that?" I asked.

"Well, Deena called. I think they're ready to settle this thing. Also I've obtained the records from the fertility clinic. They do have the proper documentation—with signatures and photo IDs. The only problem is when Serena took Parker to the clinic, he looked nothing like you." Bill laughed.

"She didn't!"

"Oh, she did my friend. She did!"

"Wow," I said.

My heart raced as I talked to Bill. Suddenly, my ears began to sear with incredible heat. I had done nothing wrong, how could I be facing my moment of truth?

"What's the likelihood that Semaj is my daughter?" I asked. And even though the words came rushing out, I wasn't so sure I was ready for the answer.

"The answer is probably gonna be yes on this one," Bill said. "We still need to wait for an official DNA test, but considering all she did, it's highly likely."

He gave me some time and I held my reaction. I closed my eyes, pinched the bridge of my nose, and swallowed back tons of regret.

"You still there?" Bill asked.

"Uh, yeah, I'm right here," I said. My voice cracked a bit and I felt like I was choking on my words. I think Bill knew I couldn't speak because he quickly started explaining.

"This woman went to great lengths. I'm not sure if the elevator goes all the way to the top floor, but I can say when she sets her mind to something, she doesn't give up."

I listened as Bill ran the scenario down to me. He also told me he was considering filing suit against the fertility clinic for negligence.

"By the time we're done, they're gonna think we're sue happy," I joked.

"These cases won't make it to a jury," Bill said confidently.

"How can you be so sure?"

"Parker, you were already the poster boy for paternity fraud when the phrase was virtually unknown. Now the fact that this woman went to such incredible lengths, stealing your sperm, finding an imposter, the cards are stacked completely against her. So this is the time for us to move in for the kill!"

LACHEZ

The text message put a smile on my face that stretched more than a mile wide. My baby was coming! He even said sorry for the *no show* Sunday night.

"Woo hooo!" I screamed and quickly texted him back.

"What you doing up in there whooping and hollering?" Toni asked. She stuck her head in as she was walking by my room.

"Junie said he's coming by," I told her.

I noticed the skeptical look on her face, but I ignored it. As I sent him a message telling him how excited I was that he was coming, I thought she would keep walking but she didn't.

"Are you gonna act right this time?" Toni asked me.

I looked up at her.

"What's that supposed to mean? How do I not act right?"

"Lachez, we had to pull you off that poor woman! I'm surprised he agreed to come back."

I got up and tried to calm myself. I even asked God to soften my words because Toni was seriously tripping.

"Are you trying to tell me you don't have a problem with Junie and Pricilla?" I asked.

"Girl, your son is not a boy anymore. She's a cougar, and everyone is doing it. If he's happy, you need to fall in line and be happy for him. He's gonna be eighteen in how many weeks? I'm saying you're gonna waste a bunch of energy and time for nothing because the bottom line is this—there's not a damn thing you can do about it. He's grown!"

"He's not grown. He's seventeen!"

"Have you checked the age of consent?"

"The what of what?" I asked.

"In Texas seventeen is the age of consent. That means if your son, who is seventeen and more than a half, wants to bang a woman his mama's age, there's not a damn thing you can do about it legally," Toni said. She looked at me like she was exasperated.

"So she won't even go to jail for molesting my baby?" I asked helplessly.

"He's *not* a baby," Toni deadpanned.

"He's my baby," I said.

"Well, that may be the case, but right now, you need to face reality, and reality is, your *baby* is doing some real grown-up stuff and with a grown-ass woman!"

When the phone chirped signaling another text message, I was glad for the interruption. The conversation with Toni wasn't going anywhere. She wasn't saying anything I wanted to hear.

Toni turned to leave and I went to grab the phone. It was Drew.

Jus thkn bout U! his text message read.

I smiled. I couldn't believe he was all into me like this. Back in the day, I looked at him as just another revenue source. It wasn't like he was balling out of control or anything like that, but he had a good job and he didn't mind sharing.

"*I'm Gd Sup w U?*" I texted back to him.

"*Hook up 2nite?*"

With Junie coming over this evening, I wasn't sure planning a date with Drew was a good idea. But I also didn't want to give him the impression that it wasn't good for him over here either.

"Damn," I said.

"What's wrong?"

I looked toward the door. I wondered why Toni didn't have other shit to do besides sit up and listen to my conversations through the paper-thin walls?

"Nothing," I yelled.

"Well, come out here. What are you doing in there?"

"Okay, I'll be out in a few minutes," I said.

When I finished texting to Drew that I may be able to hook up, but it would have to be late, I walked out of the room.

"So, besides getting ready for your boy and his woman, what else you got planned for today?" Toni asked.

I eased down on the sofa and thought about her question. That's when I realized I needed something more to do than work with Toni a couple nights a week. Of course I had to figure out ways to convince my son that he shouldn't *wife* his babysitter, but besides that, I needed to be about something else, too.

"Girl, I'm chilling. Why, what's up with you?"

The knock at the door interrupted our conversation.

Toni jumped up and rushed to the door.

"You expecting someone?" she asked over her shoulder.

"Not til later when Junie comes through," I said.

"You mean, Pricilla," Toni said as she pulled the door open.

"See, why you keep saying that bitch…?" I looked up before I could finish my sentence and it was a good thing I did. I nearly choked on my words when I saw Pricilla walking through the front door.

"I tried to handle this the best way, but it seems to me like you insist on shoving your nose where it don't belong," Pricilla said.

She stopped on the other side of the couch and I was dumbfounded. I could feel the muscles in my face flinching. As I sat there looking up at the old hag, I couldn't get over how much I hated her.

"Excuse me? What the hell are you doing here?" I asked.

"I came here to try and talk some sense into you. Junie has been sick since we left here and I thought you should know."

I looked at Toni as if to say this bitch done gone and lost her mind for real. But a part of me couldn't understand what she was thinking.

"What the hell? Where is *he* and why are *you* here?"

Pricilla seemed like a completely different person than the timid woman who was here the other week. This time she didn't seem lost and nervous. But if she thought she was gonna be able to stand in front of me talking out the side of her neck, we were definitely gonna have problems.

"I know all about you. I know about the things you've done, the things you're doing, all of it. I know you don't want me with your son, but people don't choose who they fall in love with. When it happens, it happens. If you want to continue to see your son and have a relationship with him, I suggest you find a way to tolerate me—because I'm here to stay!"

By the time she was done, her hands were planted firmly on her hips and she didn't look like she was backing down.

EBONI

"Well, I'm paying off the mortgage on my mama's house. You know that's only about fifteen to twenty thousand. Then, I've been eyeing this Bentley, so I'm gonna go see about that. After that, of course we can go shopping," I said.

"Girl, you are so lucky," Ulonda said.

I put my fork down and looked at her.

"Luck? Are you kidding me? After all I've been through with this man? I'm serious—this has nothing whatsoever to do with no doggone luck! Imagine if I had given up! I had to struggle from the moment he decided he was mad at me for not doing what he wanted," I said.

"Yeah, but if that judge had accepted that contract...," Ulonda said.

She couldn't be serious! I had no idea she felt that way.

"Contract?" I balked. "You and I both know that was *no* contract. Nia told me if the judge hadn't tossed it because he could barely read it, we would've gotten it tossed behind the fact that I was drunk at the time," I said. "And let's not forget, he was pissy-ass drunk, too!"

"Umph," Ulonda said.

I started eating again and so did she. For a while neither of us said anything and that really was fine by me.

"So I was thinking about some business ideas," Ulonda suddenly said.

She started to perk up. And I was glad she changed the subject. But even though I told her we'd go into business together, there was so much I wanted to do before we got to that point. I especially wasn't so sure I wanted to go into business with someone who was finally letting her true feelings be known. Who knew she thought it was luck that had gotten me where I was today?

"We should look at investing in some adult entertainment shops. We could do something like sell sexy clothes, toys, and offer erotic exercise classes," she said excitedly. "We don't have to be up front if you don't feel comfortable. We could hire a face of the business."

I wasn't really feeling her idea, but I didn't want to hurt her feelings. I hadn't told Ulonda that I was thinking about taking a trip, too, so I could clear my head and figure out what I wanted to do next.

As she talked, I started to think. It didn't take long for me to discover that the problem with having money was friends who had none. If I wanted to take that trip, it was not like she could go with me unless I paid her way. I couldn't even go on shopping sprees because well, she couldn't afford to hang.

"So how much money did you get right off the bat?" Ulonda asked.

I leaned in closer 'cause I didn't need everybody all up in mines.

"He gave me three hundred grand," I whispered.

Ulonda's mouth lowered like a drawbridge. Her eyes got so big I didn't know if she was shocked or thrilled for me.

"The money he promised in Vegas?" she asked.

"Yeah, girl, because we still have to wait for the test before the judge is gonna announce how much I get each month," I said.

"Damn! So you got that much money and this is *before* the judge's order?"

Now she seemed stunned by what I said. I didn't understand why.

She had to have known I was gonna get paid because Shawnathon is who he is.

"He seems like he's really trying to make up for all that tripping he did," I told her.

"You know, I never thought I'd see the day when we'd be sitting at lunch talking about Shawnathon acting right. It's so crazy. After all you've gone through running from him, the restraining order, the threats..." Ulonda reminded me.

I shook my head as she ran down our drama-filled past. She was right, and as she ran it down, it dawned on me, Ulonda had been there every step of the way.

"Girl, that's all in the past now. He was tripping, but he's apologized for all of it. And honestly, when he came by, I wasn't sure if he was up to something, but it turned out he was really ready to do right by me and his kids," I beamed.

"So he brought you all that cash right there on the spot?" Ulonda asked.

"No, silly, it was a cashier's check," I said. I thought that was a strange question, but I figured I'd see where she was taking this conversation.

"You are so damn lucky," she said again as she finished her salad. When she shook her head as if she found my new fortune hard to believe, I had finally had enough.

"Ulonda, is there a problem?" I asked. I didn't mean for it to come out the way it sounded, but dammit, so be it. She was the one tripping!

She looked up at me with surprised eyes. I watched as her eyeballs darted around as if she was confused by my question. Her face twisted as she chewed her food, then swallowed.

"What are you talking about?" she asked.

"I'm talking about how you've been acting ever since we started talking about the money. Where do you get off acting like I should be grateful that Shawnathon finally decided to do right by me and the kids?"

"Ummmm..."

I didn't give her a chance to interrupt. "You know I always knew you were just a little jealous of me, but the minute Shawnathon put that money in my hand, I said, 'Oh Lord, please don't let this cause problems between me and Ulonda.'" I was trying not to get all-emotional, but she had pissed me off with all of her dumb questions and lucky comments.

She tried to hold her finger up to stop me, but I was nowhere near being done.

"No, I'm not done yet," I snapped. "Listen, I can't help it that your sorry, wannabe-rapper-ass, baby daddy don't do shit for you or his son, but I thought we was better than this hate I'm getting from you," I told her.

"Are you done yet?" Ulonda asked. She rolled her eyes dramatically as if it was all she could do to sit and hear me out.

"No, I'm just saying, I expect this kind of hate from people who don't know what I've been through with him, but you?" I shook my head. By now, tears were burning in the corners of my eyes.

"I'm not sure where all of this is coming from," she said. "But if I gave you the impression that I'm jealous, upset, or in any way negatively affected by your newfound wealth, that's your problem and not mine! Yeah, Dalton is a deadbeat and a loser, but up until just the other day, it was me and you against him and Shawnathon, one and the same. So don't go acting brand new now because he's laced you with a few dollars! I've never been against you, and after all we've been through, it's more than insulting to me that you would even try to play me like that! Now that Shawnathon is trying to come correct, you suddenly think I'm jealous?" She tossed the fork down and threw the napkin on top of her plate.

"I don't need this shit," she said.

I watched as she looked around the restaurant. All of a sudden, she grabbed her purse, dug into it and pulled out a fistful of cash.

"You know what? I got this. Let me pick up the tab, because Lord knows, I don't want you praying to God ever again about whether *your* money will ever change me! And I hope things don't ever turn sour with you and Shawanthon again." She got up, dropped the money on the table, and stormed off. "Because this time I won't be there to save your ass!"

I didn't call or go after her because I didn't feel like I needed to. She took everything I was trying to say all out of proportion and I was not about to go running behind her to point that out.

I sat alone at the table and finished my lunch. The more I thought about it, with all my money, and especially once the judge made it official, Ulonda would need me long before I'd ever need her again.

SERENA

"Yes, this is Serena Carson, around the corner. Our daughters are, um, in the same class," I said to the woman on the other end. I had asked to speak to Madison's mother.

"What's your name again?" she asked.

Suddenly, a massive, extra-dry boulder lodged itself right in my throat. I was nervous, embarrassed, and couldn't remember a time when I'd felt so alone.

"Uh, my name or my daughter's name?" I stammered.

"Your name," the woman corrected. I told myself not to read too much into the sarcasm in her voice. How could I blame her? I'd been meaning to get over there to introduce myself to her properly, but I'd had a lot going on. Quite surely she could understand that.

"Oh, I'm Serena Carson, Semaj's mother," I said.

"Oh, yeah, I thought that's what you said, but I wasn't sure." There was no way to ignore the sarcasm in her voice that time. But I held my tongue. After all, I did need her help.

"Yes, sorry, my allergies have really been messing with me," I lied. "Anyway, I'm trying to see if Semaj is over there," I said.

"Over here?" The woman chuckled a little. At least that's what I thought she did. I couldn't really tell.

"Yeah, I'm looking for her. We...uh, you know how teenagers can be." I tried to chuckle, too, but she didn't say anything and the silence made me feel awkward.

"Ms. Carson, my daughter, Zoey, is upstairs studying with her sister. I'm not sure where your daughter is, but from what Zoey has told me, they stopped talking nearly a year ago," she said.

Bitch!

She sat on the phone and listened as I stumbled my way through this conversation when she knew all along that our damn kids didn't even talk anymore. Some people were just too damn much! Who does that?

"Oh, and Ms. Carson?" She dragged the *s* out in Ms.

"Yeah?" I was good and irritated after all of that.

"Obviously, you don't know where your child is, but seems to me like you should try to focus more on *family* and less on airing your dirty laundry for everyone to see," she said.

"Uh, obviously you don't know me that well," I said. "But if you did, you'd know that I really don't give a flying fu..."

She had the nerve to hang up on me! I was so hot, but I was also on a mission, so I had to keep it moving. I flipped through the little diary-type book I'd found in my daughter's room and continued going down the list of names and numbers.

I found another name, and tried my best to figure out who it was and whether it was the neighbor whose house was down the block and across the street.

"What the hell," I said as I dialed.

"Hi, my name is Serena Carson. I'm Semaj's mother. Our daughters took swim lessons together?" I asked more than said. I assumed Williams was the name of the girl who lived down the street.

"Oh, you must be talking about my granddaughter's little friend," the woman said. When she spoke, I could tell her voice sounded aged, but whatever. "Yeah, I remember that lil' girl," she said.

"Okay, the reason I'm calling is because Semaj was upset when she left and now I can't reach her," I lied.

"What do you mean she was upset when she left? My grandbaby is only thirteen. I don't know how old your child is, but Jessie don't go nowhere by herself," the woman admonished.

"Ma'am, have you seen my child?" I asked. Enough with the damn parenting tips.

"You probably don't even know my name, do you?" she asked.

Once again, my hatred for Parker resurfaced. I hated to be in this position. I hated that he was some local celebrity, able to do all kinds of stuff and nobody judged him and his parenting skills, while I was stuck alone doing all of the heavy lifting over here. Now I had to lower myself to being questioned by people who thought they were better than me because my kid ran off.

"Ma'am, I'm just trying to find my daughter. She took off and I want to make sure she's okay," I said.

"So you pick up the phone and start calling up strangers. How do you not know where your child is?"

"I don't need a lecture right now. We got into it and she left. So I won't win Mother of the Year, sue me!" I screamed.

"Umph, seems to me like you don't need to be inviting any more lawsuits, just my two cents," she said.

I hung up on her!

"Damn! What's wrong with these people? Can't anybody mind their own damn business these days?"

I looked at Semaj's list closely and wondered how old this mess was. But what could I do? I wasn't gonna stop looking for her, but it was obvious I needed to change my approach.

It was easy for other parents to sit up and judge me. Their business wasn't plastered all over the news or all over the neighborhood. I really didn't give a damn what they said or thought, because when it came down to it, they weren't doing a damn thing for me anyway. So what, I hadn't made it around the corner to meet that little girl's mother? Who had the time these days?

It wasn't like I didn't know where my child was back when they were friends. If anything would've happened, I would've known exactly who to point the police to. In the car, Semaj would point to their houses and tell me all about what was going on. I knew enough, but that's not what people wanted to hear. They just wanted to judge others.

The irony of my thoughts struck me hard. I was sitting there upset and worked up, looking for Semaj, and had no clue where she might be.

At least I knew not to call Latrice's house! If I was a bad mother, I wouldn't have known she and Latrice fell out last month.

"Where would a twelve-year-old disappear to with no money, no car and no one to give her a ride?"

PARKER

"So what do you think we should do?" I asked Bill.

"Don't tie my hands here. I think we should do exactly what we planned. We need to keep it very public and force her to retract everything she said. The damage her accusations could do to your brand alone is enough to ruin your professional reputation," Bill said. "Don't tell me you're getting soft on me now."

I sighed. "Nah, it's not that really, but well, I will say this, since we announced our lawsuit, membership has increased threefold, and cash donations have poured in. We're at something like fourteen thousand dollars. Men are coming by to volunteer in any way they can."

"See, this tells me the climate is ripe for us to do whatever we'd like. If we want to take this all the way to a jury, we'd do well, or we could force them into a settlement," Bill said. "We simply need to decide what we'd like to do and get it done."

Roxy looked at Bill, then she looked at me. I could tell there was something on the tip of her tongue. Perhaps she was waiting for the right time, or what she thought would be the right time. I wasn't worried about whatever it might be because lately she'd been very supportive of everything and I had to admit the new Roxy was more refreshing than her predecessor, angry, upset Roxy, and I was relieved about that.

"You okay, honey?" I asked.

"Yeah, I'm fine. Bill, would you like coffee, scotch, anything at all while we wait?"

Roxy got up from the table. That's where we'd been sitting since Bill arrived. He told us that things were going really well. It had only been two days since we came out, and my face and story were just about everywhere.

"If there's someone who supports Serena or what she did, we can't find that person and her attorney knows that. Serena may not have good sense, but her attorney does, so I expect to hear from them relatively soon," Bill said.

I couldn't help but notice how confident he was. His confidence was more than reassuring, and it made me feel empowered, not only for myself, but for the other men I came in contact with at the center.

"You've gotta make up your mind. And remember, she brought this to us," Bill said.

"Yeah, I hear all of what you're saying, but there's also something else we need to discuss. Since it appears highly likely that Semaj is really my child, Roxy and I have made a decision about her," I said.

One second Roxy was near the coffee maker, the next she was at my side. She rubbed my back while I talked to Bill about our decision.

Bill looked at me, but his demeanor had changed. His bubbly personality had disappeared. I was trying to read him before he spoke, but it wasn't easy.

"What's that?" he asked almost as if he was afraid to know.

I looked up at Roxy to make sure she hadn't suddenly changed her mind. She nodded slightly. Since the letter arrived pointing us in the direction of how Serena became pregnant, Roxy was very clear about the path we should take and she never wavered. What made me feel good about it was the fact that it was Roxy's idea.

"We want to fight her for custody," I said. Roxy's hand was rubbing my back all along.

Bill sat there and simply looked at me. I didn't know if he was thinking or whether he thought that was such a bad idea he needed to choose his words carefully.

"Are you two sure about that?" Bill asked. His dry tone of voice made his position very clear.

"We've talked about it, and we think it's the best thing for all involved," Roxy said.

"You realize that move would be opening a massive can of worms," Bill said.

"We didn't open the can. Serena did that the second she held that news conference," Roxy said.

It was almost as if Bill was trying to talk to me with his eyes.

He leaned forward, and for the first time since he arrived at our house, he seemed stressed. The visit had been easy going, and Bill had been pretty laid back, until then.

"I said we didn't ask for this, but I want you to know just what a move like that would mean," Bill said.

"How would it look that Semaj is my daughter and I left her there to suffer? Serena's got issues, and I don't want that future for my child," I said. "Besides, you have to remember, Semaj knows both Roxy and me really well. Remember, Bill, we were all close at one time."

"Okay, fair enough," Bill said. He looked at Roxy and said, "I'll take that scotch now."

"Okay, coming right up. Dinner should be ready in ten minutes," Roxy said.

"We should brace ourselves, because I have a feeling Serena is not gonna give up her kid without a serious fight," Bill said.

"How much of a fight do you think she'll put up?" I asked. "She tried to pin her kid on my best friend. She waited years later to pin it on me—that tells me she's probably desperate," I said.

"Desperate, broke or not, you can never predict what might happen when you try to separate a women from her child, even a woman like Serena," Bill said.

"Was that the doorbell?" Roxy asked over her shoulder as she stood at the stove.

I jumped up to go get the door. "I think we'll be okay. See, what you don't know is back when she was trying to pass the kid off on my boy, James, she dropped her off at his front door with her suitcases," I said as I headed for the door.

"That Serena sounds like she's something special," Bill joked.

Laughing at Bill's understatement of the century, I pulled the door open and the smile slipped from my face.

"Is it true?" the voice asked.

Instantly, my eyes scanned the front of our house. I glanced to see if a car was waiting, but the street was dark.

"How'd you get here?" I asked.

"I wanna know if it's true. I'm tired of being lied to," she said.

I could tell she'd been crying.

"Who's there?" Roxy yelled from the kitchen.

Instead of answering, I stepped aside and said, "Come on in so we can talk."

"Hey, what's going on here?" I heard Roxy ask before I could turn around to see her.

"Semaj, how'd you get over here? Your mom know you're here?" Roxy asked.

Semaj didn't answer. She kept her eyes glued to mine and asked again, "Is it true?"

LACHEZ

"I'm sorry she did that to you, but Ma, you gotta admit, you ain't tryin' to hear nothin' once your mind is made up, and you know it!"

Junie had a point there, but we weren't here to talk about me and my shortcomings. I wanted to talk about him and his decision to date that old hag.

"Why we come here anyway?" I asked, looking around the restaurant. I liked seafood, but I didn't think Pappadeaux had the best seafood. Of course I wasn't gonna say a word about that because Junie would only accuse me of being negative. I was glad to be alone with him. My plan was to try and talk some sense into him since she wasn't around.

"It's not that I don't like Pricilla," I said.

"C'mon, Ma, let it go," he said.

I shrugged. "What? What are you trying to say?" I asked him.

"Ma, you know good and well you don't like Pricilla. You should know by now that you can't lie to me," he said.

I frowned a little. Was my son trying to check me? I needed to stay in control here.

"It's not that I don't like her. I'm confused—that's all," I lied. Not only did I not like the bitch, I wanted to beat her like she stole something. But for purposes of this conversation, I decided to keep that part to myself.

"What are you confused about, Ma?"

He spoke to me like he was irritated by everything I said. I couldn't help myself. Each time I looked into my son's eyes, I still saw my stubborn twelve-year-old who thought he was smarter than everyone, including me.

"Why someone so much, more um, experienced?" I asked. I wanted to point out that the bitch was old, but he expected me to say that.

"Ma, I've always been into older chicks," he said.

My eyebrows went up because I never knew this before.

"Why do you think I used to hustle all those men with you?" he asked.

I leaned in and lowered my voice. "I didn't hustle anyone," I said.

Junie's expression never changed.

"Get real, Ma, this is me. Of course you did—that's all you did. But don't trip, I'm not judging. I'm only saying, didn't you ever wonder what I did with my money?"

"Your money? What money?" I asked him.

"Ma, c'mon now, I'd shave my cut off the top each time someone broke you off something," he said.

"I knew it!" I yelled. I caught myself and glanced around the restaurant, then lowered my voice. "I knew you were pinching off my ends," I said.

"Ma, what we gave you more than covers the little chump change you were pulling in," he said.

It was strange. He sounded like my son, even looked like him, but his demeanor, his mannerisms, had all changed. He was acting like a little man.

"What are you talking about, what you gave me?" I asked.

"The envelope Pricilla and I gave you before you jumped on her," he said.

"Oh," I said.

"You didn't even open it, Ma? Wow, that's wild," Junie said.

"You gotta remember what all happened that day. With us breaking out into a disagreement like that, it slipped my mind," I said.

"Slipped your mind, huh? Well, I hope that five thousand-dollar check is still good by the time you take it to the bank," he said.

"You slid me five grand?" I asked in a whisper.

"Ma, you just got out. Of course we gave you a few dollars. See, you wasn't listening to anything I was saying."

"Where you get that kind of money?" I asked.

"Oh, my hustle is legal," he said and winked. I noticed he wasn't talking too much about that at all, but then, I couldn't blame nobody but myself. If I knew my child like I knew I did, he was up to something.

"What's that supposed to mean?" I asked him.

"Listen, I want my two favorite girls to get along. I am in love with Pricilla and we're getting married," he said.

"You're gonna marry that ol' lady?" I asked him.

He tossed me such an incredibly nasty look I wanted to remind him that I was his *mother*!

"Ma, like I said, I've always been into older women." Junie sounded more like a thirty-year-old man than a seventeen-year-old kid. He'd be my kid for the rest of his natural life, and as I sat and listened to him, it made me even more determined to get my two youngest, Mickey, who was thirteen, and his fifteen-year-old brother, Lorenzo, back. I hated that I had missed so much with my boys while I was away.

"You've always been into older women?" He had to be kidding me.

"Ma, turn the page," he said.

"Whatever. She better be glad I didn't pounce the moment she walked in the damn door! How she gonna be texting me pretending to be you? That was foul!"

"Ma, can't you try to get along with Pricilla? What she did was wrong, but she only wanted to try and reach you, and she knew if she'd come out right and asked to meet with you, well..." He stopped talking.

"You make me sound so…" I shrugged my shoulders.

Junie flicked his wrist and looked at his watch. He looked up, then around the restaurant. "They need to come on. I've got some business," he said.

"I wish she wasn't so old," I muttered.

My child looked at me like I was the hopeless case; he finally waved his arm in the air and summoned a waiter.

"You're stressing about things that are beyond your control. I'm good. I don't need a mother trying to nurture me. Those years are gone. Besides, my daddy stepped up while you were away," he said.

The thoughts swirled around in my head, but I didn't dare ask the question that was tethering on the very tip of my tongue.

"Your daddy?"

"Yes, my daddy, as in my pops!" Junie started smiling. "Oh, that's right, you probably don't even know, huh?"

I frowned and started to study the menu again. Before my eyes could focus on anything, he snatched it from me.

"Ma, look at me," he said.

"What, boy?"

"So you didn't know for sure who my daddy was?" He chuckled a little, but there was no humor in his tone. "I guess they're right when they say mama's baby, daddy's maybe, huh?"

I started to reach across the table and slap the crap out of him, but the waiter showed up to take our order.

The minute the waiter walked away, my child looked me in the eye and said, "Julius *is* my daddy, as in my biological daddy. He had me tested right after you went to jail."

"I knew that," I snapped.

He looked at me with a smirk on his face. He didn't have to say he knew I wasn't sure, because his expression told me he didn't believe my claim.

EBONI

"You are being real extra right now!" I screamed loudly and giggled. "You really need to take your drunk behind home to your wife. I'm sure she wouldn't even appreciate it if you walked in with my essence all over your lips," I said.

Shawnathon had stopped by to see the kids, and getting rid of him was more difficult than I expected. Once the kids went to sleep, we shared a few drinks. After the blow-up with Ulonda yesterday, I had felt more than a little down and lonely. So when he called and asked if he could come through, it was right on time.

"Girl, I ain't hardly drunk," Shawnathon said.

Right at that moment, he looked so damn sexy to me I needed him to leave because I wasn't sure how much longer I could maintain in his presence.

"Seriously though, you good?" he asked.

"Yeah, I'm straight," I said. I kinda wanted to tell him about how Ulonda and I had fallen out, but I decided against it. What would've been the point really?

"So...check it," Shawnathon said. "I know you gonna be dating, if you not doing so already, and I, um, I don't know if I want a bunch of different cats running through here and hanging around my kids," he said.

I tossed my hands to my hips. I couldn't believe what he was trying to say. Didn't he know I had more sense than to parade a bunch of men through my house when I had small kids?

"I don't even get down like that," I said.

"I'm not trying to be all up in your business or anything like that. It's just that you don't know people these days. You think someone's real cool, and they turn out to be all twisted and shit. That's all I'm saying," he said.

"No, I totally understand, but I wouldn't be bringing every Tom, Dick, and Harry up in here and around my kids," I said.

"That's all I'm asking really," he said. "So we good then?"

When Shawnathon put those sexy eyes on me, it was all I could do to get out of his way. I tried to pretend like they no longer had power over me, but I'd have been straight lying to myself.

"You need to go home," I said with more meaning this time.

Shawnathon was near the front door, but it was like he kept trying to find reasons to hang around.

"What—you got a hot date tonight?" he asked.

"No dates, not yet," I said.

"Well, when you decide to start giving it up, you need to let me know," he said.

I looked at him like he only had a short time to fix his comment. He glanced at me sideways, and giggled in that way that used to turn me on.

"Get out of here," I said and playfully swung at him. He caught my arm and pulled me close. I felt uncomfortable and uneasy being so close to him. Before I knew what happened, a flood of memories washed over me.

Shawnathon's lips were just as soft and sweet as I remembered. I could taste the hint of beer on his breath just like back in the day, and I was getting caught up. He backed me into the wall and grabbed my arms, pinning each wrist against the wall.

We kissed like we were hungry for each other. He started sucking on my neck and soon, his hands were traveling all over my body.

I didn't know if it was his skills or just the fact that I hadn't been with a man in a long time, but suddenly I started to feel like I would die if I couldn't have him inside me.

We stumbled over to the sofa, still kissing and tugging at each other's clothes. He tasted good and his hard, muscled body felt even better. When we pulled apart, I tried to catch my breath.

"Oh God," I cried. "I've missed you like crazy," I said.

Shawnathon kissed me even harder. This time he grabbed fistfuls of my hair and pulled my head closer to his. We started to fumble with our clothes and struggled to undress each other.

Moments later, I was in my panties as I stood and waited for him to find a condom.

"What are we doing, Shawnathon?" I asked.

He turned and looked at me with sorrowful eyes.

"Whatever happened to us?" I asked.

"We're a mess, huh?" He chuckled.

"Yeah," I said.

He looked down at his erection and back up at me. I hated to see it go to waste too, but I had to use common sense. Shawnathon was now a married man. Our relationship was just beginning to rebound, and I had a feeling this would be a turning point.

His body was incredible.

"What do you wanna do?" he asked.

"You know what I wanna do," I said.

"Then let's do it," he said and moved toward me.

Instinctively, I moved back. "What would this mean?" I asked.

He frowned as he grabbed his shaft and stroked. "What would what mean?" he asked.

"This? Us? You think you can just come over here to see the kids, then get a little ass on your way out?" I asked.

He looked like he was a little surprised by my question, but I had to let him know I didn't want to play his game.

"C'mon," he whined. "You gon' leave me like this?" he asked.

"I'm sure your wife can take care of that," I said. Suddenly, I was in a bad mood and pissed at Shawnathon. I should've been his wife. How was it that he didn't want kids when we were together, but he got with Elisa, she got pregnant and they got married?

"You make me sick," I said and tried to turn away from him, but it was too late. He was already in my personal space. When he pulled me close this time, I felt his hardness up against me and it instantly turned me on.

"I don't make you sick," he said. We kissed again, and unfortunately for me, this time was better than the last. I missed him so much it hurt to think about it and what we were about to do.

The moment I reached for him and felt how hard he was, there was no turning back. I wanted him and I didn't care about Elisa or her baby. It wasn't like I didn't have him first.

When Shawnathon entered me, it was like he was home. He felt so good I wanted to cry. I wanted to give him anything he wanted. We were so in sync with each other's bodies. It had been so long since we'd been together, but still, it felt like it was just yesterday.

The only thing that made my stomach churn was when we finished. Shawnathon had the nerve to look at his watch. Then he jumped up from the floor.

"Shit, what happened to the time?"

I wanted to say it passed while we were making love on the couch, and on the floor, but I laid there and watched as he scrambled to pick up his clothes, rushed to the bathroom, then came walking out with a whole lot more swagger than I remembered.

"Whassup?" he asked, looking down at me.

I was still on the floor, but I had put my bra and panties back on.

"So what does this mean now?" I asked.

He didn't get mad or anything, but I felt like such a fool.

Shawnathon reached out to me and helped me up off the floor. He pulled me close and hugged me. He held me tightly like he really felt something for me.

"We're gonna be all right," he said.

I tried not to cry, but fighting the tears was harder than I expected. I knew he had to go, but I didn't want to break our embrace. I wanted to beg him to stay. What did Elisa have that I didn't have?

"Okay, I need to bounce," he said when I didn't budge.

"You have to go?" I asked.

"Yeah, but I can come through tomorrow night," he said.

"To see the kids?" I asked.

"Yeah, and you, too," he said. He kissed me on the top of my forehead and before I could say anything else, he was gone.

As I listened to his truck take off, I decided at that moment that I would get my man back so that we could be the family we should've been in the first place.

SERENA

I was frustrated, pissed, and at my wits' end. When I saw Parker's number pop up on my caller ID, I damn near dropped the phone. Why was that punk calling me? Wasn't he supposed to be calling Deena? What the hell was he calling me for? He probably wanted to see if I'd consider settling out of court to save him even more embarrassment. But I wanted his ass nailed to a poster that said, "I am a deadbeat loser!" He was wasting his time calling me. I ignored his call.

It was dark and I still hadn't heard from Semaj. I didn't want to think about how long she'd been gone. I had already gone through all of her secret hiding places, found numbers, called, and still no progress. I picked up my phone and dialed Deena.

Her answering service picked up. What's up with her? Usually, she answered anytime I called. All I could think was that if she was with Gloria Allred, I bet I wouldn't be waiting for a call back.

"This is Serena Carson, Deena's client, and I just had an emergency and I need her to call me back immediately. It's urgent," I said.

"Okay, ma'am, your message will be sent right away," the woman said.

"How long will it take for her to call back?" I asked.

"Ma'am, we don't know. We send the urgent messages with a flag and they're tagged as urgent. It all depends on factors that are beyond our control."

"Really?"

"Yes, ma'am," she said.

"But what if this was a life-or-death matter?"

"You'd be urged to hang up with us and dial nine-one-one," she said.

"I see. Well, please make sure Deena knows that I'm waiting for her to call back," I said and hung up.

Good help was so hard to find these days. Where'd that chick get off talking to me like that? She worked at an answering service center for God's sake, yet she acted like she was better than me! Umph!

Thirty minutes after I called the answering service, my phone rang three times, but neither of those was calls from Deena. I had started to get antsy.

Parker had already called twice. I wasn't sure what to do so I picked up the phone and called Loren.

When she didn't answer, I wondered if I had missed the memo on *everybody avoid Serena day*! I grabbed my cigarettes and started smoking. By the time the phone rang again, I was pissed. It was like every other call. It was a call from Parker.

By nine o'clock that night, I had thrown in the towel. I made the one call I didn't want to make, but I felt like I had no choice in the matter.

"Nine-one-one, what's your emergency?" the operator asked.

"My daughter is missing and I don't know what to do," I said.

"Ma'am, slow down," the operator said.

I took a deep breath.

"My daughter is missing. I've called all of her friends, I have no idea where she is and I'm scared," I said.

"Okay, how old is your daughter?" she asked.

"She's twelve," I said.

"I'm going to give you a number to call and talk to an officer," she said.

"But I'm talking to you," I said. "What wrong with me talking to you?" I asked.

"Ma'am, nine-one-one is for life-or-death situations. I know you're concerned about your daughter, but I need you to hang up with me and call this number," she said.

I sighed. I was tired. I was emotionally spent, and I wanted someone to listen and act like they cared about what I was going through.

"I don't understand," I screamed. "Why can't you send a detective over here to find my daughter?"

"Ma'am, I need you to calm down. I also need you to call this number because the number you've dialed is for life-threatening emergencies. The longer I'm on with you, the greater the possibility that someone who is really in need is being ignored."

I listened, took the number, and called like she told me to do.

I was more frustrated as time dragged on. I dialed the number I got from the operator and was immediately placed on hold. I didn't understand how they expected me to file a report as I sat on hold.

Thoughts of the fact that Deena never called back only pissed me off more. How could she *not* call back? I told her Parker was trying to reach out to me and it was like she didn't give a damn!

As I sat on hold with the police department's non-emergency number, all sorts of crazy thoughts ran through my mind. What if something happened to my daughter? What if some pedophile picked her up?

All of a sudden I wondered if trying to call around was the best thing to do? Perhaps I should've jumped in my car and tried to find her myself!

When someone finally answered my call, I wasn't sure how I should say what I needed to say.

"My daughter is missing and I really need to find her," I said.

"How old is she?" this officer asked. His voice sounded so uninterested in what I was saying, I was tempted to ask to speak to a woman.

The way I looked at it, if I was talking to a woman, at least she'd be somewhat sympathetic to what I was going through. This guy sounded like he had one eye on the clock and the other on whatever he was writing down from our phone call.

"What difference does her age make?" I asked.

"Ma'am?"

"I'm calling to tell you all that my child is missing and I'm being interrogated as if I've done something wrong. Can you please send someone out here to see about my child?"

"It doesn't work like that, ma'am," he said.

"What do you mean, it doesn't work like that? What am I supposed to do?"

"Well, let's finish the report. Once I get the report, we go from there," he said.

I sat there rolling my eyes as I answered each and every question he asked. I felt like this was completely counterproductive. In the time it took me to get routed to the right person, sit on hold, then explain my story, someone could've been over here and out on the streets looking for my child.

"So is there anything else you need from me?"

"No, but ma'am, it sounds like your daughter is a runaway," he said.

I nearly fell off my chair!

"What?"

"Has your daughter run away before?"

"Absolutely not!"

"Okay, well, I'm gonna have to transfer you to..."

I couldn't take it anymore! I hung up the phone and sat there trying to think about what the hell I should do. This time when the phone rang, I assumed it was the officer calling me back but it wasn't.

"Serena?"

"Yeah, who is this?" I asked the woman on the other end.

"It's me, Roxanne," she said.

Now he put her stupid ass up to calling me? What was wrong with this man? Didn't he understand that I wasn't interested in anything he or his stupid wife had to say? Wasn't it enough that I had ignored all of his previous calls? What did he think putting her up to calling would do?

Roxanne and I were kind of close back in the day. When she left Parker, it was my couch she crashed on, but the minute they made up, of course she turned her back on me, just like everyone else.

"Umph, Roxanne? What the hell do you want?"

PARKER

I could tell Roxy was getting tired, and who could blame her? I watched as she dialed the number yet again and blew out a frustrated breath when there was no answer.

"Let's give it a few minutes and see what happens," I said.

Roxy looked at me with tired eyes. I understood her frustration, but that was the stupidity that was Serena.

"If she doesn't answer this time, I'm not calling her again," Roxy said as she dialed the number one last time.

"Serena?" I heard Roxy say like she was surprised the fool finally answered.

"It's me—Roxanne," I heard her say. She rolled her eyes. I sat there as she listened. My mind thought about this woman, my wife, and how she had endured so much.

Roxanne and I hit it off nearly instantly. We met at a holiday party and the meeting was accidental.

"Is this the Reliant party?" I asked when I finally made it up to the suite inside Reliant Stadium.

The department that decided to hold our company's holiday party at the stadium following a football game should've been fired.

First off, there was no way to learn the layout of the stadium. The suites were on the upper levels, but the people who worked there must've been new because they didn't know the layout of the facility either.

After being sent to three wrong locations, I was fed up.

The woman who greeted me at the door of the fourth suite I had visited was nice and friendly.

"Oh, no, you're way on the other side. This is the South side. Here, let me show you where you need to be." She smiled. She put her glass down and led me back out to the lobby and the elevator.

We stepped inside and I was stunned.

"I don't want to put you out," I said.

"It's no biggie," she said. "I needed a break anyway."

The elevator took us down to a lower level.

"Okay, see where we are." She said as she guided me to the edge of the top of the bleacher seats. "You see that over there?"

"You mean like way over there on the other side?" I asked.

"Yup, you have to go way over there." She pointed to the opposite side of the stadium.

"How do you know?" I asked. "I mean it was someone over there who told me I needed to be over here."

She turned and looked at me. When our eyes met, I realized how cute she was. She was shorter than me, but she was pretty and nice. I couldn't think of too many women who'd leave their suite party to show me where I needed to go.

"That's a whole lot of walking, especially when I just came from over there," I said.

"Well, you're not the only one. A few of your co-workers were sent over here," she said.

"And did you give them the special directions like you gave to me?" I asked.

She looked at me and smiled.

"Well, no, I didn't give them all this special treatment," she said.

"Oh yeah? Well, what makes me so special?" I asked.

"You asked *me*," she said, then turned and started walking away.

I was hooked.

"Hey." I jogged to catch up with her. "Where you going?"

"Back to my company party," she said.

"Well, I don't feel like walking all the way over there." I pointed over my shoulder but in the direction of the Reliant suite.

She shrugged her shoulders and pressed the button for the elevator.

"You gonna leave me down here by myself?" I asked.

Roxy looked at me like she wasn't sure what her answer should be. When I noticed a smile curling at the corners of her mouth, I went in for the kill.

"Why don't you invite me upstairs to your company party and I won't even have to worry about what's going on way over there," I said.

Roxy looked liked she was really contemplating what I had offered.

"I guess I could do that," she said.

We went back up to her company party and I was glad I stayed put.

"Let me take you out to dinner, show you a real nice evening," I said as I walked her to her car after the party.

Roxy leaned against her car and smiled as she looked up at me.

"Why should I?" she asked.

"Didn't I show you a great time tonight? Imagine how much more fun we could have if you let me get behind the wheel," I joked.

Roxy and I exchanged numbers and I walked back to my car that was way on the other side of the stadium.

It gave me plenty of time to think about the women who hadn't made the cut with me and why they hadn't. The women I dated had to be educated, upwardly mobile, and more importantly, they had to have something going for themselves other than a deep desire to get a man. I was very selective and had been very careful. I felt it deep down in my bones; she was a possibility.

I thought about some of the women I've had and they had to be the best of the best; there was no doubt about that. For a long time I thought I'd wind up alone because I didn't think many women could even measure up to my standards, but I refused to lower them.

There was Jeanine; she had wanted to get married so badly that she had accepted anything I had thrown her way. Sometimes, I'd do shit to see if she'd complain, and she never did. I suspected it was because she was holding out for my last name.

Andy was another one who thought she had found her Mr. Right in me, but she had too many damn issues. I liked a woman that was strong-willed, but damn, know when to let a man be a man. She was so hell-bent on proving to me that she had balls, she had lost sight of the fact that no straight man wanted another set when he had his own.

Then I thought about some others whose names I couldn't remember, but either their faces or bodies or skills between the sheets made them memorable.

I never believed in messing with women beneath my level. I wasn't about to rescue no woman, and didn't want a ready-made family either. Some brothas got a kick out of moving females out of the projects or even out of the hood. None of those places were anywhere on my radar. Those were the kinds of women who had illegitimate kids, and then tried to sue you for child support. My mother had drilled that into my brother, Preston, and me the moment she thought we were out there screwing.

That night I was with Serena, I never thought she was trying to get at me like *that*. I was seeing another female at the time and she was out of town or something. Serena offered to come cook me dinner, but I wasn't feeling her like that and didn't think she was feeling me in that way either.

I knew we hadn't screwed, but she did give me head. Once I remembered the head job, I remembered being glad I was strapped up. But who thought about what happened to the condom once the deed was done? I guess I should've thought more about it. There had been no sex between us—that much I remembered, and for a long time, I didn't realize exactly what had gone down between us. She wasn't my type and I didn't think I was hers.

A long while after I had met and started dating Roxy exclusively, James brought Serena around. When I saw how into her he was, I figured it was best to leave the past in the past. At the time I didn't think our past would have a reason to come out, but I was sadly mistaken about that.

Never in a million years would I have guessed where we were today.

"Your daughter is over here," I heard Roxy finally scream into the phone.

This told me our headache was just beginning with Serena—again!

LACHEZ

"I can't believe you had the audacity to do a DNA test on my child without my permission!" I yelled into the phone. Ever since that conversation with Junie, I was counting down the minutes until this phone call.

"What the hell is your goddamn problem? I guess you didn't wanna take care of your kid, so you figure test results could possibly free you, huh?"

"And hello to you and welcome home, Lachez," Julius said sarcastically.

"Don't give me that shit," I snarled.

"I heard you were out. I should've known sooner or later you'd be ringing my phone," he said.

"What the hell is that supposed to mean? How you figure you should've known I'd be ringing your phone? You act like it was some kind of forgone conclusion that I'd be reaching out to you. Umph!"

"Lachez, all these years later, you coming at me talking about me doing a DNA test on Junie? Are you for real?" he asked. He sounded like he had changed.

"Hell yeah, I'm for real! Junie told me all about the stunt you pulled! You know damn well if I was here the shit would not have gone down like that!" I stressed.

"Do you not remember all the shit you had going on? You were running men like a busted faucet. You were selling cigarettes, beating the system, and apparently you were running one helluva possible baby daddy operation," he said.

"Julius, if you had paid your damn child support the way you were supposed to, and on time, I wouldn't have had to be out there grinding as hard as I was. But that's neither here nor there. I'm offended that you had the nerve to test my child without my permission," I hollered.

"Your mother gave me permission and that was all I needed at the time. You better be glad the test came out in your favor because that would've been your ass for real!"

"Julius, you don't talk to me like that! You knew damn well Junie was yours! He walking around with that big, melon-ass-shaped head, just like you. What you expect! Besides, when I was getting down with you, I wasn't all out there like that with anybody else," I lied.

"Save it, Lachez. I know you better than you know yourself. You and I both know you ain't been faithful a day in your life! Now, unless you want something else, I need to run. My wife is calling me," he said.

"Your what?" I laughed.

He held the phone and waited for the laughter to die down.

"Who the hell don' married you?" I joked.

"Shiiit, you wanted to," he tossed back at me.

"You a damn lie," I said. I rolled my eyes, even though there was no way he could see me through the phone.

"Yeah, okay, Lachez. You and I both know I could come over there and get *it* right now if I wanted to," he bragged. "I could probably bring my wife, too. Ain't no telling what you into these days after being locked up with all them desperate-ass women," he said.

"Whatever, Julius, whatever," I said.

I had no idea why news of him being married made me feel a certain kind of way. It wasn't like I wanted a husband or anything like that, but there were some men who I knew would be there until the day I died, and I always thought Julius was one of them for me.

"All joking aside, though," he said, "I was trying to give you some time to get settled before coming to see about you."

"Oh, really, is that right?"

"Yeah, really, Lachez, you know we've been through too much for you to be acting like I'd just leave you hanging," he said.

That touched my heart. Julius had sent a few letters and he put some money on my books while I was down. He never visited, but he did enough to let me know he hadn't forgotten about me while I was gone.

"So you coming to see about me, huh?" I said.

"Girl, you know I am! I wanna see what the few years have done to you." He laughed.

"Oh, don't trip. It's still all tight over here," I boasted. "Everything is still together just like you remember!"

"I'll be the judge of that," he said. "I may shoot through there this weekend, that is if you and Toni ain't putting on no butt-naked parties." He laughed. "I could only imagine what's gonna be going on over there with the two of you under the same roof!"

"I'ma' tell her you said that, too," I threatened.

"Girl, don't go starting no shit," Julius said.

"Yeah, that's what I thought," I told him. "Seriously though, I'd like to see you, so why don't you come through Saturday or Sunday evening?"

"Okay, sounds cool. I'll call before I come through," he said.

"Yeah, that would be wise," I said. "Oh, and Julius," I called out before he hung up.

"What's up?"

"Don't bring your wife," I said and hung up to sounds of him laughing.

"Who you all giggling and laughing with on the phone in here?" Toni asked when she walked through the living room.

"Girl, that was Julius' simple behind," I said.

"Oooh, talk about a blast from the past," she said. "What's he been up to?"

"Married now! Can you imagine?"

"He's what? Married? Who done went and did that?" she joked.

"Girl, that's what I said. Imagine Julius being married! I wonder if he goes home every night," I said.

"For a long time, I thought the two of you would end up together," Toni said. "I mean—think about how long the two of y'all had been kicking it off and on. I figured when it was time to finally settle down, y'all would do it with each other."

Toni and I sat around and talked about the old times. As we talked my mind thought about Julius being married to someone other than me. It was strange, and thinking about it made me feel was even worse.

"So he coming through?" she asked after a long while.

"Who, Julius?" I asked.

"Who else?" she asked sarcastically.

We both started laughing.

"You gon' give him some, huh?" she asked.

"Girl, didn't I tell you Julius is married now? Naw, I ain't giving him nothing," I said.

As I said the words aloud, I didn't even believe them myself. All I could hope was that Julius wouldn't make good on his promise to come by for a visit. Drew was good and all, but Julius?

Well, he took it to a whole new level. There was a reason we were off and on for years. I couldn't leave him alone for good. He may have worked my very last nerve every chance he got, but when it was time to handle the business in the bedroom, Julius brought a special skillset to the party.

Julius was hung like a stallion, and he knew every bit about how to use what he had.

For a woman like me who had been on hiatus for quite some time, his talents would come in handy, regardless of who had papers on him now!

EBONI

"You want any more kids?"

I glanced toward the door. Our kids were sleeping.

Shawnathon's question caught me completely off guard. We'd just finished making love for the second time that evening and were spooning in my bed.

I turned to face him.

"I don't think so. Two is enough for me." I smiled.

I loved being with him. Even during such stolen moments, he knew exactly what to say and do to make me feel special and wanted.

"Why'd you ask?"

"I'm tired of wearing a condom with you," he said.

Now that nearly stunned me to silence. It wasn't that his statement was so incredible, but it was the fact that I had been dreaming about the exact same thing! I hated him having to use a condom with me. I wanted to feel as close to him as possible, and the condom simply got in the way.

"What about HIV or AIDS?" I asked.

"You get tested regularly, don't you?" he asked.

"Well, I hadn't been since I had the kids, and everything was fine then. But it hasn't really been a priority to me since I haven't been with anyone else since then," I lied.

"Testing isn't the biggest concern. I have three kids. I think I'm done," he said.

"Yeah, but how does your wife feel about that?"

"Oh, trust me, I don't think she'll be having any more. She's miserable. She's always complaining about the weight, her ankles, how sick she is. She hates being pregnant," he said.

"That must be miserable for you, too," I said sweetly.

My pregnancy wasn't awful at all. As a matter of fact, the only horrible part was not having *him* around. But I didn't share that part with Shawnathon. I took extra pleasure in knowing that Elisa was having a difficult pregnancy. That day we saw her she looked great, but she was probably only putting on a show for us.

He seemed like the thought of her difficult pregnancy impacting him hadn't crossed his mind.

"Well, not really," he said. "I just try to stay out of her way. She's all emotional and shit, so I stay clear of her."

I decided I'd tuck that bit of information away for later use. If he didn't like being around her while she was pregnant, that meant my home needed to be an oasis for him.

In the nearly two weeks since we'd been to court, Shawnathon had really been stepping up to the plate. I thought about that after he left my house.

He hadn't been coming over every night, but he did come over more, and I didn't feel as lonely as I thought I would without Ulonda.

The sex had also gotten better and better. It was so intense and so incredible I hardly ever wanted him to leave. I tried to build up the courage to ask him if we could take a trip somewhere together, but I'd have to ease into that.

I was in bliss when I thought about us being alone on an island together. I decided I'd plan the trip myself and sort of surprise him with it. I figured a Thursday through Sunday or Monday would be great. That way he wouldn't have to be away from home for too long. If I could set it up before the season started, he'd be more inclined to agreeing to go.

Did I just hear someone cry? Sometimes my kids laughed or cried a little in their sleep. I stopped and listened trying to make sure my ears weren't deceiving me. When I didn't hear another sound, I figured it was one of them giggling or laughing in their sleep.

I also thought about getting a nanny, or someone to come in and help me with the kids. Once I explained my plans to Shawnathon, he'd be more than supportive. Here recently, he had been close to perfect.

"You need anything?" he'd call and ask before he came over.

"No, I'm good."

"What about the kids?" he'd ask.

"Everyone is good on this end, so just hurry," I'd say.

I was so glad we'd made up and things were getting back to normal with us. If he wasn't married, there was no doubt that our *normal* would include us being under the same roof as a family. But I had a plan. I simply needed to be patient.

He was already spending more time with the kids and me. He called whenever he couldn't make it over, and when we were together, he seemed really comfortable.

Because of Shawnathon's situation, we'd have to go to a really exclusive and expensive vacation spot. We didn't need to run the risk that nosey ass people would recognize him and run back with pictures for his wife to see.

One of my kids woke up right when I was about to get my laptop so I could figure out where Shawnathon and I should go. I put the baby back down, grabbed a glass of wine and the laptop.

"Now where could we go and spend some quality alone time together without being disturbed?"

I had heard a few people taking about the Belizean Keys. I had never been before and that would be secluded enough for us to be able to really enjoy ourselves.

I hopped online to look up the destination, and picked up the phone to call and get some information. The plan was to get everything in place so that when I presented him with the information, I could answer any questions he might have.

I dialed the number and put the phone to my ear, but instead of it ringing, a voice greeted me.

"Hello?"

"Ah hello. Is this the Belizean Shores Resort?" I asked. I wondered why the woman who answered didn't talk with an accent.

"Eboni, it's me…Nia," she said dryly.

Her voice had me scared. She sounded different. I couldn't really put my finger on it, but the way this call came about left an unsettling feeling in the pit of my stomach.

"Nia?" I questioned. "What are you doing on my phone?"

"I must've called while you were trying to call out," she said.

"Oh, okay," I said.

I wondered what was so important that it couldn't wait until business hours the next day. Nia and I weren't cool like that. Ours was strictly a business relationship. That was why I never told her about the money Shawnathon gave me or about how we had reconciled. I figured she'd want a cut, even though she never lifted a finger to make anything happen.

"So what's going on?" I said.

I wanted her off the phone so I could plan my vacation.

"We have a problem," she said slowly.

My heart nearly stopped. Damn! What if she found out about the money? I had already put some in my mom's account for safekeeping, and I got caught up on a lot of bills, but there was still more than 100 grand left. I didn't feel like she was entitled to any of that money. I handled that on my own.

"What's the problem, Nia? More importantly, what can we do to fix it?"

I didn't have time for this foolishness. I had things to do, and I didn't need her *problem* getting in my way.

"Eboni, Shawnathon is not the father of your children," she said.

Eboni, Shawnathon is not the father of your children.

Eboni, Shawnathon is not the father of your children.

Eboni, Shawnathon is not the father of your children.

She only said it once, but that's how many times the words seemed to echo in my brain.

"Eboni? You still there?" she asked.

"Mistake, this is some kind of..."

"Eboni, listen to me carefully, DNA doesn't lie. There is no scientific possibility whatsoever that Shawnathon could've fathered those kids. None!"

SERENA

I tried to focus on the police cruiser in front of me. Crying was never my thing. I had always been real strong, but lately now, when everything seemed to crumble down around me, I couldn't stop the tears from flowing.

What pissed me off the most was the fact that I had to go to the damn police station myself. When this mess was over, I planned to sit down and write a series of letters ripping everyone involved in this nightmare.

Trying to calm myself as we stopped at a traffic light, I knew I needed to pull it together real fast. There was no way in hell I'd let them see me falling apart.

When the cruiser pulled into their driveway, I decided to park on the street. It was bad enough they had those damn sirens blaring. I wanted to sneak up on their simple behinds, but I wasn't running the operation—the cops were.

Of course, their neighbors were just as nosey as mine. But this time, I didn't mind putting on a show. I stepped out of my car after I noticed the two officers climbing out of the cruiser. I reached back in to grab my bundle of tissues I brought along for what I was certain would be an emotional reunion between Semaj and me.

"Ma'am, we'll need you to stay back here," one of the officers said.

"But my baby is in there," I said, looking toward the door.

"Listen, ma'am, this is official police business. The charges you're making are serious. If these people did what you say they did, we've gotta handle this delicately."

That's when I saw the other officer had pulled his gun from his holster.

"Whoa! Hold on a minute here! What's he doing?" I pointed toward the officer who was now crouched down on the side of the front part of the house.

"Ma'am, get back in the car and let us do our job!"

I didn't get back in the car, but I stood at the walkway and watched as the officer left me and walked up to the front door and knocked.

The door swung open and I saw Roxanne. The officer said something I couldn't hear, but all of a sudden, Roxanne looked over his shoulder at me and then said, "Really, Serena?"

The bitch had the nerve to wrinkle her nose when she spoke to me. I crossed my arms over my chest and tapped one foot as I waited to see what would happen next.

Soon, Parker was in the doorway. Before long, all three of them had turned and stared at me.

"Kidnapped your child?" Parker balked.

"How else would you explain how she got over here then?" I asked.

The other officer stood up straight and put his gun away. He tossed a disgusted look my way, but I didn't care.

"Ma'am, come here, please," the one closest to Parker said.

Reluctantly, I moved up the walkway. I felt like a troubled kid being sent to the principal's office. All eyes remained glued to me with each heavy step I took.

"Ma'am, it is against the law to file a false police report," the officer said once I stepped onto the porch.

"I did not file a false report. I want you to arrest them, both of them!" I demanded.

"Ma'am, your daughter was not kidnapped. Why did you come down to the station behaving as if you feared for your daughter's safety?" he asked.

Before I could answer, he said, "You gave the impression that these people had a reason to want to kidnap your daughter, and that is not the case."

"I didn't give you any kind of impression. I told you all that my missing daughter popped up in the house of a person who is trying to sue me! I told you that I had no idea how she wound up there! I also said one minute she was at home, then the next she was gone and I had been going out of my mind trying to figure out what happened to her!"

"Ma'am, you need to calm down. You are in some serious trouble right now," he warned.

"I'm in trouble?" I hissed. "How the hell does what I just explained translate to me being in trouble? I'm not the one who kidnapped a child. That is my child! Why wouldn't they be in trouble? Why aren't you arresting them?"

I was burning up mad. This stunt told me that Parker was probably in my neighborhood trying to spy on me when he saw Semaj and convinced her to go with him! I didn't understand why Deena hadn't called me back, but someone needed to do something about him! I was sick and tired of being treated like what I had done was so criminal, but yet he was able to do whatever the hell he wanted.

"Lemme guess—so you guys are not gonna do a damn thing to him, right?" I asked.

"Ma'am, you are really pushing it. These people did not kidnap your child and you knew they hadn't when you came into the station hysterically claiming that they had."

"I knew no such thing," I said with an attitude.

"Did Mrs. Parker here call you to inform you that your daughter was in fact over here?" the officer asked.

"She called me, but when she said that, an alarm went off in my head. These people are suing me, so why would they have my child? All I could think was they were gonna try and hold her hostage," I said.

"Cut the crap!" Parker yelled. "The gig is up, Serena. You're lying like you always do, like you always have, and now this is gonna finally come back to bite you in the ass!"

I swung at him, but the officer caught my arm and twisted it behind my back.

"Ooww! Let me go," I cried.

"Ma'am, do you want to add an assault charge to what you're already facing?" he asked.

"Let me go!" I struggled to free myself from his grip, but he held on tightly. "I'm pissed that you would take their word over mine! This fool is suing me and suddenly my daughter pops up over his house, but I'm the one being treated like a criminal?" I yelled.

"Ms. Carson," the officer said. He finally released me.

"I'm calling your supervisor! Where's my daughter? Where's my child?" I started yelling.

"She is upstairs watching TV. We finally got her calm and settled. She was very upset and hurt when she showed up at our front door," Parker said.

"I'll bet she was upset. You would be, too, if someone snatched you up and tossed you into their car," I yelled. "Semaj!" I started screaming. "Semaj, Mama's here, baby!"

"See, this is what I was telling you about," Parker said to the officer.

"I think you have a great case. I'll be sure to add all of this to my report. I can't see any judge in their right mind choosing her as a parent over the two of you," he said.

I froze where I stood.

"What did you say?" I asked the officer.

"If you would've listened when I was on the phone, you wouldn't be learning about it this way," Roxanne said.

"Bitch, who's talking to you?" I snapped. When I charged in her direction, she flinched and Parker jumped between us. I hated her with a passion.

"No, get out of my way Parker. I don't want to miss the look on her face," Roxanne said.

"What are you talking about?" I asked.

"We are fighting you for full custody of Semaj!" Roxanne said.

The last thing I remembered was tumbling to the ground and scuffling with the officer who struggled to get handcuffs on my wrists.

As the police cruiser pulled out of the driveway, I looked back to see Semaj looking out of an upstairs window. Did my child roll her eyes at me?

PARKER

The phone call from Bill came bright and early the next morning. He sounded jovial as he sang his greeting in my ear.

"Well, aren't we in a pleasant mood this morning?" I said.

"Yes, we are, and it's only going to get better, my friend," he said.

"What's going on?" I asked.

Here lately I had learned to brace myself for anything when it came to Serena. Her antics could've given screenwriters a run for their money.

"We got the call I said we'd get," Bill boasted. He was beside himself, giddy with laughter.

"What call is that, Bill?" I asked.

"Serena's attorney just called. She says they want a meeting. I guess the night in jail did her some good because it appears she's come to her senses," Bill said.

"Oh? What kind of meeting is this?"

"She wants to talk about dropping her lawsuit and about Semaj," Bill said.

"Oh, that's great news!" I said.

"I'm not done yet," Bill laughed.

"Oh, excuse me, sir, please finish. My mistake," I joked.

"Before she called I got off the phone with an attorney from the Houston fertility clinic. They want to know what it's gonna take to make this go away—without them admitting any fault, of course," Bill said.

"You have got to be kidding me!" I screamed.

"What?" Roxy walked into the room.

I put up a hand to quiet her.

"Didn't I tell you this one wasn't going anywhere? Didn't I tell you this case was the best one for us to move forward with? And didn't I tell you to trust me?"

"Yes, Bill, you told me all of those things! And I'm glad I listened to you."

"So when can you get in here so we can talk? I want to get back to both of them as quickly as possible. I have a feeling if we drag this thing out too long, things could fall apart."

"I agree. Give me about an hour. I'm wrapping up breakfast with Roxy and the baby and I'll stop by before I go into the office," I said.

"Great, see you then," Bill said. "Say hello to Roxy and the baby, will ya?"

"Yes, sir," I said.

"What?" Roxy stood in front of me like an impatient kid waiting on candy. She looked excited.

"Bill says hello," I joked.

"Don't make me hurt you," she threatened.

"Wwwhat?"

"I know he said more than hello. So tell me…what's going on?"

"They want to settle," I announced.

Roxy's eyes grew wide. When I saw the smile curling at the corners of her mouth, I started to get excited, too.

"What do you mean, they want to settle? So Serena is dropping her ridiculous lawsuit?" she asked.

"Yes, she wants to talk about dropping it and Semaj's future.

Bill suggested we pick Semaj up from school today, and he'll meet us at Serena's," I said.

Roxy swatted the thought away. "I don't wanna be nowhere near that fool. What do you think would've happened if that cop had not been here? She really hates me. You two can handle it. I don't want you going over there alone," Roxy said.

"No, I won't," I told her. I started to get up from the table.

She walked over and rubbed my back.

"Last night when I took Semaj to buy clothes from Walmart for school, she told me she still loves her mom, but she can't handle the drama anymore," Roxy said.

"She said that to you?" I asked.

"Yes, she said she'll probably stay with her mom, but she wants to spend time with us and the baby, too. She also said she's not mad at you."

"Oh, well, that's good to know." I laughed.

"No, seriously, I don't want this to be about Serena. I want it to be about Semaj. She's a very smart child and she's seen far more than any kid her age should have to. So when talking things out with Serena, I want you to remember, despite how much you can't stand her, this is not about her. It's about a little girl who deserves some stability in her life," Roxy said.

"I agree, so what are you saying? Do you not want to fight her for custody?" I asked.

"That's what I'm trying to say. Fighting is not the way to go. When you and Bill talk to her and her lawyer, work something out where Semaj stays at home, but comes over here, too. This shouldn't be a battle. She's been through enough."

"You're right, honey. I'm glad she took a cab over here versus to a friend's house or God knows where else," I said.

"And that's what we have to do, be a peaceful alternative to her mother's house. I don't want to come between their relationship, but I want her to know we're here for her."

"How'd I get so lucky?" I asked.

"Because I chose you," Roxy said. She pecked me on the lips, then walked away.

Later that afternoon Bill and I were sitting across from Serena and her attorney, Deena.

"So I want everyone to be clear," Bill said.

"You will drop your suit, make a public apology and agree to only seek joint custody for Semaj if an agreement can't be worked out," he said before looking up from his notes.

"That's correct. And once we drop the suit, you'll drop yours, agree to immunity in any possible litigation against the fertility clinic, and you stop mentioning Serena's name during your public appearances," Deena said.

"Sounds like we have a deal," Bill announced.

I was thrilled. I had so many other things that needed my attention and this was not one of them. Now that she was going to make a public apology, I could return my focus on the men at the center and not my own personal drama.

As we were filing out of the office, Serena looked over at me and said, "I just have one question."

"What's that?"

"How did you find out about the clinic?" she asked.

I looked at her and then said, "We hired a private investigator."

She nodded as if she understood. It didn't really matter. She was not named in the suit against the clinic because, at the time, we were already countersuing her. This agreement meant that she wouldn't have to worry about that, so Bill said there was no need to inform her that we were already in negotiations with the clinic.

On the ride back to the office, Bill looked over at me and said, "What do you think would happen if she knew her boyfriend, JahRyan, sent us that letter?"

"Oh, there'd be hell to pay for him!" I said.

We laughed.

"No way in hell I'd let that loose and turn that wrath onto that good man!" I joked.

"Yeah, JahRyan will never know how close he came to a tsunami," Bill said.

"But I wish he did know how much his information meant to us and this case," I said.

"I have a feeling he knows. It's why he called and later offered to back up the letter if needed."

LACHEZ

I had racked up a nice little stash of paper and it felt good to have my own. Toni and I had talked about another lick that she was sure would put us over the top. We had started taking turns on the set-ups after I showed her how to do it. I was going along for the ride, regardless of what she had planned.

A month of freedom had crept up on me swiftly, and while I could probably stay with Toni forever, that wasn't even my style. I needed to start making plans because we couldn't keep hustling like this forever.

"What's so special about this one?" I asked.

"We're taking the show on the road," she announced.

I was very surprised. Up to now, our little hustle had been going exactly the way I said it would. We only targeted executives who always traveled with lots of cash. Then all of them were married.

"What do you mean, we're taking the show on the road?" I asked. I didn't want her to think I was second-guessing what she'd worked hard to organize, but I didn't want to take unnecessary risks either.

"I found out about this convention going on in New York. I think it's the perfect place for us to slip in, handle the business, then go and hang out for a few days before bringing it back home."

"We don't know the lay of the land in New York," I said.

"I've got it all worked out. I know the host hotel and I know who our target is already," she said.

"Well, I'm not gonna start questioning you now. You know what's up. I trust you," I said.

And I did trust her. Toni was serious about this hustle. If it was up to her, she'd do this for the rest of her life. While I liked making the fast money, I didn't like all of the risks we had to take.

The success of everything we did relied on none of these men going to the cops. If only one went and ratted us out, we'd be screwed. So far, our luck had been working out pretty well.

"I'm excited about going to New York. You know me, I'd thrive in the city that never sleeps," I said.

"Girl, we can go to Jay-Z's club, rub elbows with some celebs, you know, show 'em how we do it in the dirty South," Toni said.

She didn't have to do all of that to sell me on the idea, because I was already sold.

"When do we roll?" I asked.

"This Sunday night," Toni said.

"Okay cool. Julius is coming tomorrow night, so what's up, you got plans?" I asked her.

Toni smiled. "I thought you said he was married now," she said.

"He is…at least that's what he told me." I giggled.

"You know you wrong, right?" Toni said.

"What? I haven't done a thing! I don't know what you're talking about," I said.

"On a serious tip though, you and Julius, y'all probably need to leave well enough alone. Why go backward?" Toni asked.

"Are you serious?"

"Yeah, girl, I never go backward. If it didn't work out before, we're not gonna revisit it," Toni said.

"Are you trying to tell me you ain't never hooked up with an ex?" I didn't believe her. I had never met an ex of mine that I didn't want to let hit it for old time's sake.

"I don't believe in going backward. Leave the past in the past," Toni said.

That was the mantra she lived by, but thoughts of me and Julius did nothing but bring back the best of the best memories for me.

Sure, Julius and I had our issues and problems. Because we were off and on for years, sometimes our *ons* didn't quite match up perfectly, but we always connected in one way or another. I was looking forward to seeing him.

"I'm not as strong as you. If I had chemistry with someone and sparks flew when we connected, he could always hit it!"

"Eewww," Toni said.

"We partying tonight or what?" I asked.

Toni looked lost.

"All we do is work. We might go shopping a little, but think about it. Ever since I've been out, all we do is work, work, work. And what makes it so bad is it's not like we can mix a little fun in there," I said.

"You got a point there, but honestly, I wouldn't know where to find a party. It's not that we're old, but when I think of clubs these days, I think of hip hoppers, and who wants to do that?"

"Are you trying to tell me you can't find anywhere for us to go have a good time here in Houston?" I wanted to clarify. "What happened to the Texans, the Rockets, the Astros?" I asked. "Isn't there a hockey or soccer team here?"

"Really? Hockey or soccer?" Toni asked.

"Think about it, Toni, we used to do it up back in the day. We barely had two nickels to rub together but that didn't stop us from going to Vanessa's shop, dropping a grip on some hair, getting dolled up, then hitting the Galleria for some expensive gear and strutting up in everywhere turning heads! What happened to us?"

"I don't know. Aren't you a little embarrassed about going to jail?" Toni asked.

"Embarrassed? Girl, please, shit happens. Is that why we've been huddled up in the place like some lepers?"

"I feel like so many people knew us and how we carried it, so when we took that fall, you know everybody was talking about it and us," Toni said.

"Are we in middle school now? I can't believe you've been carrying on like we some old, broken-down, tired broads ready for the nursing home because you think people been talking about us!" I got up and strutted across the room. "Girl, you should look at it like this. If we can look this hot, after being in a place that usually breaks people, and we still standing and looking fabulous, let them talk shit. Let's just make sure we give them something to talk about," I said.

Once I had gotten to the bottom of Toni's problem, we agreed we should hold off and step out the weekend after we returned from New York. Anyone who knew us knew we were far from average chicks, so when we did it, we always did it big, and I didn't want this time to be no exception.

The next night I had gotten Toni out of the house. The place was clean and candlelight flickered all around the living room, giving off a surreal setting. I had gone to Victoria's Secret and picked up a raunchy yet sexy little outfit that I was sure would help break some vows.

"Oh damn. I didn't pick up any Crown." I looked around and was pleased with everything I had set up. Toni kept Patrón so I didn't have to worry about being without liquor. It simply wasn't what he used to like back in the day.

Ten minutes before he was supposed to arrive, I went and searched for the KY Jelly I'd bought just for the occasion. An hour later, I was still waiting. Because Julius was married now, I couldn't pick up the phone and call him up for fear his wife would intercept the call.

Nearly two hours later, the ringing phone pulled me out of a deep slumber. At first I thought it was in my dream. Once I realized my cell phone was ringing, I wiped drool from the side of my mouth and snatched the phone.

"Hey, Lachez," said Julius.

Damn. I had dozed off, with candles still burning!

"What the hell is wrong with you?" I snapped.

"Chill out. I can't make it tonight, but maybe we could hook up tomorrow night," he said.

"You got me twisted! Do you know what all I had to go through to squeeze you in my schedule tonight and your ass don't show? What—you think you should get some props because you decided to pick up the phone and call me two fucking hours late? What the hell?"

"Damn, sounds to me like you were expecting something more than just a little visit." The bastard laughed.

I hit END on the phone, turned it off, then blew out the candles before I burned the place down. We had an early flight the next morning, so I probably needed my rest more than I needed Julius anyway.

EBONI

In a matter of days, life as I had known it was completely over! My world had flipped upside down and back again! The kids and I were in hiding. I had to get out of there and try to get my thoughts together.

When I fell asleep, I dreamed about Nia's phone call. Then I'd dream that she called back laughing hysterically, telling me this was all a bad joke.

Although the initial call was on instant replay in my head, that second call never came. I didn't have much time before Shawnathon's attorney would be calling him with the news and I needed to get the hell out of dodge.

This time I didn't have Ulonda to act as a human shield for me. I was truly alone. I had gone from making plans for a romantic getaway to running and hiding for my life. The moment Shawnathon got the news, he'd flip out and murder would be front and center on his mind.

"How long will you be staying with us?" the hotel clerk asked.

"Uh, a week, maybe two," I said.

All the damn questions were making my head hurt.

"Will you need cribs for your entire stay?"

"I need to get to my room. The kids and I have been on the road. Can we move this along, please?"

"Oh, absolutely, Ms. Brown. Right away," he said.

Later, once we settled in the room, I couldn't stop pacing back and forth. What was I going to do? I didn't have a plan B. I was supposed to be working on bringing my family back together. How could this have happened?

I spent a restless night, crying. I tossed and turned and even woke to my kids crying. I wanted to join them but that would do me no good.

Suddenly it hit me. I had to call Nia, but I didn't want her to know where I was staying. I was certain she was probably worried about how she'd get paid, because now, so was I.

I picked up the hotel phone and blocked the number. I dialed Nia's office number and was stunned when she answered the phone herself!

"Ah, Nia?" I wanted to be wrong. Maybe all of this was really a dream.

"Eboni, where the hell are you? My phone has been ringing off the hook. I need you to come into the office. We need to figure out what we're gonna do," she said.

I couldn't think straight! She was rambling and talking about what I needed to do, but I wanted to tell her all she needed to do was listen to me!

"Nia!" I screamed.

That was when she stopped talking. I finally had her attention.

"Nia, I know what happened! I know what's wrong," I said.

When I heard her sigh loudly in my ear, I knew she had to be part of the conspiracy.

"Eboni, what are you talking about? What do you mean, you know what happened? Everyone is looking for you. The media is all over this!"

"He got someone else to take the test," I said.

You could've heard crickets. That's how quiet it was on the other end. Had she hung up?

"Nia, are you there? Did you hear me? I said, he got someone else to take the test!"

The kids started crying, both of them at once! My head never stopped hurting, but the pain had intensified and had started up again.

"Eboni, DNA doesn't lie!"

"Nia, you don't understand. Shawnathon used to hate me. He tried to kill me several times. He didn't want our kids, but we've made up. He's been over after we left court. You can't tell him this. You need to give me some time to figure this all out! If you tell him, he's gonna kill me for sure. He's gonna want his money back. Please, you've gotta listen to me." I was crying right along with the kids at that point.

"Eboni, where are you? You need to come in so we can talk this thing through. We need to give the press a statement. We need to clear Shawnathon's name and we need to do it quickly. If we come out in front of this thing, it will help to mitigate the damage," she said. "Wait, what money?"

Soon, her words sounded like she was under water. She wasn't listening to me. There was no way I'd tell anyone anything except that Shawnathon McGee was my baby daddy! I needed her to understand what I was trying to tell her. But it was useless.

"DNA doesn't lie," she repeated. "If he gave you money, you need to return it now!"

I wanted to reach through the phone and slap her. She was supposed to be on my side! She was my lawyer! Why couldn't she believe that it was possible for him to send someone in to test for him when he hated me?

Visions of my perfect life as Shawnathon's wife, or even his mistress, began to fade from my mind. All of the money, all of the nice things, what would I be without him?

When my cell phone rang, I looked at the caller ID and wanted to scream.

Strange numbers popped up left and right. Did people think I was completely stupid? No way in hell was I gonna answer some random number.

I sat there in my hotel room on the bed, crying with my kids for hours.

If Shawnathon wasn't their daddy, then who was? Didn't they look like him? How the hell was I gonna get out of this mess?

SERENA

I was comfortable with the way things had turned out. I wasn't quite at the point where I could consider the Redmans *friends* just yet, but I could see myself working with them. My daughter was back at home, and we were talking again. We had been through so much. In addition to my night in jail, Semaj had fallen sick and was rushed to the emergency room. Those scares opened my eyes and made me realize the bickering wasn't worth it. Both she and I had started seeing a counselor.

I desperately wanted to break the cycle. My mother was a bitter, angry, lonely old woman and I didn't want to wind up the same way, nor did I want my daughter to take on those traits. I didn't want to mess things up with Semaj, and over the last six years, she'd been through so much that I was worried.

Because I wasn't the type who ran from a challenge, I was talking to a counselor myself. I was trying to get to the bottom of my own anger.

When I sat down and did some self-evaluation, I realized that I was angry about every aspect of my life. I didn't like my neighbors; I felt like they were too nosey. I didn't like Loren anymore because I felt like she tried to judge me behind that whole thing with Parker.

I was tired of disliking folks and being pissed off all the time. It took too much wasted energy to keep up with who I didn't like and why I didn't like them. I even tried to get in touch with JahRyan, but he sent my calls to voicemail and never called back, so that told me he didn't want to be bothered either.

After a few sessions with the counselor, I could already tell a difference. The other day, I went to buy a cheeseburger. When I got home, I realized there was a piece of hair on top of the tomato. I was upset, but still I got back in my car and pulled up to the drive-thru.

"Ma'am, is your manager available?" I asked the lady who had served me not even fifteen minutes before.

The manager walked over to the window with a nasty scowl on her face. She didn't greet me or anything.

"What's the problem?" she asked.

"Oh, I was here a few minutes ago and I found a piece of hair in my food when I got back home." I gave her the burger.

Instead of her tossing it into the trash, she unwrapped the burger, and removed the bun as if she was inspecting it herself. After close scrutiny, she looked down at me and said, "I don't see no piece of hair in here!"

The old Serena would've been through that tiny window with my hands wrapped around her chubby throat before she had a chance to finish that sentence. I didn't ask her to verify whether there was a piece of hair there. I knew what I had seen.

"Are you sure it wasn't one of yours?" she asked, still inspecting the burger.

I looked at her and calmly said, "Ma'am, I can assure you, it was not my hair because I'm not blonde. Also, please believe that I would not make up something like that, jump in my car, waste my gas to drive all the way back here if there wasn't a problem with the burger." I said all of this in a slightly irritated but very calm tone.

"Well, where's your receipt?" she snarled.

She behaved as if she was mad at me for finding hair in my food!

"If it's not in the bag, I'm not sure," I said as I tried to look around on the passenger seat.

"Ma'am, we can't give you a refund without a receipt," she insisted.

Again, I looked up at her and calmly said, "Ma'am, I was here ten minutes ago, I bought the burger here. I have no reason to try and steal $2.65 from you."

When she rolled her eyes, opened the cash register, and all but threw my money at me, I took a deep breath and drove off. The old Serena would've made the news in a story that would've gone viral about how badly a burger joint manager was mopped up by an angry customer.

They may have been baby steps, but I was glad progress was being made. I also tried to deal with the bitterness I held on to when it came to Parker. I had lots of issues, but I was trying to work some of them out.

"So, Mom, what's gonna happen when I go to take this test?" Semaj asked.

"Nothing major. They'll take a long Q-tip, ask you to open your mouth, and they'll tickle the inside of your jaw with it," I explained.

"Is that all?"

"Yup, that's all," I said.

"Mom, how is it that you don't know who my father is?"

She asked the question so innocently. I couldn't do anything but remember the progress I had been making. There was no need for me to haul off and slap my child in the mouth for a question that obviously had her genuinely puzzled.

"Semaj, when you grow up, you'll discover that some things in life are far more difficult than we want them to be. Sometimes adults make choices that aren't the best, but all we can do is try to make up for our mistakes and try to do better."

When she looked at me, I could see the question still in her eyes. She shrugged her shoulders and went back to texting on her cell phone.

I couldn't go back in time, but the fact that I wanted to, in hopes of trying to undo some of the mess I had created, told me the future would be better and brighter.

PARKER

"Paternity fraud has got to end now! Men cannot continue to reward women for fraud and neither should the government!"

I wrapped up an impromptu press conference inside our offices. The press conference was thrown together at the request of Shawnathon McGee. He had been hounded by the media when the news broke.

His paternity case had already made international news because of his status in the sports world, so now this was fuel to a smoldering fire. I felt for the young brotha because I knew how he was feeling.

"Parker," his gruff voice called out to me.

At first I had no clue who had called. The number was blocked on caller ID. Shawnathon didn't sound like himself. As a matter of fact, he sounded like a broken man. Years ago, I had experienced the same thing with my best friend, James. Ironically, it was his then wife Serena who lied and told him Semaj was his daughter. She was extra dirty with it, evening naming the girl after him by spelling his name backwards.

I knew how Shawnathon was feeling.

"I can't talk to the media. I need your help. I can't believe this shit! I wanna kill her ass, man."

"No, come on in, bruh. We can do whatever you need. I don't want you to be in contact with her because, at this time, you don't want to do or say anything you might regret later. I'll be at the office in an hour," I told him.

"Can I go there and wait for you? I'm not feeling too good right now," he said.

"Yeah, I'll call and let them know to expect you. I'll have my assistant open my office for you. I'll be there as quickly as I can," I said.

I saw no signs of Shawnathon's entourage when I pulled up, so at first I thought he had changed his mind about coming in.

"Hey," I said to the receptionist as I walked in.

"Shawanthon McGee is in your office. He's been in there for almost an hour with his bodyguard," she said.

"Okay, no problem, hold all my calls." I looked around. "Where's everyone else?" I asked her.

She shrugged. "That's the strange thing—this time he came alone. The bodyguard just got here about ten minutes ago," she said.

"Okay, don't disturb us okay."

I walked into my office and Shawnathon was on the sofa. His bodyguard stood off to the left with his arms crossed over his massive chest.

"Parker…man." His voice cracked as he tried to greet me.

"What do you want to do?" I asked.

Shawnathon and I worked on a statement together. An hour after we announced the press conference, the office was jam-packed with reporters. TV and newspaper cameras littered my little lobby area.

I read the prepared statement and answered a few general questions. While this was going on, Shawnathon was watching from my office.

After I said goodbye to the last reporter, Shawnathon and I cracked open a couple of brews.

He sent his bodyguard for food and we sat back.

"I'm sorry this happened to you," I said.

He shook his head. He seemed lost in deep thoughts.

"I gave her three hundred grand," he said.

I raised an eyebrow.

"I should have her taken out. You know how many people would be willing to snuff her out for less than half of that?"

"Not the way to handle this," I said.

"I know, Parker, I know. But it gives me crazy pleasure to think of ways I could have her dealt with," he said.

"What did your lawyer say about getting the money back?" I asked him.

He shook his head.

"That was between me and her. Lawyer didn't even know about it," he said.

"You gave her three hundred thousand dollars without telling your lawyer?"

Shawnathon nodded his head in response to my question.

"I *knew* those kids were mine," he said. "I thought they looked like me! Did I just want to see what I thought I saw?"

"It happens man! It happens."

"She could keep the money for all I care. I don't ever wanna lay eyes on her again. I don't know what I'd do man. I don't even trust myself around her right now."

As I listened to him pour out his frustrations, I was glad my own nightmare had finally come to an end.

The results came back and showed that Semaj was, in fact, my daughter. I attended counseling with them one day out of the week and we knew it would take some time, but we all wanted to do what was best for Semaj.

"I could kill..."

I looked up from my computer to see tears running down Shawnathon's cheeks. I stopped typing for a second and sighed hard.

"Killing her," I said softly, "will mean the end of life as you know it. Your career will be over, your new family. It seems like a viable option, but really it's not. It doesn't seem like it now, but this too will pass."

I sat quietly and allowed him his moment. He'd speak when he found his voice or when he felt like it. Soon, I started to think about all that was possible with our new arrangement.

The clinic had already made an offer, but Bill said they'd need to come back at least twice as high before he'd be ready to sit and talk.

Roxy and Semaj were becoming closer, and business was thriving at DFF.

LACHEZ

We didn't fly first class or anything like that, but to say I was thrilled to get on that plane would be an understatement. Between Junie and his worthless daddy, I needed a break!

When we touched down at JFK International, I felt like more like a businesswoman than a crook. I told Toni I didn't believe in dressing in jeans and tennis shoes when I traveled. I liked to look and dress the part.

Actually, I bit off Pricilla and bought a navy St. John pantsuit. I grabbed like five pairs of string pearls and stacked them around my neck.

When I walked out of the room and pulled my suitcase behind me, Toni frowned.

"Where the hell are you going all dressed like that?" she asked.

"To the airport with you," I said.

She eyed me up and down, then looked down at the simple capris and matching top she had on.

"Are you serious with that outfit? And with your hair all pinned-up like that, I'll look like a little kid next to you," she complained.

"Well, go change! We are about to go work a job. You never know who you will encounter while on business," I said.

"Umph, I guess not, huh?"

"Are you gonna go change or what?" I asked impatiently.

"I don't think I have much of a choice," she said, pulling herself up from the sofa like it was a task.

Nearly thirty minutes later I screamed toward her bedroom door.

"Toni, we're gonna miss the flight if you take much longer!"

"I'm coming!" she yelled back.

When Toni walked out this time, I felt a lot better. She wore a pair of designer slacks that looked like they were tailored specifically for her body. She had on a crisp white Anne Fontaine shirt, and she looked polished with silver accessories.

"Now, don't you feel better?" I asked.

"C'mon, before we miss our plane," she said.

My theory proved to be true. From the moment we arrived at the airport, we received the star treatment. We even slid into the President's Lounge with no passes, and I explained to Toni it was all because of how nicely we were dressed.

"I think you may be on to something," she said.

Once we checked into our hotel room, Toni called for a car service.

"The car service will take us to Hotel 3030. We'll go in there and see if they have any vacancies. While we try to figure that out, we'll take a taxi from there to the host hotel."

"Why do we need to check for vacancies?" I asked.

"The idea is to give the impression that we're searching for a room—that way no one is paying too much attention to us and the fact that we're not staying there," she said.

"Once we leave the host hotel, we'll go back to 3030 and have someone hail us a cab. He'll take us to the Fairfield Inn on 37th, then we can walk over to Courtyard on 5th Ave."

"Walk?" I asked.

"Yes, walk. The two hotels are not far from each other at all. Trust me on this," she said.

"Okay."

From the moment Toni was dressed like we were headed to a picnic instead of the Big Apple, I should've known she was a little off her game, but I didn't pay it no mind. I simply wanted to handle the business, and then get to partying.

We arrived at the host hotel, the Doubletree on Broadway, and went our separate ways. I walked up to the front desk and greeted the clerk.

"Yes, there should be a key for me. My name is Heidi," I said.

The way the clerk looked at me made me uncomfortable.

"Umm," she said. But I already knew the drill. I never gave any more information that what was required.

"Oh, yes, Heidi, I see right here. Do you have identification..." her voice trailed off. I suspected it was after she read her notes, which said *no ID required*, she knew what was up. I didn't know why she was playing games.

I snatched the key from her, and tossed back a dirty look as I sashayed up to the room and waited for my date. I got a text message from Toni.

"U in Yet?"

"Yup! Where R U?"

"At Bar!"

"K, what's his name?"

"Walter. Filthy Rich!"

"Emm. My Fav!"

I ended with Toni and slipped into a body-hugging sheer dress, minus underwear. I put my other clothes into the large hobo I carried on jobs and got the cocktails started.

About twenty minutes after I settled into the suite and began to sip my drink, there was a knock at the door.

"Coming in, Heidi. I hope you're ready for us," a boisterous voice announced.

My heart nearly skipped a beat. *Us*? Toni didn't say anything about two men.

I quickly grabbed my phone and texted her the room number, a sign to her that there was a problem.

Then I text another message saying, "*dbl fun?*"

Before I could prepare myself, they rounded the corner, drinks in hand, and when I locked eyes with one of them, I nearly dropped my drink. He didn't react right away, so I figured he didn't recognize me.

What the hell is *he* doing here? I'd never forget those hazel eyes. Both men were drunk and still drinking.

I was so nervous I didn't know what to say or do.

"You ready for a good time?"

I couldn't tell who had asked because I was busy trying to look at my phone. I was waiting for Toni to text back.

"Hey, who you callin'?" one of them asked.

"Looks like I'm gonna need backup. I have the perfect person. She's friendly, discreet, and she loves to party!" I smiled.

"Backup?" They looked at each other as if neither knew whether it was a good idea.

"Let's get you two fresh drinks first," I said.

"Now you're talking," Barron said.

I took two glasses over to the kitchenette and turned my back to them. Once I fixed their drinks just right, I strutted over and served them. They were already in the midst of a mind-numbing industry conversation, and I feared they'd bore me to tears before Toni showed up.

Since they seemed content drinking and going back and forth in the verbal battle, I fell back. The last thing I wanted was for Barron to catch a familiar glimpse of me.

By the time Toni's knock came, words were slurring and they both seemed less lively than when they had arrived.

"Gentlemen, I'm Trixie, but my friends call me Sexy," Toni announced.

She didn't even finish her introduction before the two of them were snoring.

"Barron!" I called out.

I walked over and nudged him, but he didn't move.

"Damn, they're out like light bulbs," I said.

"C'mon, let's get this going," Toni said.

"Umm, I don't think this is such a good idea," I said.

Toni's eyebrows shot up.

"What do you mean, not such a good idea? Look at these two geriatrics. They'll probably be out for days!" Toni started looking around the room. "Come on! Let's shake 'em and bounce!"

"Toni, chill, this is not their room! Look around! I think they rented this extra room just for the romp! There was nothing in here when I got here," I said.

For the first time since I started talking some sense into her, she slowed her roll and looked around.

"Damn! What the what?"

"Yes, let's cut our losses and get up outta here," I said.

"Empty-handed?" she balked.

"Toni, there's nothing here, no bags, no luggage, no safe. This is not their room!"

"Let's at least empty their pockets," she begged.

"No, let's bounce!"

"Why? Why you tripping? We didn't come all this way to leave empty handed!"

"Toni, this one right here..." I pointed to the salt and pepper haired man. "This is Pricilla's daddy! If he wakes up with empty pockets and his jewelry gone, I don't want my face to pop into his head.

"Damn Pricilla. Pricilla?" she asked.

"Let's go!"

I was done with this hustle. That's what I thought about as we rushed up out of that hotel. Now I had to sit in fear hoping Pricilla's dad wouldn't rat me out!

As we made our way back to our hotel, I turned to Toni and told her what was on my heart.

"I'm done! I'm going legit," I said.

Toni looked at me like I was speaking French.

"I'm serious, Toni. I can't live like this. I ain't tryin' to go back to jail!"

"So that's it? You tryin' to tell me I'm on my own?" she huffed.

"If that's how you wanna look at it. I don't know about you, but I'm tired of taking chances. What happened back there, that was a straight wake-up call for me, and I'm answering the call!" I said, right as our cab pulled up.

EBONI

I didn't know where else to turn. Suicide had crossed my mind several times, but that wasn't an option for me. It would probably push my mom over the edge, and I definitely didn't want to do that!

I sat and thought all sorts of thoughts as I waited for her to pick up the phone. I had no right to even think about calling her, but what else could I do?

"Hello?" My heart raced like I was the frontrunner on a NASCAR track.

"What the hell do you want?" her voice asked nastily.

"Ulonda, I know, I know you probably hate me. I am so sorry," I sobbed.

"Eboni, you're not sorry. You're scared and alone. You probably only called me because you can't call another damn soul. Remember when you were riding high, your money was your only concern. But now, lemme guess, you're probably hiding out somewhere unable to rest 'cause you're looking over your shoulder at every turn."

"Ulonda, I was wrong for the way I treated you. I'm sorry," I said.

"Yeah, I accept your apology, but I'll never forget. You and I were digging together, but the minute you thought you hit a gold mine, you dropped me like a bad habit. That—I can never ever forget or forgive."

She was right about everything she had said. I wanted to bust out and cry, but I didn't have any tears left. I decided I'd let Ulonda get it off her chest, but I wasn't about to sit on the phone and let myself get dumped on even more.

"So are you telling me our friendship is over?"

"I'm not telling you that. What I'm telling you is that it can never be the same. So to me, you should take that and do with it what you want. Also, Eboni, you should call me after you've worked this all out. I gave everything to our friendship. I was there with you from day one when we schemed on how to hook ourselves some ballers. You lied to me then, and obviously you don't know how to stop lying. Right now, I'm trying to get my shit together. I don't have enough energy to solve my problems and yours!"

That was it. She had her say, and then she hung up.

I sat there, dumbfounded. What was I going to do? I was nothing without Shawnathon and his money. I was even less without my best friend. Unfortunately for me, I learned all of this far too late.

I lay back on the bed. The kids were in the corner quietly playing together. I had no idea what the future would hold for us, but I had to leave Houston. There was no way I could face Shawnathon, Elisa, or even Ulonda again.

"I have enough money for a fresh new start. Maybe I'll go to L.A.," I muttered as I watched the kids.

My kids are cute. I'll go there and focus on making them stars. That way Shawnathon will beg me to call him their daddy!

"Yeah, I may be down, but I won't be for long!"

I jumped up from the bed, declared this pity party over, and decided to put my plan in motion.

I planned to call my mom, tell her about my plan, and urge her to come West with me. If she didn't want to go, that would be okay, too. I didn't need to hang around constantly looking over my shoulder. The move would be best for us all.

READER'S DISCUSSION GUIDE

1. Which character did you relate to most and why?
2. Why do you think Parker was so passionate about his work?
3. Were you surprised that Roxanne didn't spend much time doubting her husband?
4. Do you think it was wrong for Ulonda and Eboni to hunt for rich men the way they did?
5. Do you think a man should have to pay child support if he and the woman agreed on no kids?
6. Do you think Shawnathon's popularity made him feel like he could behave any way he wanted?
7. Do you think Ulonda grew jealous of Eboni?
8. How should Eboni have dealt with it if she thought Ulonda was jealous?
9. How much of an impact do you think Lachez's disapproval will have on her son's relationship with the older woman?
10. Was Lachez and Toni's new hustle really foolproof?
11. What should Eboni have done when she got the test results?

12. Was Serena's case one that Gloria Allred would've taken on?

13. What should Eboni have done differently?

14. Should Parker and Roxy have fought for full custody?

ABOUT THE AUTHOR

Pat Tucker is the author of eight novels and a participant in three anthologies. She is a radio news director in Houston, Texas, and co-host of the *Cover to Cover* show with *Essence* bestselling author ReShonda Tate Billingsley.

Printed in the United States
By Bookmasters